Meeting Ms. Right

A novel

By

Richard Jeanty

RJ Publications, LLC

Newark, New Jersey

D1511093

The characters and events in this book are fictitious. Any resemblance to actual persons, living or dead, is purely coincidental.

RJ Publications
rjeantay@yahoo.com
www.rjpublications.com
Copyright © 2005 by Richard Jeanty
All Rights Reserved
ISBN 0-9769277-0-5

Printed in Canada

May 2005

2-3-4-5-6-7-8-9-10-11

New Introduction

Why do most women feel that they are Ms. Right? There's nothing wrong with feeling that way, however, you cannot be Ms. Right if you're dating or married to Mr. Wrong.

You're probably wondering what I mean by the above statement, right? Well, let me explain. There are so many Black women out there complaining about the lack of good available Black men, and that can be true in some way, but most of the time what they think are good men are completely the wrong men for them. The educated sistas, most of the time, are looking for their educated male counterpart because they feel they might have more in common with an educated brotha. Well, that's not always the case because many of these educated brothers feel like they are God's gift to women and the cream of the crop as far as available men are concerned. Just because two educated people come together, it doesn't mean there's going to be perfect harmony.

The same can be said about the women who love thugs and hustlers. If you're not part of that world, chances are, these men would be wrong for you as well. If a man is beating you everyday and you stay with him because you think you're in love, you're in love with the wrong man because abuse is not part of love, whether physical or emotional. Women need to know exactly what they want in order for them to find the right man and become Ms. Right. There's nothing wrong with having standards, requirement and prerequisites, but make sure those things that you desire in a mate comes with compatibility as well as interest in other areas.

If you're dating Mr. Wrong, you can never be Ms. Right.

Satisfying My Needs

Thank goodness for XXL magazine. I was getting tired of getting my groove on using Playboy magazine most of the time. Sometimes, I really had to work very hard to get an erection because the skinny white centerfolds in that magazine just did not have enough booty to get a rise out of me. In addition, the sisters, who made their way into the pages of Playboy, might as well have been white because most of them had the same type of body as the white women. Who really gets off on these skinny women, anyway? A brother needs some meat on the bone.

When XXL came on the scene, it was like a blessing from above. Although it was not considered a nude magazine, the models in there were damn near naked and they had bodies that I could identify with. There were everyday, normal looking sisters in that magazine that a brother could really appreciate. These sisters did not have to be completely naked for a brother to get an erection. Masturbating became easier for me when I bought my first copy of XXL. I signed up for my monthly subscription after I purchased my first copy. It was like clockwork after a while. My bathroom saw a lot more action thanks to that magazine.

Don't get me wrong, I am not into exploiting women in any way, but I had needs as a thirty year-old man without a girlfriend. I knew these women were posing in the magazine for their own personal reasons, but I bought the magazine for my own personal reasons as well. I could only imagine seeing Halle Berry naked so many times in front of me, and after a while, I needed more of a variety. It wasn't like I had ever seen Halle Berry completely naked anywhere, anyway. I got a glimpse of her bare breasts a couple of times briefly while watching one of her movies, and I was only able to get off on that for a little while with my remote control in hand rewinding the scene over and over. However, these sisters in XXL came in all shapes, sizes, and flavors. I could have the woman I wanted everyday of the week by flipping through a few pages. If I was going to have sex by myself, I might as well have had the variety that I wanted.

When Gabrielle Union first came on the scene, I was masturbating with my eyes closed and her in my mind almost three times a week. She filled a big void in my life for a while. She was the epitome of sexy and class to me and I imagined she and I doing things that if she was aware of she would have me put in jail. How can you blame me? She was one of the sexiest women that I had ever seen on the big screen. She did not have to reveal her naked body for my imagination to run wild. She was just as sexy fully clothed, as she probably would have been naked

Being a single man at my age did not leave me too many choices when it came to sex. My hands were my favorite girls and sometimes I had more fun with them than any other parts of my body. It should not be shocking that I masturbated to satisfy my needs because ninety five percent of married men masturbate too. I believed that fifty percent of married women masturbate and ninety five percent of single women masturbate at least once a week. I had no data to prove this, but I knew I was not the only person getting my thrill with me, myself and I.

Some people have likened me to A.C Green, the ex-player for the Los Angeles Lakers, but I was quick to tell them that if I had the opportunities he has had as an athlete; my virginity would have been history a long time ago. I was not a virgin because of religious beliefs, there was a lot more to it than that as you will find out. Besides, masturbating was the safest form of sex for me.

The Ultimate Experience

I never thought the two most beautiful women in the club would ever leave with us. Whatever Dexter must have said to them had to be amazing because we were in for one magical night. All eyes were on us, as we left the club with the women. Nikki was the finer of the two; she was brown skinned with bone straight hair down her back and a body that would put any video hoochie out of work. Maria was Puerto Rican with long curly hair and a sexy accent that could make a man melt in her hands. She had a real petite body that could take a man's imagination to places that the Lord would deem forbidden.

The smiles on the ladies' faces confirmed the fact that they were down for whatever we were planning on doing with them that night. Maria kept flirting with me; she told me that she was turned on by my shyness while we were sitting in the back seat of Dexter's BMW on the way to his house. I could see that Dexter and Nikki were getting along great. She was sensually massaging his neck as he put the pedal to the metal to get us to his place as quickly as he possibly could without crashing. Nikki was licking Dexter's neck and sticking her tongue in his ear, creating a tingling sensation that almost sent him flying off the road a couple of times. My heart was beating a mile a minute with fear. However, when Maria glided her way over to me and rolled up her mini dress pass her thighs to reveal that she was not wearing any underwear, my other head took over the fear, as it stood erected. She started groping me and my tool got harder and harder. By the time we got to Dexter's place, I had Maria's breasts in my mouth sucking on them as if I was a baby looking for milk.

We all went upstairs to Dexter's pad and at the girls' suggestion; we started playing "Truth or Dare." I could not recall anyone who took more than one truth, but the dares were coming out of the woodwork. By the time we came around to Dexter the second time for a dare, we were all butt naked ready to start an orgy that was out of this world. At first, I was a little uncomfortable getting naked in front of Dexter because as cocky as he was, I thought he was packing twelve inches or something. I did not want to get embarrassed in front of the girls. However, when I saw his eight inches dangling like a ripe banana in front of the two women who seemed too eager to take a bite, I pulled off my underwear exposing my nine-inches for the ladies to salivate over. Not that it made a difference that I was slightly bigger than Dexter was, but it gave me a lot of confidence.

All four of us were sitting butt naked in Dexter's living room with a couple of hard and erected bananas ready to take part in a banana split and a couple set of tits waiting to be caressed. We were waiting for Maria to take the next dare, as it was her turn. It was as if the ladies had planned the whole thing. Nikki double dared Maria to deep-throat my nine-incher without gagging on it. And that she did. She took every inch very slowly in her mouth and by the time the head of my penis reached the back of her throat, it felt like I was hitting her sugar walls. The look on Maria's face alone as she slowly deep throat all of me, must've sent enough blood rushing down to my meat, causing it to grow even bigger. The fact that she was massaging my balls as she took me in her mouth almost caused me to have one of those quick orgasms and embarrass myself in front of everyone.

Maria went to pull my Kielbasa out of her mouth and Nikki ordered her to keep it there until she said otherwise. Nikki continued to instruct her to suck it, and that she did. While I was trying my best to keep from exploding in Maria's mouth, it was Dexter's turn to take a dare and Nikki dared him to penetrate Maria from behind. Without hesitation, Dexter wrapped his "Grade A" beef in a condom, inserted it inside Maria and slowly started stroking her from the back while she juggled my nuts in her mouth as I stood in front of her. Nikki was a spectator for all but five minutes while Maria tried to take us both on.

Nikki's turn to take a dare had finally arrived and I dared her to stand on the couch and stick her ass up to Dexter's face so he could eat her while stroking Maria. It seemed like Nikki could not wait to be eaten. She jumped on Dexter's leather couch still wearing her heels and stuck her ass up as high as she could near his face without falling over. It was almost awkward; somehow, she managed to get in the right position for Dexter to stick his tongue in and out of her. He ate her out until she started shaking in a trance while he was still stroking the hell out of Maria. All I could hear was the moaning and groaning of the two women.

By the time Dexter and I switched positions with the two women, we had ignored the fact that we were playing "Truth or Dare" it had become a free-for-all orgy. I could not wait to pick up Maria's little ass and start banging her around the room. She jumped on me like a little kid who had not seen her father in years. She wrapped her legs around my body as she took all my nine inches inside of her in the middle of Dexter's living room. After about ten minutes of stroking her with all my might, I laid her down on her knees on the chair and started banging her from behind.

I could see Dexter on the other side of the room with Nikki's ass hanging upside down swallowing him whole while he ate her to ecstasy with her legs wrapped around his shoulders. Dexter appeared to be an oral expert from all the moaning that Nikki was doing. Nikki got me turned on even more and I wanted to get a piece of her as well. Therefore, I picked up Maria's little ass while still inside of her and brought her over to the other side near Dexter and Nikki. Dexter sat on the couch as the two women stood with their asses sticking up in the air sucking him off. I grabbed a hold of Nikki's ass and slowly penetrated her from behind and inserted a couple of fingers inside Maria. I developed a rhythm that was both Latin and R & B the way I was pleasing these women. By the time I was ready to climax, my phone rang and it was Dexter calling to see if I wanted to hang out with him later that evening.

I woke up almost drowning in my own semen and sweat like I had just run a marathon. It was weird for me to talk to Dexter in my position, so I told him I would call him later. I had a long day at work earlier that Friday and I came home and dozed off. Other than beating my meat, my wet dreams was the only other way I ever got my thrills and someone seemed to always interrupt my flow with a phone call.

About Me

My name is Malcolm Davis and I feel like I'm the last guy left with a conscience on the planet. I try to be very honest and straightforward in everything that I do; and I'm hoping to meet a wonderful woman who is as honest and straightforward as I am. I am honest about a few issues in my life, like being a masturbator and not being God's gift to women. I do not do the cyber-dating thing because I do not want to disappoint anyone and I do not want anyone disappointing me. Most people in cyberspace have high expectations as well. If they were so hot, they would not be in cyberspace in the first place. Also, cyberspace has produced more weirdoes than I have room in my life to accommodate right now. I have heard the stories.

For example: One of my cousins drove all the way down to Maryland from Boston to meet this girl he met on the Internet, her picture was hot and she seemed perfect in many ways. She had a college degree, a great professional career, witty and appeared smart online. However, when he met her, she looked like she had added five more women to the picture she had posted on the Internet and to top it off, she could not hold a conversation even if it was with President George W. Bush. When my cousin told me the story, I could not keep from laughing in his face. It was just as well because he had just gotten divorced two days before he met the girl. Karma is alive and well.

I never believed in a dollar and a dream. I am the type of person who believes in making things happen for myself. I don't wait for opportunities to come to me I create my own opportunities. After graduating from Brandeis University with a BA in

Education, I taught for a year at the local high school to get a feel for teaching. After a year of teaching, I realized that teaching was in my heart. Therefore, I decided to go back to school at the University of Massachusetts in Boston and enrolled in night classes to pursue a Master's degree in Education while I taught full-time during the day.

Presently, I teach Social Studies to ninth graders at the Jeremiah Burke High School. I am not one of those conventional teachers who force my students to listen to a lecture everyday because I think I speak well and I'm more advanced than they are. I'm engaging with my students; I allow them to question historical facts. Almost all of my lessons are related to current issues. I teach ancient history with a mix of today's related topics. The students in my classroom are very fond of me and they always look forward to coming to my class.

During my first year at the high school, I had the highest attendance rate of students in my classes of all the teachers. I feel I bring something to the classroom that the students have not seen before. The fact that I show great interest and care in my students makes them very comfortable in my classroom. Although, there are boundaries set within the classroom, I treat my students as if they are my colleagues. There is mutual respect between teacher and students. The classroom is the only place where I am confident. My students are like sponges that absorb my every word and it feels great to know that I am having a positive impact on their lives.

I'm very satisfied with my teaching gig and I look forward to going to work every morning. After having been a teacher for the last six years, I am still excited about my profession. Every time I attend a graduation, it reinforces my dedication to teaching. I'm always proud of my students for their achievements. I'm also one of the few positive reinforcements that the school has left. Most of the older teachers at the school don't show any special interest in the students. I find that they give up on them too easily. Sometimes we have to fight to make these students see a brighter future.

There was one particular day, young Shawn Daily came to me and told me that he wanted to drop out of school because he felt he wasn't smart enough to make it through school. I set up a special meeting after school with Shawn to show him all the positive attributes that he possessed. By the end of our meeting, Shawn was thinking about which college he was going to apply to in two years when he would become a senior. That's the kind of teacher I am. My aim is to change my students' lives one at a time. Teaching is the most fulfilling job in the world. My students are like clay and I get to mold each one of them to a masterpiece whenever I'm given the opportunity.

The Conception

I have never met my dad. Before I was even born, Michael Francis, my dad, also known as the coward, decided that he no longer wanted anything to do with my mother, Anita Davis, anymore. They started dating at the end of their junior year in high school. My mother and the sperm donor, as I call him, were supposedly high school sweethearts. My mother was dating Michael Francis for half a year before she became pregnant with me. Everything was going well between them, however, there were rumors circulating around the school about Michael sleeping with half of the girls at the high school. My mother ignored the rumors because Michael was a sweet talker who made her feel like she was a queen when they were together.

He was also a football star at the school, which drew a lot of attention and rumors. He rarely went to class, but he excelled on the football field. He only attended school when there was a football game scheduled. His coach didn't make a big deal about him not going to class because the team needed him on the field. The coach figured as long as he got what he wanted out of him, who cared about my father's life. There was a lack of interest regarding Michael's education from everyone except my mother.

While Michael was older than my mother was, he lied about the huge disparity between their ages when they first met. During her senior year in high school, which was actually Michael's third year as a senior as well, he pressured her into sleeping with him and promised to marry her if anything happened as a result. My mother fell for his conniving lies and she got pregnant the first time they had sex. My mother was one gullible chick. One of the reasons Michael claimed he was going around sleeping with every girl at the school was because my mother was not sleeping with him earlier in their relationship. It was the typical guilt ridden argument that he brought against her.

Whenever I hear my mother talk about my father I can never grasp the reasons why she was ever attracted to that fool, much less date him. From what she tells me about him, he was a complete loser with no future. She tried her best to get him to finish school, but he wasn't interested. I figured my mother must have been going through the phase where she was attracted to bad boys. She never described him as handsome, intelligent or well mannered. He seemed to have been on the road to becoming a high school drop out who did not want to make much of his life from the time she met him.

My mother became pregnant with me in December 1973 during the Christmas break from high school. She told me it was the first time that she had seen Michael for three straight days since they had been dating and during that week he came by her house everyday while her parents were at work. He was relentless in his quest to sleep with her. He talked her into watching porno films to convince her that sex was not painful. He told her that everyone at the high school, except them, were having sex and also told her that if he didn't sleep with her soon, he couldn't marry her. I don't know what my mother was thinking because all those lines sound weak to me. I guess because my mother was in love, she fell for anything that came out of Michael's mouth. My mother finally gave in to him after three days of nagging.

She slept with Michael for the first time and he didn't even bother to bring a condom. I know that half the responsibility should've gone to her, but she never anticipated sleeping with him. On the other hand, he knew he wanted to sleep with her all along. She didn't have anything pleasant to say about the experience. She could only say he was rough, careless and very selfish. It felt weird sitting there listening to my mother describe her sexual encounter with my dad, but that's the kind of relationship we have, my mother is more like a comrade.

After my mother slept with that fool, she didn't see him again until they went back to school a week later. My father was a very convincing liar who was able to talk his way out of anything. When my mother asked him, why she didn't see him after they had slept together, he told her he was home sick with the flu. I don't know if she was truly that gullible or if her better judgment was clouded by what she thought was emotional love, but I'm glad she came to her senses sooner rather than later. My father continued to try to sleep with my mother after their first sexual encounter, but she refused. A month had passed and she did not see her menstrual cycle. She was nervous and hoped that it was just off schedule because she only had sex that one time.

Unfortunately for her, she found out she was pregnant. When she told Michael that she was pregnant, he told her there was no way I was his child because they'd only had sex once. My mother didn't know what to do, so she went to her mother and told her what happened. My grandmother was shocked, but she told my mother everything was going to be fine. My grandmother also spoke with my grandfather who went looking for Michael with his 45-caliber shotgun. Back then, it was customary for the girl's parents to get involved and he had intended to bust a cap in Michael's ass.

Word had gotten around school that my grandfather was looking for Michael, and just as quickly he came into my mother's life, he disappeared. My mother graduated from high school later that June while still pregnant. She gave birth on September 15, 1974 to a new baby boy, which is I. My grandparents had three other kids who lived in their three-bedroom house and after I was born, it seemed like there was hardly any room to breathe in that house. The house seemed more crowded than ever.

My grandparents were in their early forties when I was born. They were working hard trying to prevent their other two daughters from becoming pregnant. They did not seem overly concerned with my uncle, though. The old proverb "Boys will be boys" was silently adhered to in the house. My grandparents watched me as much as they could when my mother needed a sitter, but they hated the idea of my mother raising me on her own. They felt that she was too young to be on her own with a child. My grandparents tried their best to help raise me, but when I was old enough to start school, my mother decided to get her own place and we lived together until I received my Master's Degree in college.

Young Dexter

Dexter is the son of an auto mechanic and an administrative assistant. His father Dexter Little Sr. was known and loved by everyone on our block. Dexter Senior is everyone's mechanic and he charged his neighbors very little money when they needed work done on their car. Dexter Sr. has been working at this guy's auto mechanic shop his whole life. He never wanted to be his own boss. The only time he ever worked for himself was when his neighbors asked him to work on their cars on his days off. Dexter Sr. was also a father figure to all the boys on the block who grew up in single parent homes.

Dexter Jr. was an only child and the apple of his parents' eyes. He was very close to his dad. He would spend hours helping him work on the neighbors' cars ever since he was three years old. He was always by his father's side in the run-down garage located in the backyard of the house. His father kept spare parts for every car known to man in that little garage. It was hard for Mrs. Little to get young Dexter to leave his father's side when they were working on a project together. Young Dexter admired his father and they were very close. By the age of six, Dexter Jr. was building his own little cars made out of aluminum cans.

He was a very bright boy who absorbed everything about cars that his father dished out. His passion for cars grew into an obsession. By the time Dexter Jr. turned sixteen years old, his father helped him put together a Toyota Corolla that he would later keep for seven years. Young Dexter and his father formed an unbreakable bond. They were like two best friends and they talked about everything. Even Mrs. Little sometimes would get jealous of their relationship. Don't get me wrong, young Dexter loved and adored his mother too, but he spent most of his time with his father.

Young Dexter and his dad shared the kind of relationship that was so close and comfortable that no subject was ever off limits. Dexter Sr. took pride in schooling his son about being a ladies' man. He used to brag to his son about how his mother was the luckiest woman among many who tried to get him to settle down as a young man. Mrs. Little would always tell her son that his father embellished more than he told the truth and that he in fact had to beg her to marry him. Young Dexter found it amusing when his parents spoke about the old days.

Mr. Little is a very dark skinned man who thinks he's an African god. He stands about six ft two inches tall and weighs about two hundred pounds. It's easy to tell that at one point in time, Mr. Little was very fit and muscular. He never developed a beer belly like most men in his age group. Even as an older man, his good looks never completely faded. He has strong facial features that still stand out today. His high cheekbones and pearly white teeth are probably his best features. Mrs. Little is also a gorgeous woman. She is light brown complexion of petite stature and probably weighs about one hundred and twenty five pounds, and she could've easily been mistaken as a Toni Braxton clone in her younger days.

Dexter Sr. made sure that his son was not kept in the dark when it came to sex. He started talking to Jr. about sex when he reached puberty at the age of twelve. Dexter was an overly developed twelve year old with a deep voice and his father took notice of the change. While working on the cars in the garage, Dexter Sr. would casually talk about sex with his son and the possibilities of fatherhood. But, he also taught his son how to talk to the ladies. Dexter Sr. in his own mind remained a ladies' man even though the only woman in his life was his wife.

Dexter Sr. couldn't walk into a room without thinking that all eyes were on him. Though he was still a sharp dresser for a middle-aged man, he exaggerated his whole image to his son when he talked about his younger days. He had helped Jr. develop the kind of confidence around women that was sometimes unbearable. Sometimes, it would take the intervention of Mrs. Little to bring Dexter Jr. back down to earth.

Dexter inherited most of his father's physical characteristics. It was almost as though his mother didn't contribute to his physical attributes. He was definitely his father's clone; they even shared the same walk. Mr. and Mrs. Little also wanted to have a daughter, but they were unsuccessful in their attempts and they cherish the fact that they were able to have young Dexter. They reared him to respect other people and be compassionate to his fellow human beings. Mr. and Mrs. Little weren't religious, but they instilled strong values in their son to help him develop into a decent young man.

A Lifetime Meeting of Friends

Dexter and I have been best friends most of our lives. He's an auto mechanic and a ladies' man. He and I grew up on the same street just a couple of houses away from each other. It was weird how we became friends. When I was younger, I never played with the rest of the kids on my block. My mother didn't want me hanging out on the street because she knew I was a little chump who wouldn't know how to defend myself if I ever got into a scuffle. I never thought that Fuller Street was a bad street, but my mother always feared the worst. I spent most of my time indoors reading books that my mother brought home from the library. My mother made me read a book a week and I had to submit a book report for every book I read at the end of that week. This was one of my mother's attempts to make me somebody.

It was during the summer of 1984, Dexter saw the book titled The Autobiography of Malcolm X in my hand on my way to putting the trash out in front of the house. We were just ten years old the first time we met. He wanted to know what the book was all about. When I explained to Dexter who Malcolm X was, his interest in the Civil Rights leader grew and he wanted to learn more about the man. That summer Dexter and I spent most of our time at the library reading about Malcolm X and the Black Panther Movement of the sixties. We also formed a bond that would never be broken and we became best friends for life.

I remember once, Dexter got into a fight with a couple of the other kids from our block and he ran to my house and rang my doorbell. When I answered the door, I saw him standing there with a big knot on his head. He asked if I wanted to help fight the two kids who had jumped him, I handed him the biggest book I could find and told him to hit them as hard as he could over the head with it. I could always throw a book or two, but I was never a fighter. He laughed at my suggestion and told me to stop acting like a schoolboy. He, however, took the book from me and went back outside swinging the book as hard as he could at the kids and scared them off.

Dexter was always tougher and wiser on the streets than I was. He was a product of the Boston Public School system. He learned how to fight and was street smart while I learned how to act like the proper Negro around my White classmates at my suburban school. My mother wanted me to have a better education than the Boston Public School offered. She signed me up for the METCO program in Boston when I was a toddler. The METCO program offered students in Boston the opportunity to attend school out of their school districts. As a result, I never slept passed 4:00 in the morning during the school year because I had to get up early everyday to catch a bus to my school at 5:00AM just to make it on time. It was all part of the bussing program established in the seventies. I stayed in the METCO program through high school.

I graduated from high school in the top 10 percentile of my class and that made my mother the happiest woman on this planet. She was very proud of me and my attending college was non-negotiable. My mother had worked hard all her life to give me a better life and I was not going to disappoint her. Over the years, my mother became a very tough parent and she made sure that I never crossed the line with her and I appreciate her for that.

I went away to school at Brandeis University in Waltham right after I graduated from high school; Dexter visited with me as frequently as possible during the weekends. He opted to go to trade school to become an auto mechanic after high school to pursue his love for cars. It only took Dexter two years to become a certified mechanic and he received one of the best job placements that his school had to offer. His job placement was at the local BMW dealer in Boston working as a mechanic earning about thirty thousand dollars right out of school. Although, Dexter entered the workforce two years before me, he drove his Toyota Corolla to the ground for seven years and most of the wear and tear came from the weekend drives from Boston to Brandeis University.

Dexter's visits continued even after he started working and each time, he would leave me fifty dollars at the end of his visit. He always found a new hiding place to put the money without handing it to me directly. He would call me later from his house to tell me where to find the money. Dexter knew that I wouldn't take the money from him directly and he didn't want to shatter my pride. He also knew that Brandeis was an expensive university and with my limited scholarship, my mother couldn't afford to give me an allowance on top of the high tuition that she was helping me pay. A certified nursing assistant at Beth Israel hospital in Brookline, my mother worked the 3:00- 11:00 pm shift. In addition, she was going to school to get her Bachelor's Degree in Nursing. The fact that I came from a single parent home taught Dexter to appreciate his own parents more. Dexter saw firsthand how hard my mother had to work to provide for our family.

Dexter and I are like brothers because both of us are the only children of our parents. He doesn't have any siblings, as he was a miracle child who was conceived late in his parents' lives. Dexter has always been the tougher and more outspoken of the two of us because of his experience, but he has tried his best to school me about the streets every chance he got. He enjoyed visiting me at Brandeis because the girls at the school thought he was so fine. He always got lucky with the ladies when he came up to Brandeis for a visit. Sometimes, I would only find notes on my door that said he wouldn't be coming back to the room until the next day. I guess those were some of the perks that came along with the visits.

I was overly consumed with my studies; I didn't have too much time to dedicate to chasing skirts on campus like most college guys. My rap with women was weak and I was always able to find a way to destroy a good conversation with the opposite sex. I liked intelligent women and most of the intelligent women I knew were into bad boys and that, I was not. I guess that's why Dexter was always so busy during his visits at Brandeis.

I went through four years of college watching my best friend bang more women than I cared to know about. Sometimes, I was a little envious of Dexter, but I couldn't be angry with him for who he was. Dexter and I are different in many ways and that somehow strengthened our relationship. We don't quarrel much about anything. We occasionally have minor disagreements, but for the most part, we get along well. We both like the Celtics and the Patriots and we always root for the home team no matter what. We are so much alike that people find it hard to believe that we're not related. DNA is the only thing that separates our brotherhood.

After I graduated from college and entered the workforce, Dexter and I only got a chance to hang out together on Saturday nights and Sunday afternoons. Our conflicting schedules didn't permit us to be flexible. On rare occasions, Dexter would convince me to disregard the fact that I had to wake up early for work on Fridays so we could go to the Harbor Club on Thursday nights. His excuse was always the same, "The women are fine and I have to get up just as early as you," he would say. Dexter worked six days a week while I only worked five. As a teacher, I got a lot of time off, unlike Dexter who worked almost sixty hours a week. We were both social drinkers who only drank when we were out somewhere at a social gathering. Even when we watched football games at his house on Sundays, we didn't drink. According to a bunch of lushes that we once invited to join us to watch the football game, no liquor made the whole event less exciting. We didn't indulge in alcohol, and we didn't need it to have a good time.

Dexter is the total opposite of me physically. Dexter spends a lot of his spare time at the local gym where he works endlessly on perfecting his physique. He has the abs of a middleweight boxer and the toned body of a sprinter. Dexter is 5 feet 11 inches tall, weighs 195 pounds of solid muscles, dark smooth skin with bedroom eyes, dangerous enough to make women melt in his hands like ice cream. Dexter also inherited his father's pearly white teeth and bright smile, which is like some kind of magnet for the ladies. Dexter is overly concerned with his hygiene and appearance because he is an auto mechanic. He doesn't want to reinforce the stereotype that mechanics are greasy and dirty most of the time. Dexter takes pride in his looks and frequents the barbershop every week to make sure his low fade style haircut and his well-proportioned goatee look fresh and clean all the time.

Me, Myself and Women

I may have been a great teacher, but I was not always so lucky with the ladies. I couldn't even get a female corpse to spend time with me at the morgue. Even women at the morgue, I thought could mysteriously find a way to disappear when I was around. All right, maybe I contributed to the reasons why I couldn't get a woman, but I refused to change who I was as a person just to get a woman. I am an average looking guy and I admit that I never went the extra mile to make myself stand out in a crowd. I wouldn't know how to do that anyway.

My favorite outfits were my khaki pants and Polo shirts. I must've had at least ten pairs of the same style pants and ten pairs of the same style shirts in different colors. I liked what felt comfortable to me and I may have been challenged in the fashion department. I didn't get very excited about spending a lot of money on the latest fashion and I still don't today. Where the hell was I gonna get the money to spend on high fashion anyway? My favorite places to shop were Marshall's and TJ Max. After all, I was just a teacher who taught kids how to get ahead in life.

While I'm beating myself, I must also admit that there was nothing exciting about my appearance. I was not athletic, I had no bulging muscles on my arms and chest and I was not suave or confident in any way. I was a simple, brown complexion man of average height and average weight. To be more specific, I was 5 feet 9 inches tall and weighed about 160 pounds, and I don't know how much of it was fat. I didn't have a protruding gut or skinny legs or anything like that. I have always been told that I had the biggest eyes that god could have bestowed upon somebody and a warm smile. I wore my hair low and neat and had no facial hair. I have been trying to grow a goatee for the last ten years, but to no avail. I could've always used a haircut more often than the ones I got once a month. To me, once a month sufficed, only women need to see a hairdresser more than that. I was a cultured man who enjoyed reading, the museum, plays and Afrocentric artifacts.

I was the type of person that most women considered having as a friend because I am insightful and I can hold intellectually stimulating conversations. Most women couldn't stand to be around me for too long because I enjoyed talking about issues that affect the world. Many of them didn't think those issues were relevant and found the conversations boring. I was always the outsider looking in. I could sit with a woman for hours listening to her rant about other men in her life without saying a word. It was never personal with me. I usually took myself out of the equation before the women got a chance to do it for me.

I have one female friend named Jessica that I met when we were freshmen in college. She was the apple of my eye but I never had enough guts to tell her that I wanted to be more than friends. Jessica didn't exactly shut the door of romance on me totally, but I was just not confident enough to ever crack the door fully open. It could've also been a figment of my imagination that she had any interest at all. Either way, I didn't want to risk losing her as a friend. I saw the type of guys she dated and they were totally opposite of what I was; Jessica was into guys like Dexter.

Jessie as I affectionately called her, came to me with all her problems and I was always the one person she could count on for solid advice. Most of the time, I think Jessie already had the answers to her problems, but she liked the reassurance of my opinion. When Jessie's parents divorced during her sophomore year in college, I was the shoulder that she leaned on for support. She wanted to drop out of school to spite her parents, but I was able to convince her that she was only denying herself something that she'd always wanted. I think deep down in her conscience, Jessie knew that she didn't want to drop out.

With some encouragement from me, Jessie decided to stay in school. She eventually got her bachelor's degree in finance and later went on to pursue an MBA in finance.

She was a very bright girl who hadn't yet learned to look beyond the physical. I was concerned that she would never meet the good-looking, intelligent guy with the bad boy flavor that she had been searching for. She had been looking for a total package that might not have existed, or so I thought.

Jessie once introduced me to this guy she met at her gym. His name was Dante and his second home was the mirror. He would glance at himself on any reflective items-drinking glasses, silverware, car windows and even a hubcap if he had to. I couldn't understand how she could date a moron who was so preoccupied with the way he looked. I know I don't have the right to judge Dante because my best friend Dexter is one calf muscle away from becoming a Dante. At least, Dexter is more subtle with his obsession. Dante wanted people to know that he was pretty. He'd often make comments to Jessie like "Baby, Am I your every dream physically?" and she would patronize that fool. I was so happy when she finally caught Dante with a wannabe super model that he was cheating on her with. And when she caught him, he had the audacity to tell Jessie, "Look how fine she is, I couldn't help myself." It was a humiliating situation for Jessie. As a matter of fact, he and that girl belonged together. If you ask me, Jessie is three times more beautiful than that girl.

Jessie is so gorgeous that when she applied for a job with IBM after getting her MBA from Harvard, the women in the office thought she was doing special favors for one of the executives in order to get the job. She is the ultimate triple threat; she is beautiful, intelligent and driven. Jessie is about 5 feet 7 inches tall with a body that only the man upstairs himself could've drawn from his own sketchpad. She is a perfect size 6 and weighs about 120 pounds. She has perfected her body by making sure she makes the best of her membership at Bally's. Jessie is of brown complexion with killer light brown eyes that most men drooled over. She has the most beautiful smile and the sexiest lips that a man could lay eyes on. Looking at her long legs is like a long visual voyage up and down a beautiful, Italian Byzantine column.

The school where I worked didn't offer any opportunities to date women, as most of the female teachers were married. However, I was well liked by everyone at the school and many of the teachers thought I was a good enough catch for a well-grounded woman. In other words, I was the perfect loser for someone who was looking for a loser. What the hell did well-grounded mean in that context, anyway? I figured it meant, a desperate woman who probably went through all the pretty boys to fulfill all her vanity desires, but doesn't mind settling down with the former loser because he might be a good provider. People always had to dress me up with words. Everyone who thought I was a good catch was already taken, and not everyone I wanted to catch was interested in my bait.

I never really had a male role model in my life other than Dexter and his dad. I considered Dexter a role model because I liked his confidence and when I was younger, I wished I could be as confident as he was. No one could tell Dexter that he was not a handsome man. I was always the guy who was "not that bad looking" after you really got used to seeing me. It was almost like when people first saw Wesley Snipes. At first, the women didn't really break their necks over him, but after a couple of movies and a few million dollars, he became a stud. All I was asking for was a chance like Wesley without the camera capturing my every move. I'm sure I could've been a very attractive guy to many women, but they were not taking the time to dress me up with their eyes like they did Wesley.

My mother always tells me that I am handsome and I look just like my father. He must've grown on her too because my mom's beautiful. Why couldn't she sleep with a man who was good looking at first sight? Not only was the bastard unattractive, he didn't even stick around to help me build my confidence. Talk about a double whammy! I do believe that certain unattractive men can develop a swagger that can make them attractive to the opposite sex. When my mother describes my father, I think he had that swagger.

My Two Best Friends

Dexter had the ultimate bachelor pad and he had earned enough money as a BMW mechanic to buy himself a two-bedroom condominium in Jamaica Plain, Massachusetts. His place was very eclectic. Dexter's bedroom was very contemporary; his money was well spent at Ethan Allen and Pier 1. He enjoyed open spaces, so he had a big canopy bed right in the center of the room with a contemporary wooden dresser on the left side of the room and a chair in the right corner. He remodeled his whole kitchen after he bought the place. He also added all modern stainless steel appliances with an island in the center of the kitchen and a couple of stools that served as a breakfast area.

Dexter purchased one of the most beautiful dining sets that his money could buy. Stainless steel chairs covered with leather cushions and a stained glass table with a wine rack to match sat in the corner of the room next to the kitchen. His living room was very large; he had a big screen television in the middle of the room against the wall, a contemporary yellow leather couch across from the TV and a red suede chair near the entrance of the room. In the center of the room, he had a funky adjustable coffee table with a magazine rack built in at the bottom. He also had a few abstract paintings on the walls that he bought from the local artists at an art show.

Dexter used the extra bedroom in his condominium as an office. He didn't like women spending more than one night at his house. He only had room on his couch for one night and he made it very clear to every guest. He had a couch, a desk, a computer and a chair in his office. Dexter was very meticulous about the way his house was kept. He cleaned his house once a week. Unless Dexter told someone he was a mechanic; no one would ever peg him as such.

Dexter has always been a sharp dresser for as long as I've known him. He visited the fashion district in New York for the latest fashions at least once a month. Most of his clothes look like they were tailored to fit him perfectly. Dexter also knew the importance of wearing a nice pair of shoes. His closets were always filled with more shoes than one would find in Imelda Marco's closet. In addition, Dexter also lavished himself in the latest cologne that his money could buy. He never left his house without wearing some type of cologne after stepping out the shower. Dexter tried his best to have me conform to his sense of style, but I was just too practical to change my ways. I was a true believer that outer appearance was a vain thing that people with no self worth were caught up in. I just couldn't justify paying too much money for anything. I may not have been as confident as Dexter, but I felt I was more down to earth. I didn't make my appearance as much of a priority as Dexter did. Maybe I should have.

In comparison to Dexter's place, my apartment was modest. It was decorated with furniture purchased from Jordan's Furniture. My good friend Jessie had to convince me to throw away an old couch that my mother gave me when I graduated from college. Dexter offered to help decorate my place, but after going through his price list for furniture, I ran back to Jessie who had offered to help decorate my place with furniture from Jordan's. I have to admit that I was not the neatest person on the planet. Jessie couldn't believe that all the effort she'd put into decorating my place was futile a few weeks later. Unlike Dexter, I spent my time reading at the house and I had tons of books everywhere. Dexter was never anxious to spend time at my house because it was never clean enough for him and he didn't really like the way my apartment was decorated.

Dexter and Jessie never got along from the time I introduced them. It was always a tug of war when I was around the two of them. Jessie thought Dexter overcompensated for his looks by dressing up all the time and Dexter thought Jessie was just an average girl searching for Mr. Corporate America. Dexter's arrogance got on Jessie's nerves and Jessie's high standards irritated Dexter. I felt deep in their hearts they both really liked each other, but neither of them was willing to admit it at the time.

Jessie and Dexter acted like two siblings who were always at each other's throat. Jessie was well educated and polished while Dexter was a homeboy who thought he had more to offer the world than people gave him credit for. The clash between them was comical and constructive at the same time. I thought their little clashes forced them both to strive more because of their animosity towards each other. They both wanted to prove to each other that they were better than they each thought.

Bosom Buddies

Dexter was well aware of my deficiencies when it came to women, so on Saturdays when we hung out together at the Cotton club on Massachusetts Avenue, he always went fishing for both of us. My bait was always left hanging at the club. It seemed like my worm and Dexter's worm came from different earths. Women were always trying to cling on to him. A bad night for Dexter at the club was when he only got phone numbers from just a couple of women on a rainy or snowy night when the club was half-empty. Dexter always looked out for me at the club, though.

I never developed any Mack Daddy vibe with the ladies. My whole ensemble couldn't carry a Mack Daddy vibe even if I borrowed one from Dexter. He was more abrasive with the women and his arrogance was welcomed by most. I said arrogance because I have heard women describe Dexter as very arrogant, but that only happened when he didn't give them a second look. Occasionally, Dexter had his run-in with women who found him repulsive as a man too, but those were rare occasions. Most of the time, women adored his confidence.

Whenever Dexter and I hung out, he made sure he only accosted women who came in pairs. He was always careful not to bring along a third wheel that could possibly ruin the fun. Dexter knew that if he were able to convince one of the women to go with his plans, the other would follow. I honestly thought that these women agreed to meet me because they were for the most part, both hoping that they would end up with Dexter. Even after we were introduced, they still overlooked the fact that I even existed. His game was so smooth, he never staked claim on any woman when we went out; he always made them believe he was available to all takers. Dexter was the player of all players as far as I could see.

Even with Dexter's help, I was still unable to score with the women because I was so different in contrast to Dexter. Most women automatically assumed that I was as flashy as Dexter was when he told them about his friend "who was somewhere in the club." Usually, I was not within the vicinity of his encounters because Dexter's best moves happened on the dance floor. I loved watching the scenery from the bar and it was the best place for me to enjoy the ambiance.

The Harbor Club offered the best view out of all the clubs we used to frequent. I have watched so many men get dissed from the bar. I especially liked to watch the corny guys who thought they were ballers get their egos crushed by high maintenance women who were looking for true ballers. There weren't too many guys out there who looked like me with the confidence of Michael Jordan and the balls of Mike Tyson. Guys like me have to develop confidence one day at a time. It's almost like Alcoholic Anonymous, we're grateful for every little bit of progress we make.

I once saw this poor guy get caught up in a spectacle with this pretty girl who had a stink attitude. She created this big commotion with the poor guy just so she could get the attention of one of the Patriots defensive players. This poor guy asked her to dance, she turned to him and told him "You can't afford me and you must have gotten your clothes from the same pile that Steve Erkel donated to the Salvation Army" and she said it loud enough for the whole club to hear. I felt bad for the guy, but he should've known better than to approach a woman who was wearing her skirt so high up her thighs that if she bent over the club would've been shut down for not having a license for adult entertainment. I don't care how much liquor I had to drink, my balls would never grow big enough for me to approach a woman like that in public. My balls knew their limitations. I saw that same girl coming out of the back of a limousine wiping her mouth and fixing her hair on my way out the club at the end of the night. I was almost certain there was at least one football player from the Patriots in the limo. She had just serviced someone who thought nothing of her, but was more than willing to shut down the guy who would probably treat her like a lady.

It was easy for me to detect when things were going to go right on any given night when Dexter and I hung out at the club. I was always on cue when the shallow women were going to be disappointed after our introduction; it was as if they almost wanted to say, "Show me the money." I'm sure if they had time to go to an ATM with me, they'd know that I had a little bit of money saved and I would get more than a piece of ass from them. These women operated on the notion that "Birds of a feather flocked together." Sometimes, I found the look of disappointment on their faces amusing. Dexter knew that when we went out I never had high hopes for some of the low life women we met at the clubs. Dexter shared the same sentiments. He knew half the women at the club were looking for their next meal ticket and all they got from him was usually one meal before he disposed of them. Dexter was willing to invest in one meal before he slept with any woman and she had to be fine with no children. Dexter didn't want to deal with the baby mama drama. It wasn't that we put every woman at the club in a bunch, but the minority of them ruined it for the majority.

Dexter thought that I focused too much on people's perceptions of me. I know that was because he was not on the receiving end of the looks I got from women. I always felt that women didn't think I was cool or hip enough. If only Dexter had to walk in my shoes for one day, he would have understood my pain. When I was out with Dexter, most of the women who ended up keeping me company on his couch were mad at themselves by the end of the night for allowing her friend to get with Dexter first. I once heard a woman say that she wished she were more aggressive in her pursuit of Dexter. I never thought women could be so cruel. The one thing I admired in Dexter was the fact that he stood up for me no matter the outcome of the situation. I have watched Dexter dis some of the most beautiful women he's met when they had something cruel to say about me. Dexter never thought ass was more important than our friendship. He treated me like the nerdy little brother that he had to protect.

Dexter never allowed an opportunity to pass him by when it came to gloating about his accomplishments. He enjoyed letting the women he met know that he was a successful man and he worked hard for it. I never blamed him for it because I knew how hard he had worked to get to where he was. Dexter has always been a very ambitious person. He mapped out a plan to own his own garage by the time he turns 32 years old and he was well on his way. Most of the time, women were so impressed with Dexter's car alone that by the time they got to his place; their panties were uncontrollably wet. Dexter bought a 1995 528 BMW the last year after the model was introduced. He was able to get a great deal on it from his job at the BMW dealer. That car was his first love.

Everything about Dexter was clean except for his bad reputation as a man who had slept with over 300 women. At first, Dexter appeared to be every woman's dream. He could sweet-talk Martha Stewart into sleeping with him. He made it a rule not to sleep with any one woman more than three times no matter how good the woman was in bed or how gorgeous she was. Dexter was not looking to settle down anytime soon. He wanted to have his fun for as long as he could. In the public's eye, he was probably a perfect catch but little did they know...

I couldn't really blame Dexter for not wanting to settle down. After all, he was only thirty years old and hadn't yet accomplished the goals he had set for himself. What I did have a problem with was the fact that Dexter led these women on when he first met them. Dexter's game was just as cruel as the women who dissed me at every opportunity. He'd promise them the world and every imaginable dream that came with it. Most women thought of Dexter as Prince Charming until they slept with him for the third time and the phone calls stopped. That was how he went about his game. Dexter hated the fact that most women prayed for a man to bring them happiness. He had never met a woman who was happy with herself.

I never understood how he was able to sever ties with a woman after sleeping with her three times. He was able to control his emotions like no one I have ever known, he made his rules, and I guess he was sticking to them. Dexter also took every precaution not to have any children out of wedlock. He enjoyed the family life that his parents gave him and he wanted to do the same for his children in the future. The fact that Dexter saw how my mom struggled to make ends meet on her own may have played a significant role in his decision as well. Dexter loved my mother like his own and we both felt like we had two homes growing up. Dexter's dad was somewhat of a father figure to me too, but I always felt like I was intruding on his relationship with Dexter. It was my own shortcomings that made me feel that way.

At first glance, people could easily assume that everything in Dexter's life came easy for him. However, I knew how hard he had worked to get to where he was, and some things in his life did come quicker for him when compared to the rest of us. Like the time when he was promoted to a managerial position at his job, Dexter was running the BMW service department five years after he was initially hired. At the age of 25, he was earning over seventy five thousand dollars a year. He achieved success on merit and hard work. Being in his shadow all the time was tough on me at times. I spent six years in school to earn a master's degree and I was earning far less money than Dexter was. I couldn't get a woman if my life depended on it. In addition, no one noticed me unless I had toilet paper stuck to the bottom of my shoes coming out of a public bathroom. My life was just pathetic compared to Dexter's.

Life and Its Surprises

Life works in mysterious ways. For as long as Dexter and I have been friends, I have always lived in his shadow. To be honest, I was getting tired of living in my best friend's shadow. I didn't want it to strain our relationship, but I needed to reevaluate my life as a person and figure out why my life was the way it was. Dexter was living the life that most men dream of and I couldn't even get mine started. He had tried his best to make me part of the dream life and I couldn't fit it in; I had never learned to live like him. I had been playing it safe most of my life and it had gotten me nowhere. I was tired of finishing last all the time. No more Mr. Nice guy! I figured maybe if I lived on the edge a little, things might change. I didn't really want to change who I was as a person, but I wanted to improve the outlook on my social life.

Life on the edge was going to be a big change for me. I had to bury away the old conservative ways of living. However, I needed to take small steps towards my new life and I had to crawl before I walked as the old proverb says. I decided that I was going to start changing my life the week after that woman from the club crushed my ego. I felt like crap for a whole week after that incident. The first thing to do on my list was to invest $10.00 in that new Powerball jackpot that was over one hundred and fifty million dollars. Everyone was making a big deal of it, so I figured why not join in the fun. The old me would've never gambled my money away no matter how small the amount. What were the chances that a Black man in the hood would win this jackpot, anyway?

I have to admit that it didn't feel refreshing at all giving my ten dollars to the Indian clerk at the gas station for some damn lottery tickets. I started to think that I was too cheap to live on the edge after I handed him my money. I wondered if he would take the tickets back and reimburse my money after I bought them. I was sure I could have invested my ten dollars in a way where I would be guaranteed a return. Why did I waste my money? I thought. This new attitude I was trying to carry might have been just too costly for me. As much money Dexter spent on wining and dining women, he had never once complained about it. I couldn't do that; I would have had to limit my dates to once a week if I were dating as many women as he did. I didn't think this new life on the edge was going to be successful for me.

The end of the school year was fast approaching and I was looking forward to having a great summer in 2002. I was going to do things that summer that I had never done in my entire life. I wanted go to Jamaica for a week to hang out with Dexter for our annual getaway vacation. Dexter and I plan a week-long trip out of the country every year. We have visited quite a few countries since we entered the workforce. Our favorite place to visit was Barbados because the Barbadians were especially nice to tourists. We felt like we were in the motherland when we visited Barbados. Everyone there was very cordial. The folks in Barbados also knew how to party. Dexter especially loved Barbados because of the score of beautiful women that inhabited the island. Before I could do any vacation planning, I had to write myself a note to remind me to call Dexter to plan our vacation.

Before I got a chance to call Dexter, he called me to tell about this new girl that he had slept with who blew Halle Berry away with her beauty. Most brothers use Halle Berry as the barometer by which to judge the level of fineness in a woman. Sometimes I felt like Dexter was just rubbing in my face the fact that he was always sleeping with a new beautiful woman, but I knew honestly that was not at all his intention. Dexter, like most guys, couldn't keep his mouth shut about his new conquests and since I'm his best friend, I had to sit there and listen to every graphic detail about the dirty deeds. Yes! Most guys do kiss and tell. Since I was not really in the mood to listen to Mr. Braggadocio, I changed the subject to the Powerball jackpot that everyone had been talking about. Dexter however, quickly shut down my dream of ever winning the jackpot by asking me where I played my numbers. When I told him that I bought my ticket from the gas station on Massachusetts Avenue in Roxbury, he dismissed my chances of winning to none.

It was a well-known fact that most lottery winners were old couples that lived in rural America. It's not like they need the money most of the time because most of them are usually halfway to their grave. I would have been pissed if I won one hundred million dollars at eighty-five years old. God plays too many games. He'd allow people to go through their whole life suffering and all of a sudden decides he wants to bless them on the way to their grave. Forget about the saying that "it's never too late," it would be too damn late! What would I do with that kind of money when I'm either going to be battling Alzheimer's disease or some other terminal illness? Not to say that all elderly people succumb to these illnesses.

God must have known that I wouldn't have welcomed his blessings when I'm 85 years old, so he resolved to bless me while I was still a young man. After Dexter crushed my hopes of winning the lottery the night before, I went to bed regretting that I ever wasted my ten dollars on a dream. It was the first time I had ever gambled in my life and I did it as a way to prompt change in my life. So much for me trying to live on the edge, right? When I got to school the next morning, there was this big uproar at the school amongst the teachers about how someone from Roxbury had the winning numbers to the Powerball.

There was a lottery pool at the school that the teachers organized and they didn't even bother to mention it to me because I had turned them down each time in the past. Everyone at the school was happy that someone from the hood had finally won a big jackpot. I didn't have time to check my numbers as I had class successively for three periods that day. I had to wait until my lunch break to check my numbers. I always had an early lunch period since I started teaching and usually spent my time in the teacher's lounge reading the paper. My lunch period always came during fourth period for some reason and that was way too early to eat lunch.

Here I was a thirty-year-old teacher hoping that ten dollars worth of lottery tickets would change my life. I couldn't stop my hand from shaking as I pulled the lottery tickets out of my pocket. I had no clue what my numbers were because I had bought ten dollars worth of quick pick cash tickets. Also, I had never been so nervous in my life. My whole body was shaking as I read the newspaper. I had already turned the newspaper to the page where the lottery numbers were listed and I had glanced over the numbers a couple of times before reaching in my pocket to pull out my tickets. I set the paper on the table as I checked my numbers row by row. The first ticket containing five dollars worth of play was not a winner; I didn't even get one number out of five dollars worth of tickets. I threw the first ticket in the trashcan near the door. It was the first time that I ever swooshed anything in that trashcan. Whenever I tried swishing something in the trash before I always missed. I still had another five dollars worth of lottery numbers to go through.

I took the other ticket out of my pocket and started checking row by row once again. When I got to the fifth row, I noticed something very familiar to what I saw in the paper just minutes ago. The numbers seemed to be aligned the same way they were printed in the paper. At first, I could only remember five of the numbers and I knew for sure they all matched. It was the final and sixth number that I wasn't sure about. Therefore, I took another look in the paper to check the sixth number and to my surprise, it was the same number as the sixth number on my ticket. It was the Powerball number. I couldn't believe the numbers were 9-12-17-19- 23-30. I was actually sitting in the teachers' lounge holding a one hundred and fifty million dollar lottery ticket in my hand. I couldn't believe it and I didn't know how to react.

I calmly placed the ticket in my wallet, ripped out the winning numbers from the newspaper, and stuck it in my pocket. I went back to my classroom and continued with my lessons for the day. Something inside me still made me feel like I couldn't deprive my students of the opportunity to learn their lesson for the day. It was a Wednesday and I still had two more days left before the weekend. I was contemplating whether I would go back to the school to teach for the next two days or use two of the many sick days I had earned since my tenure at the school to think my situation through. The logical dedicated side of my brain won the argument and I settled to go back to the school the following day. I thought that my good fortune shouldn't be my students' misfortune.

I couldn't wait to get home to call my mother and tell her to quit her job. My mother had always been first in my life and I always dreamed of providing a better life for her. I knew working as a teacher made it close to impossible to realize that dream, but the man upstairs had other plans to make it happen. I wanted to keep my winnings as quiet as possible. Since my grandparents passed, only a couple of my aunts came around annually to check on my family. We weren't close to too many other family members and I knew once they found out that we were the winners of a $150,000,000.00 jackpot, they would start popping out of the woodwork.

Right after school let out, I went straight to my bank and obtained a safe deposit box where I placed my winning ticket along with the winning numbers from the paper. I wanted to make sure I kept the proof of the winning numbers from the paper. I never trusted the White institutions of America. They have a way of changing the rules on Black people with good arguments. I wanted to cover all the bases. I didn't want the winning numbers to change all of a sudden because I'm a black man. I have watched enough Court TV to convince me that any great lawyer can present a convincing enough argument in court that the winning numbers were announced by mistake to void my winnings. I was not taking any chances.

If police officers can be exonerated for crimes committed against people on videotapes in cities around the country, there was no telling what a good lawyer could do to take away my winnings. As many brothers as I watched get their ass whipped on videotapes, made me believe that white people see things in a whole different light than black folks. My winning numbers weren't going to be changed under no circumstances. I almost called Johnny Cochran to put him on alert just in case. Johnny is the only Black lawyer who has been successful against the justice system. I bet OJ still thanks God everyday that he invested in Johnny.

Life's Regrets

Winning all this money got me thinking about things that affected my life that I wished never happened. Why couldn't I win all this money a few years earlier when my grandmother was sick in the hospital? My grandmother went through a period of turmoil in her life when she was diagnosed with breast cancer and her illness took a toll on the family. My grandfather spent his whole life savings on treatment for her and needed more money after he sold their house to pay for her chemotherapy treatment at the hospital. Everybody in the family except for Uncle Pete chipped in to help with my grandmother's hospital bill.

Uncle Pete's excuse or theory as he wanted to call it was that he didn't want to see my grandmother suffer anymore, but most of us knew that he was just too cheap to contribute financially. He didn't mind spending lavishly on his high maintenance wife, but he had a problem helping to take care of his ill mother. My grandmother was a strong woman and watching her deteriorate was excruciating. I tried spending as much time with her as possible when she was in the hospital. Since my mother was already a nurse when my grandmother was diagnosed, she dedicated most of her time taking care of my grandmother after work. My aunts tried their best to help out the best way they could. My grandfather was my grandmother's pillar of strength throughout the whole ordeal.

We lost my grandmother to cancer because of money. The insurance company stopped paying for her medical bills after the hospital revealed the possibility that my grandmother might not ever have a full recovery. After my grandfather sold the house to offset some of the medical bills, his heart couldn't take her suffering anymore. Everything they had worked so hard for all their lives had diminished because of a disease. The chemotherapy treatment my grandmother was receiving at the hospital was just too expensive for the family to bear. She died eight months after her admission into the hospital. And even today, I still ask why I couldn't have won the lottery before she fell ill. I would give up the money in a minute to have my grandmother back.

The family had to come together again to bury my grandmother, Rose who was the matriarch of the family. Everyone pitched in to give her the best going away party and funeral that we could afford at the time. My grandmother died in peace knowing that all her children had made it in this cruel world. She went to a better place where she would be setting the foundation once again for her family. Her husband Willy, her four children and six grandchildren survived her.

A few months after my grandmother passed, my grandfather's heart couldn't withstand the loneliness anymore. He'd missed his life companion so much; he stopped eating. Life no longer had any meaning for him, he had come to live with my mother, and I after my grandmother died. My aunts Leslie and Anne came by to see him as often as they could, but Uncle Pete last saw him at my grandmother's funeral. Uncle Pete always felt that my grandparents did more for the girls than they did for him. He harbored a lot of resentment towards my grandparents. We thought my grandparents were easier on Uncle Pete because he was a boy. As a boy, he was given more freedom. However, Uncle Pete never quite understood that and he misinterpreted their treatment of him as neglect.

Soon after we buried my grandmother, we had to bury my grandfather as well. The old man just was not the same after his beloved wife died and he died in his sleep probably of loneliness. My grandparents had been together for over forty years and they were definitely bound at the heart. Like my grandmother, grandpa, went home to a better place to join his beloved wife. My mother bore most of the expenses for his funeral because he was living with her. I also helped out as much as I could, but my graduate tuition limited my ability to help. I was in my last year of graduate school when my grandfather died. My mother financed some of the cost of the funeral because we didn't have the cash to pay for it all up front. I had promised to help her with the payments after I was done with my degree and I started soon after I graduated.

My grandparents instilled in all their children, the importance of family, but after their death, I felt that most of it fell on deaf ears; the family was not as close anymore and Uncle Pete alienated everybody. Sometimes, I feel like my grandparents are turning over in their graves when they see what's going on with their children on Mother Earth. I learned a lot from my grandparents and I hope that I can develop the resilience that they both had. I know that they're both watching over the family even though we're not close anymore. Maybe I won the lottery because it was supposed to bring my family back together. You never know why things happen in life but I'm sure the money will bring a lot of family members back to the house.

I stayed with my mother until I received my master's degree from the University of Massachusetts in Boston. It was hard leaving her alone in the house after I graduated, but I needed to become a man and be on my own. I continued to go by her house everyday for six months straight until I settled into my condominium. I got a bargain on my condo in the Jamaica Plain section of Boston and I couldn't pass it up. It was a once in a lifetime deal that Dexter had discovered for my mother and me understood why I had to get it. I had to get used to being on my own without worrying about my mother, but over the years, she's appeared to adjust well without me. My mother still tells me everyday how proud she is of me and I'm just as proud of her.

Planning a New Life

One of my first concerns after I found out that I won the money was the fact that I hadn't been so lucky in the past with the ladies. I wondered how that aspect of my life was going to change and how I could keep things in perspective. I heard the stories of millionaires like MC Hammer who went broke after having so much money and I didn't want to fall into that trap. I planned to remain as frugal as ever, but I was sure that Dexter was going to try to beat the frugality out of me once he learned that I was a multi-millionaire. Being my best friend automatically earned him the right to some fringe benefits. Planning my next move was the most difficult thing that I had to do. I didn't want the whole world to know that I was rich, but the lottery had a requirement that all their winners make a public appearance to accept their winnings.

I think the lottery commission folks want the winnings to be spent as fast as possible. They make it a requirement for people to appear on TV to claim their prize so the whole world could have an idea who the winners are. They know that the more people who knew that I had money, the more that would come and ask for a loan. There's a motive behind everything done in America. What's wrong with anonymity? I wanted to remain anonymous, but there was no way around it or, so I thought.

Since I didn't want the whole world to know that I was about to become a rich man, I only had one other choice for a claimant. I know you're not thinking that I was going to ask Dexter to claim my prize, right? He and I are best friends, but I would never trust his flashy behind with one hundred and fifty million dollars. Can you imagine the havoc Dexter would wreak on the world if he got his hand on that kind of money? Sure, he would hook me up, but Dexter would still have to be Dexter. The only person I could trust with something of that magnitude was my one and only mother. She sacrificed her whole life for me and I was willing to bet my whole winnings on the fact that I could trust her. But first, I had to tell her about my winnings. I was hoping that she wouldn't get a heart attack from the good news. I bought as much Bayer aspirin as I could because I heard they could prevent a heart attack. Like I said before, I don't like taking chances. I certainly didn't want to have a misfortune offset my good fortune. I didn't want my mother dropping dead on me.

I called my mother's house the evening after I learned of my good fortune. She wasn't home yet, so I went over there and waited for her. I always had an extra set of keys to my mother's place and her car keys in case of an emergency. First, I stopped by the flower shop on American Legion Highway and Walk Hill Road to get her a set of dozen roses. I waited for a half hour watching television in my mother's living room, the same way I used to when I was a kid. When my mother finally got home, she was happy to see a fresh arrangement of roses on her table along with a card telling her how much I love her. My mother didn't make anything of it as she was used to me buying her flowers for no special occasion. She was the type of mother who deserved more than roses and flowers, but I couldn't afford to give her too much on my teacher's salary. My mother was always appreciative of the gifts she received from me and she never forgot a good gesture.

What my mother wasn't used to was my black ass being at her house at 11:00 at night on a school night. My mother knew that I was a hermit who went to bed early every night so I could get up early for work in the morning. I pulled my mother towards me as she made her way from the dining room to the living room. I hugged her as hard as I could for as long as I could without suffocating her. She didn't know what was on my mind and she assumed the worst. My mother, with tears welled up in her eyes, started ranting about how she would still love me no matter what. She continued on about how she's always sensed that I was homosexual and she didn't really have a problem with it and the fact that I never brought a woman home to her; raised her suspicions since I was an adolescent.

She went on to say that, she also thought that Dexter was my lover because only a homosexual would pay so much attention to the way he looked, referring to Dexter. She said, "I knew you and Dexter had a funny and weird relationship from the time that he used to visit you at school and leaving you money. Also, no man that I know is so overly concerned with the way he looks. At least he's the girl in the relationship, right?" I had to step back and tell mom to chill with all that homosexual crap. I couldn't believe my mother thought I was gay because I never brought a girl home. She had misinterpreted my friendship with Dexter my whole life. I wondered what she must've been thinking when I used to have sleepovers with Dexter as a kid. Maybe that's why she insisted we kept the bedroom door open at all times.

Here I was thinking about how surprised my mother was going to be when I told her that we were millionaires, but instead, she shocked the hell out of me. I wondered how many other people thought I was giving off gay vibes. I'm sure Dexter would find this little episode amusing. As much as Dexter thought of himself as a man's man, he'd be surprised to find out that a fifty-year-old woman thought he was gay. I had to set my mother straight on this whole gay notion about me. I told my mother that I wasn't gay and I've never been gay, and if I were gay I'd be more concerned with my appearance too, not to discredit Dexter's masculinity. For some reason, I didn't buy that my mother believed me because her response to me was reminiscent of what she used to tell me when I was scared as a little boy. She said, "Sure you're not gay. You don't have to pretend for me." Only she used to say, "Sure you're not scared, you don't have to pretend for me." My mother was tripping!

My mother threw me totally off track and I completely forgot the purpose of my visit. It was getting late and I knew she was tired, so I decided to let her get some rest and I headed out the door. As I was walking to the car, I remembered that I was there to tell her she didn't have to report to work the next day because we were rich. I also remembered that Thursday was my mother's day off from work. So, I proceeded to go home hoping to tell my mother the good news the following day because she was off work. On my way home, I kept replaying in my head the conversation I just had with my mother and I couldn't help but laugh it off. My mother is one funny lady and it was also reassuring to know that my mother loved Dexter and I unconditionally.

After I got home, I couldn't hold my winnings a secret anymore; I had to let somebody know of my good fortune. My mother should've been the first to know, but I was derailed while I was over her house and she was tired. After taking my shower, it was a little past midnight and I couldn't sleep. I kept tossing and turning in bed. Finally, I decided to go down the list and call the next most important person to me, which was Dexter. I dialed Dexter's number knowing he was probably in deep sleep. The phone rang about four times before the answering machine finally picked up. Dexter had a habit of screening his calls through his answering machine because of all the women harassing him. When the answering machine came on, I screamed "Dexter! Dexter! Yo! Leave that ass alone and pick up the phone." He must've rolled over a few times before he picked up the phone and said, "I hope this is an emergency." I said, "You better believe it." I knew Dexter would welcome my good fortune because as my best friend he would benefit just as much from it. I knew Dexter was planning to open his own auto shop in the near future; I was hoping to make his future plans happen sooner than later.

By the time Dexter fully woke up out of his sleep, I had been yelling in his ears to wake up a million times. He finally confirmed he was awake by saying, "What you got to tell me at this time?" I said to him "Man, you can't believe what happened to me today!" He responded, "You finally got to see what ass taste like, I'm happy for you, man. Now, let me go to sleep." I had to convince him that it was more important than that and he had to be fully awake and braced himself for what I was about to tell him. Dexter grew very impatient with me and screamed through the phone "What man! Say it already!" I was like "You ready for this? I won the Powerball jackpot!" Dexter must've jumped out of bed the instant he heard my news. He screamed through the phone "Get the hell out of here! You're pulling my leg." I said, "I'm serious, bro" He said, "You mean we're rich!" I said, "Yeah bro. We're about one hundred and fifty million dollars rich." I told Dexter he was the first person to find out about it.

I wanted to hang up the phone after I told Dexter the good news, but he was too excited to go back to sleep. I told him I needed to go to sleep so I could wake up for work the next day. Dexter yelled through the phone "You're out of your mind? You better tell those bastards to kiss your ass. Even I, ain't going to work tomorrow." I told him that I owed my kids that much. Dexter told me that I didn't owe my kids a thing and that's why they had substitute teachers. Dexter wanted to hop on the first plane to the Caribbean to start enjoying life. I had to slow him down and told him that I needed to sit down with my mother and him to figure out what to do with all this money. Since my mother was off the following day and Dexter convinced me to call in sick at work, I decided that I'd meet with my mother and Dexter in the morning. Dexter and I hung up the phone feeling very excited about our future.

I must have lain in bed for another hour after I hung up the phone with Dexter trying to figure out what I was going to do with my life. I knew I was going to get a check for at least seventy million dollars after taxes, but I didn't know how to be fair with Dexter. I didn't know if Dexter still wanted to pursue his dream of being an auto shop owner and I didn't have any plans of my own other than teaching. I didn't have any kind of entrepreneurial sense. I knew my mother wasn't going to be so difficult to please. All I needed to do for her was to buy her a new house, a new car and give her a couple of million dollars to enjoy. My mother was just as frugal as I was and she could make a couple million dollars last a lifetime.

I knew that I also had to hook up the immediate family members, like my mother's two sisters who tried to stay close to our family via telephone. I planned to give away about twenty million dollars to friends and family. Five million of that twenty Million was going to Dexter and his family. Dexter's parents always treated me as if I was their second son and I wanted to show my gratitude. Sometime during the night, while I was doing all this thinking and sorting out my plans, I dozed off.

The Big Misinterpretation

I woke up the next day thinking that everything that I ever dreamed of giving to my mother was about to come to fruition. Lady Luck had finally blessed us after all these years. It was early that morning around 6:00 and the first thing I did was call my job to tell them that I wasn't coming in so they could request a substitute teacher for my classes for the day. I cleaned my house; read the morning paper for a couple of hours then called my mother around 8:30 to tell her not to go anywhere until I arrived at her house. I told her it was very important that I saw her and I would be by her house in an hour or so. My mother normally ran her errands on her days off and it usually took all day. I didn't want her to disappear on me for the whole day. It's always good to give my mother a heads up when I need her time because that woman is always on the go. My mother's like the Energizer Bunny, she just keeps going and going and going...

Dexter showed up at my house at 9:00 AM sharp. That marked the first time that this Negro had ever been on time for anything. A lot of money can erase that whole "Colored People Time" concept to "Can't wait to be on time to see the money." I guess he was just as anxious about the plans as I was. I hadn't even gotten dressed yet when he rang the doorbell. I stepped out the shower and went to open the door with a towel around my waist. Dexter went to the bathroom as I went to the bedroom to get dressed. Not a moment too soon, my doorbell rang again and I still had the towel around my waist. This time, my mother came by to find out why it was so important that I see her. I opened the door to let my mother in and as she came in, Dexter was just coming out of the bathroom zipping up his fly. The look on my mother's face said it all.

The situation as it was, could have easily insinuated that Dexter and I had just gotten busy. However, the reality is that neither of us is gay nor would we ever engage in homosexual activities. To make the situation worst, the first words out of Dexter's mouth as he came out the bathroom were "I needed that." Of course, he was referring to relieving himself, but my mother drew her own conclusions. I don't know why my mother didn't just wait for me to come to her house as planned. It was a scene that I didn't even want to bother explaining to her.

Even though my conscience was clear, my mother made me feel dirty. She looked at me with this look of disgust in her face. It wasn't disgust because she thought I was gay, it was the kind of look she used to give when I lied to her as a child. My mother still thought I was lying about being gay. I gave her a kiss on the cheek, as it is customary in our family. Dexter was surprised to see her too and he went over and gave her a hug. My mother took one look at us and asked, "Are you boys happy?" I was thinking to myself "What the hell did she mean by that?" It almost sounded like she was sarcastically asking us if we were gay. Dumb ass Dexter jumped in to say, "Of course we're happy. We've been happy since the day we met each other." That knucklehead had no idea how deep a hole he was digging for us. How was I going to convince my mother that her only son was not lying to her? I used to lie to my mom when I was a kid to avoid punishment, but that was a long time ago. I was now a man and my mother still thought I was the same little lying bastard that I was as a child. God help her!

I had to hurry up and get dressed, so I went to my room and left my mother and Dexter in the living room. While I was in my room, I could hear my mother and Dexter conversing. Dexter asked my mother if she heard the good news yet. My mother asked "What good news?" At this point, my mother was thinking the good news was about Dexter and me taking the next step in our "supposed" homosexual relationship.

My mother asked Dexter how he felt about me and his reply was "Other than my parents, Malcolm is the most important person to me." My mother continued, "At least you guys truly love each other. Whatever next step you guys take, I'm sure it will be the best for you two." Dexter replied, "We plan on keeping this relationship tight till death due us part." My mother looked at him and said, "I see. I'm happy that you guys are confident that this relationship can last a lifetime." Dumb ass Dexter turned to her again and said, "No doubt!" The final piece to the puzzle was when my mother asked Dexter if his parents knew about our relationship and he told her that his parents have known about our relationship since we were boys and they always treated me like their second son. My mother told Dexter "You know you've always been like a second son to me too." Dexter answered " I know that Ms. Davis." My mother told him that he could call her mom since he's been part of the family and was planning to be a permanent part of it.

I couldn't believe that my mother and my best friend were sitting in my living room having a conversation that neither of them had any idea about. They were both on different subjects drawing different conclusions. Eventually, I was going to have to have a sit down with both of them to explain the little misunderstanding between them. For now, my mother was going to believe what she believed and there was nothing I could do about it.

After I finished getting dressed, I walked out to the living room and the first words out of Dexter's mouth were "I'm tired of you wearing those khaki pants." My mother asked him "Why don't you show him how to dress better?" He answered, "I've been trying to make this man more stylish for years, but he never wants to listen." That statement couldn't sound gayer. Dexter put the metro in metrosexual way before the word was invented and I had enough of all these gay innuendoes. I wanted to change the subject to my lottery winnings. I asked for everyone's attention, my mother and Dexter stopped talking long enough for me to address them.

As I began to tell my mother about my lottery winnings, she interrupted me saying, "I already know the good news. Dexter made it clear to me that you guys are gonna get married." Dexter turned to my mother and exclaimed "What!" My mother looked at him and said, "You just told me you two are gonna take your relationship to the next level." Dexter turned to me and asked, "What is she talking about?" I told him that my mother thought we were a gay couple. Dexter couldn't believe what I just told him. My mother turned to him and said, "You gave him money when he was in college, you guys go away every year and you get your nails done and a haircut every week. If that's not gay, I don't know what is. You are as fruity as Little Richard to me." Dexter was speechless and the only thing he could say was "What?" I told Dexter not to worry about it and that I would explain it to him later.

The Plan

At that time, I felt we needed to move forward with more important things other than Dexter's and my sexual orientation. I told my mother not to interrupt until after I said what I had to say. I began by telling her that I wanted to see her because I wanted to tell her that I was the winner of the $150,000,000.00 Powerball jackpot that everyone was talking about. My mother told me that she had no time for jokes and I better not had been playing a joke on her. I told her I wasn't joking that we were millionaires. I told my mother she didn't have to work a single day for the rest of her life anymore. She worked two jobs as a CNA (Certified Nursing Assistant) for 17 years in order to provide for her family and had only quit her second job after I graduated from high school.

My mother was also my inspiration because she went back to school to earn a Degree in Nursing right after I left for college. She and I were in college at the same time. My mother took advantage of the tuition assistance program offered at her job. It took her three years to complete her Bachelor's Degree in Nursing because she attended school year round. I couldn't ask for a better role model. She inspired me a lot in life and it was time for her to sit back, relax and start enjoying life.

I may have been happy about my newfound wealth, however, I had a problem with the fact that people would learn that I was wealthy through the media. I didn't have anybody special in my life and I knew the kind of money I was about to get, everyone who came into my life was going to play the special role. I wanted to find a woman who loved me for me, not my wealth. My whole life, I could not meet a genuine woman and I didn't want money to change that. If I were going to meet anybody, it would have to be genuine. I decided I was gonna let my mother accept the money because she had no problem brushing people off and not too many people knew I was her son. At least, the greedy female vultures didn't know I was her son anyway. My mother agreed to accept the money and listed me as a beneficiary just in case something happened to her. My mother had always added my name to all her accounts since I was a kid so that I would always have access in case of emergencies. However, as far as the world was concerned, I was just a working man.

On the day my mother went to pick up the check, Dexter and I rented tuxedoes, a limousine and dark sunglasses, and acted like we were her bodyguards. I told my mother to tell the Powerball people that I picked up the tickets for her from the gas station on Massachusetts Avenue in Roxbury. We opted to get the cash instead of the payment installments. Who has that kind of time to be waiting for a check every year for twenty years? Besides, too many illnesses ran in my family, I was not even guaranteed the next day. After my mother collected the $70,000,000.00 check from the lottery commissioner, we drove straight to the bank to deposit the check into her account. Afterwards, we drove to this little posh restaurant on Newbury Street. The three of us had a great dinner while the limo driver waited in the car for us.

Newbury Street in Boston is the equivalent of Rodeo Drive in Los Angeles or Fifth Avenue in New York. There, you could find some of the hottest designer boutiques Boston has to offer. Such as, Armani Exchange, French Connection, Versace, Prada, Gucci, Burberry, Guess, Ralph Lauren just to name a few. I had a few thousand dollars in my savings and so did Dexter and my mother, we all decided to visit some of the upscale boutiques on Newbury Street and splurged a little. We didn't have access to the check yet, but we sure as hell used all the money we had access to in our savings.

My mother couldn't get used to the prices on Newbury Street, so Dexter and I secretly bought her a few things with our own money. To tell you the truth, I was a little disturbed by the prices on Newbury Street myself. I was so used to getting my clothes from Marshall's; it took great convincing from Dexter for me to spend about seven thousand dollars on Newbury Street on designer items. Dexter must've spent his whole lifesaving because we hardly had any room left in the limo to fit his bags.

After we were done, we went back to the limo a few hours later. During the ride on the way home, all we could think about was the sudden change in our lives. I was with the two people I loved most in the world and I was wealthy beyond my dreams. I sat through dinner thinking about what I was going to do with all that money. After dinner, the limo driver dropped us home, as we were tired and beaten from all the shopping. We gave the driver a five hundred dollar tip for spending the day with us and sent him on his way.

Most people would think that our lives would be easier from then on, but they couldn't be more wrong. I knew Dexter always wanted to have his own business and I wanted to encourage his dream. I offered Dexter five million dollars as a friend and he was gracious in accepting my offer. I also told him that he had to look out for his parents from his share of the money. I didn't care how much he gave them; my conscience was clear as long as I knew that I told him to take care of his family. I knew Dexter loved his parents too much to neglect them.

My mother knew that I was going to take care of her; however, I also wanted my mother to take care of the rest of the family. I knew my mother could do a better job handing out money to the family than I could. I also had to include a few thousands for Jessie even though I hadn't heard from her in a while. Jessie was the kind of friend that I only heard from when she wasn't involved in a relationship with a man. She wasn't a million dollar friend. Nevertheless, she was still a good friend. After Jess and I graduated from college, our relationship was not the same.

We had to wait a few days for the check to clear in my mother's account before we could start handing out gift checks to friends and family. Dexter gave his two weeks notice at his job and my mother did the same. Dexter wanted to make the best of his time by spending most of his free time looking for a good location for the new shop that he wanted to open. Dexter was probably the most ambitious person that I have ever met. His immediate reaction to his share of the money was to make it work for him. Meanwhile, I continued to go to work without saying a word to anybody at my job. I wasn't ready to give up my job just yet. Besides, I only had a couple of weeks left before summer vacation began.

At night, I reflected on the new changes that were going to take place in my life. There was so much I wanted to do for my community and the deprived children of Boston; I didn't even know where to start. I wanted to donate about five hundred thousand dollars to the Dana Farber Cancer Research Institute in honor of my grandmother. But more importantly, I wanted to offer the kids in Boston an alternative to the streets. I wanted to open an Art Center for kids. Those were my future plans, but first, I had to take care of me.

It had been ten days since we deposited the check and it finally cleared. Since my name was already on the account, I could start splurging right away. My mother insisted on writing me a check for forty million dollars leaving thirty million in the joint account. She wanted me to have the money in my account because she didn't trust having all that money in one account. My mother was also a very frugal woman and I didn't know how much money she'd planned to give away to the family. She told me that I could use as much as twenty five million of the thirty million dollars that was in the account that I shared with her if I needed.

My mother was planning to spend no more than five million on herself and her family. My mother had her reasons for being frugal. As hard as she worked her entire life, she found it difficult to waste money. My mother was not raised with a silver spoon in her mouth and she wasn't about to hand anybody a silver spoon. She's always wanted the best for me and she worked hard to make sure that I grew up to be a respectful, intelligent and educated man. The first order was for her to get a new car because her eight-year-old Toyota Camry had been acting up. I took her to a few dealerships in Boston to pick out a car, but she was having a hard time choosing one. Instead, I surprised her with a brand new BMW 745 IL. Although my mother had upgraded her car, she refused to move from her neighborhood.

I asked Dexter out to dinner on the day that the check cleared. We went to this Thai restaurant on Commonwealth Avenue across the Boston University Bridge. Dexter and I always enjoyed Thai food and this little restaurant on Commonwealth Avenue offered the best Thai food. As I sat there with Dexter waiting for the waiter to come by with our drinks, I felt the need to open up to him about the complications in my life. Other than my mother, Dexter knew me best and sometimes I think that he even knew me better than my mother did. She thought I was gay after all.

Dexter and I were close enough to talk about anything. I wanted to express to Dexter my concerns regarding my luck with women. I felt destitute and desperate. I was thirty years old and I hadn't had sex, not by choice, but because I hadn't found anybody who found me cool enough to give me some ass. I have to be somewhat honest here. I also had my own standards too when it came to sex. Dexter didn't know that I hadn't had sex because he always assumed that I was getting it on with some of the girls he brought along for me when we went out. That was not the case and I'm not sure if I would have accepted pity booty anyway.

Dexter recognized our differences, but he focused more on the commonalities. As far as he was concerned, I was a good guy who hadn't yet found the right woman. I wanted to find the right woman before I needed Viagra to get an erection. Dexter hinted that the women would start rolling in the minute I got my new Benz and the big house in the suburb. I told him that wasn't how I intended to find a woman. Dexter has always had a nice car, clothes and a condo, and I'm not even sure if he knew the reasons why so many women flocked to him. Most women have a tendency to look at the superficial first before getting to know a person and I didn't want to meet those kinds of women. Dexter suggested that I stepped up my game in order to get a good woman.

For starters, he wanted me to start dressing better so I could be more appealing to the opposite sex. Dexter also made a valid point that as much as we'd like to kid ourselves that aesthetics are not important to us, the world judges most people on aesthetics alone. I guess I never looked at it that way. Dexter also suggested that I go to the gym, not because of women, but to gain confidence in myself and to improve my health. I also agreed with him on that. I hadn't exercised since I left college and I was truly out of shape.

Dexter vowed to get me into shape and get me out on the dating scene successfully in no time. However, I wanted to add one condition. I didn't want to get a Benz and I didn't want to get a big house until after I met my dream girl. Dexter got very blunt with me and told me that if I wasn't going to get a new house, I at least needed to make my place look better for my prospects. He told me that women didn't like slobs and a woman would always respect a man who has something to offer. Dexter told me "Women are no different than men. We're all looking for someone who has something to bring to the table, and why can't we accept that they want the same thing?" I saw his point.

The whole time I was looking for a woman, I never took the time to take a look at myself. Beside my education and sense of humor and my good manners, I really didn't have anything else to offer a woman and it took Dexter to make me realize that. I decided to donate the furniture in my apartment along with $20,000 to Goodwill and hired a decorator to do my apartment over. I wanted to keep it modest with no extravagance.

I made the decision to stay at my job for another year and keep my apartment until I met Ms. Right. I also changed from driving my 1989 Toyota Corolla to a modest Honda Accord. I had actually become the middleclass man that I should've been before my good fortune. Dexter on the other hand, couldn't be anything but himself. He went and bought the best-looking CL600 Mercedes Benz that his money could buy and the nicest house in Norwood, MA. Dexter also opened his new auto shop on Blue Hill Avenue where his service was in high demand. Dexter's plan had also changed from owning one shop to owning a chain of them in the inner city. He rented out his old condominium to a kid who had just graduated from law school who fell in love with the apartment. Dexter's game with the ladies was about to reach another level and I thank God everyday that I was there to witness the whole thing.

Dexter didn't wait too long to get us in the gym at Bally's in Cambridge, MA. We settled on a three-day work out schedule. Dexter already had a membership at the Reggie Lewis Center where he used to work out regularly, but the center didn't offer the kind of beauties he was looking for. The fact that he had slept with most of the good-looking women at the center already factored into his decision to join Bally's. It was all about starting over. Even though Bally's was a little bit out of the way for both of us, Dexter enjoyed the platoon of women who frequented the place. Again, Dexter would have a much better time working out than me because he was already muscular and the women at the gym were just as lost in the men as we were in them. Dexter wore tank tops and muscle shirts while I tried my best not to expose anything at all for the first few weeks.

Let the Good Times Roll

The final day of the school year came and as promised, I threw my students the party of their lives. I had five periods of classes that day and I wanted to reward all my good students for their hard work for the school year. I had this local catering company cater a small party for each of my classes. Each period I had a new group of students and with each group, we had fresh food. In the past, I handed out candy and other affordable goods that the kids could take with them. This time around, I brought a nice portable CD player to the school and I partied all day long with my students. I rewarded some of the best students with parted gifts, which consisted mostly of electronic educational items they could use to do their homework. I bought a few planners, calculators, laptops, and books for my better students. We had a lot of fun and at the end of the day; I gave the portable CD player to one of my students who had complained that his family didn't have a stereo at home. I made sure that an adult was able to pick the students up from school to help carry the gift items home. I didn't want to risk having anybody get jumped on the street by the jealous thugs. We ended the school year with a bang!

Some of my students questioned how I was able to throw them such a lavish party, I told them it took planning and I had been saving for it for a while. I enjoyed watching the joy of a goodtime on their faces. For a while, they were able to forget about all the troubles of the world and just act like children. Most of my students came from low-income families who could not afford anything beyond their basic needs. It was hard for some of my smartest students to concentrate on their homework because they were hungry most of the time. I believe that no child can reach his or her potential on an empty stomach and I tried to eliminate that to an extent. There were times when I bought lunch for some of them because hunger was written all over their faces. One of the reasons I wanted to go back to the school to work for another year, was to ensure that the kids who couldn't afford lunch had a way to eat. I wanted to pick up the tab for all those kids who weren't qualified for free lunch at school. I wanted to encourage a few more kids and give them hope for a brighter future.

Since I was no longer in a financial bind, I could afford to get my haircut every week as Dexter suggested. I changed my hairstyle all together. I cut down the messy low Afro that I had been wearing for years to a close faded hairstyle with the waves going around my head in a circular motion, which required a lot of brushing and maintenance. I went all out with my new hairstyle; I bought hair products, brushes and a wave cap. I have to say that that new hairstyle brought out my features better than before. I also decided to grow a goatee, which added to my maturity. I felt more distinguished as a man with my new look. My goatee finally fully grew after trying for more than ten years.

One of the things I was reluctant to change about myself was my wardrobe. I always felt comfortable wearing my khakis, but Dexter introduced me to a couple of new materials that were just as comfortable as my cotton khakis. I discovered linen for the summer and I loved it. I went crazy buying everything made of linen that summer. I bought pants, shirts, shorts, hats, drawstrings and any other accessories they offered at the stores. I also discovered wool for the winter and fall. I bought quite a few outfits to bring me up to date with the times. I was in vogue and it felt good. I had a complete makeover and I loved it. However, there was one limit to my makeover; I refused to get a manicure and pedicure. It was bad enough that my mother thought I was gay, but I didn't want to actually add to her suspicions. I did cut my own nails every week to keep them looking neat.

I can honestly say that my confidence as a person started to increase after I made those minor changes in my life and I have Dexter to thank for that. It was the first time in my life I felt like I was a desirable person. I didn't want to flaunt anything that would attract the kind of attention that I wasn't looking for, so I restricted my wardrobe to mostly conservative colors close to my old style. I wore a lot of tan, off-white, blue, white, cream and other soft colors during the summer and the regular dark colors for the winter. I also bought a few light scented colognes to accessorize my new look. I didn't want to be overly conspicuous.

I always liked the idea of going to Starbucks to have a latte while reading a good book, but in my former situation, I was too cheap to spend that kind of money on gourmet coffee. Starbucks was about to gain a new customer in me and I was looking forward to the peace and quiet and a different environment. I didn't want to act like a buppy, but I enjoyed reading. I was overly conservative with my spending as a teacher. I didn't realize how cheap I was until after I won the lottery. I started hanging out at the local Starbucks down in Copley Square during my summer vacation from work. It was refreshing to finally get a few glances from the opposite sex. People made me feel like I had cosmetic surgery or something. I guess I had a complete makeover without realizing it.

I read a couple of good books for the better part of the first two weeks of the summer after school closed and I was getting tired of the routine of going to Starbucks everyday. I can't stand monotony for too long. I wanted to do something fun and exciting. I hadn't heard from Jessie in a while, so I decided to give her a call to see what she was up to. It was an early

Wednesday afternoon when I decided to call Jessie at work to arrange a meeting for lunch. Of course, I told her it was my treat. Jessie was one of those women who always had pity on me when it came to spending. Because she had her MBA and was earning top dollars at her job, she always wanted to pick up the tab when we went out. I insisted on treating Jessie to lunch before I went to meet with her.

She was surprised to see me pull up in my brand new Honda Accord when I picked her up. She knew as miserly as I was, I wouldn't have spent money on a new car unless I got a major raise at work. As she approached the car, I got out of the driver's side to go to the passenger's side to open the door for her. Jessie stood there, looked at me, and said, "Are we making Principal money now? When did you become Principal?" I could only laugh at her comments. I may have been driving a Honda, but it was the top of the line Honda SE with the leather interior, V6 engine and all the other perks. Jessie was happy to see me, as I was to see her.

While it may be true in most cases that teachers don't earn enough money for the rigorous work that they do, but some people take the salary thing to the extreme sometimes. They act like we're close to being homeless or something. At least, I was able to live comfortably on a teacher's salary. Sometimes, I wonder if Jessie made her comments out of concern, or to ridicule me because she thought I was beneath her. I could never quite read her approach to the whole situation. I also didn't care what she thought in the past because she always picked up the tab when we went out. As long as she was paying, she could've thought about it anyway she wanted to as far as I was concerned.

Anyway, I made plans to take Jessie to one of the restaurants at the Copley Mall for lunch. I pulled up to the valet, surprising

Jessie even more. I left my car with the valet and took Jessie upstairs. Jessie hadn't noticed my new look yet. Out of the blue, she told me that something about me was different. I asked her, "different how?" She said she couldn't pinpoint what it was right away, but it was refreshing. I wanted Jessie to figure out the changes in me without giving her any clues.

It had been a few months since Jessie and I saw each other and I was sure that was her reasons for not recognizing my new style at all. She was so used to the old dull Malcolm she didn't know how to react to the new one. Jessie had always been a concerned friend who made sure things were okay with me. She pressed on about if I could afford to do what I was doing and I assured her everything was fine. The waitress came around and we ordered our lunch. I told Jessie that she could have anything on the menu, and not to worry about a thing. She was hesitant at first, but when I pulled out a couple of crispy hundred dollar bills out of my pocket, she felt more at ease. I ordered the shrimp scampi and Jessie ordered her favorite steak and potato. While we were eating, Jessie unexpectedly screamed, "You had your hair cut!" Embarrassingly enough, half the people at the restaurant turned around to look at the bozo with the new haircut, who happened to be me. I almost went under the table to hide permanently.

Throughout lunch, Jessie and I tried to catch up on what was happening in our lives. I allowed Jessie to talk first because I enjoyed listening to her tales about her sexual escapades with some of these so-called players who couldn't deliver, according to her. Jessie was seeing this guy who supposedly was a doctor and she was still trying to feel the guy out to see if he was a potential suitor. He seemed like a great guy on paper. He was a thirty-five year-old doctor with a PHD in Psychology. He had a practice in Cambridge where he grew up. I could tell Jessie was feeling this guy, so I reserved all comments until I saw Dexter. Even though Dexter claimed he couldn't stand Jessie, he didn't mind talking about her. She said a few things about this guy that raised my suspicions but I didn't want to dash her hopes, so I kept quiet.

By the time Jessie and I finished our lunch, it was almost time for her to return to work for a meeting she had scheduled at 2:30. I wanted to spend a few more minutes with my friend, but she had to go. We went back to the valet to retrieve my car so I could take her back to work. As we stood there waiting for the car, Jessie noticed I was wearing drawstring linen pants and a v-neck short sleeved linen shirt. She commented that she liked my clothes and after a close examination of my body, she finally discovered that I was sporting some newly developed muscles on my arms. She complimented me on my new look then we got in the car and left.

On our way back to Jessie's job, I told her that I had won a huge sum of money from the lottery and I had a check for two hundred and fifty thousand dollars for her. She looked at me like I was crazy at first, then she asked "Really?" I told her, "Yes." Not that she needed any money from me. She was already living the high life on her six-figure salary. Jessie was very independent and self-sufficient. She was a homeowner and drove a convertible BMW. I only gave her the money because we were friends and I knew she could always use some extra cash. Who in the world would turn down a quarter of a million free dollars anyway?

Jessie was happy for me and even happier for the gift I gave her and she gave me the biggest hug. I didn't tell her how much money I won because I knew that I was going to be buying a lot of expensive gifts for all her future birthdays and holidays. We hugged once more as she made her way back to work. I told her not to forget to give me a call later that night because I wanted to talk to her about something important. Because Jessie was pressed for time, I didn't get a chance to talk to her about what I really wanted to talk to her about. I should've known that we had too much to catch up on and there was no way I was gonna get around to asking her about coming to Jamaica with Dexter and me for a week.

I knew it was going to be a hard sell getting Jessie and Dexter to go to Jamaica with me for a week. I wanted to go somewhere and have fun with my closest friends. Dexter hated being around Jessie and she hated Dexter even more. I knew I was going to have to lie to each one of them and con them into going to Jamaica with me without either of them knowing about it. Early that evening I called Dexter and told him to pack his bag because we were going to Negril, Jamaica for a week on an all-inclusive paid vacation. I knew Dexter wouldn't think twice about my offer because he needed a break from his daily routine and a breather from the new business that he was trying to get off the ground. Dexter also could never resist the temptation of the beautiful women of the Caribbean. Dexter was just as excited as I to go to Jamaica and the first question out of his mouth was "When do we leave?" I hadn't booked the vacation just yet, so I told him I'd get back to him. Dexter asked me to give him a couple of days to get his business in order before setting a definite date for the trip.

Now that Dexter was on board for Jamaica, I had to wait for Jessie to call me to see about her availability. No sooner did I lie down in bed; Jessie called to see what was so important that I needed to talk to her about. I picked up the phone and the first thing out of Jessie's mouth was "How are you doing, rich man?" She was being sarcastic and I played along as I told her to call me "Mr." Rich man. After Jessie and I finally got through our sarcastic episode, I told her that I wanted to take her to Jamaica for a week on an all-inclusive paid vacation. There was silence over the phone for about ten seconds and I knew why.

Jessie and I had never gone away together and I knew she was worried about whether or not I was asking her to go away on a romantic vacation with me. Jessie asked, "What am I supposed to tell the guy I'm seeing?" I told her she could tell him whatever she wanted because she was going to have her own room and that I was bringing her along just for company. I assured her that I was not contemplating any romantic moves and to get off her high horse. I could feel a sense of relief in her voice after I made my comment. Jessie had totally misread my invitation. She asked if she could get back to me the next day with her availability. I said it was fine.

Before we got off the phone, I wanted to hear more about this new guy she was seeing. Earlier when we had lunch, Jessie had vaguely mentioned that she couldn't call this guy because he was still living with his ex-wife trying to sort things through with her. That raised a red flag for me. I may not have been a ladies' man, but I knew a player when I saw or heard about one. I had been around Dexter for too long to not be aware of the game. Whenever Dexter was trying to keep a woman from calling him when he sensed she might be a bit off, he'd tell her he was living with a woman and was in the process of leaving. However, in Jessie's situation I sensed that the guy was not planning to leave his wife at all because she could only see him twice a week and only after work.

They never got together on the weekend because the guy claimed he was too busy. I told Jessie she might want to go to Anywho.com to check this guy out and find out how true his story was. I was always overprotective of Jessie. She'd been involved with so many jerks I always felt the need to protect her heart. I knew the right guy for her was not me, but it definitely wasn't the jerk she was seeing either. She liked men who were suave, a bit rough around the edges, street smart, intelligent and successful. She was basically looking for all the characteristics that Dexter possessed, except for the fact that he was a player.

Covering My Tracks

A couple of days had passed and I was able to confirm the dates of our vacation with Dexter and Jessie. At first, it was hard for Jessie to go because her new friend was making a big deal of her going away with me. This guy seemed like he was possessive and overly jealous. To be honest, I could see where he was coming from, however, she knew that I was no threat and nor did I intend to be. From the way she talked about this guy I felt he was two-timing her. I learned not to judge Jessie based on her standards. She had a different outlook on life and she wanted to make life happen for her the way she's always dreamed of, and I respected that. Sometimes, I wish she didn't plan everything in her life with so much detail because over-planning can sometimes lead to disappointment.

Dexter and I were set to depart on Sunday morning at 9:00AM on a direct flight from Boston to Jamaica. However, Jessie's flight was to leave at noon later that same day. I made up a story about the 9:00AM flight being overbooked and she couldn't get on it with me. I wanted to make sure that Dexter and Jessie didn't run into each other until we got to Jamaica. When I booked the flights, I didn't think about first class because I had always flown coach in the past. When I handed Dexter his confirmation number to pick up his ticket from the customer service desk, he was pissed that we were traveling coach. When he tried to upgrade to first class, he was told that first class was booked. Dexter couldn't believe that I had booked us coach tickets. While he was at the front desk, he decided to upgrade our return flights to first class. He offered to pay the difference.

While we were in the waiting area waiting to board the plane, Dexter was trying to talk to this beautiful young woman. She was feeling him until she asked where he was seated and he told her coach. The conversation changed from amicable to cold and Dexter was angry. Things would get worse when they announced over the PA that all first class passengers would be boarding first. Dexter couldn't believe that he was sitting there with all the money in the world and waiting for other people to board the plane before he could. As if things weren't bad enough, we were seated way in the back of the plane.

As we boarded the plane, we couldn't help but notice how the native Jamaicans tried to carry on as many bags as possible on the plane. All the overhead compartments were full by the time we boarded the plane. These people brought so many luggages on the plane we were forced to check our bags in with the customer service person at the front desk. Dexter had to walk by the woman he was trying to talk to in first class twice because there was no room left for our bags in the overhead compartments in the back. Each time he walked by, she didn't even acknowledge him. By the time we were seated in our cramped seats next to this big woman, everybody on the plane was ready to go. As if it were our fault that these people brought everything in their homes on the plane. West Indians act like they can carry everything in their homes back to their native land when they travel.

Our 9:00 AM flight landed in Montego Bay, Jamaica at 1:00PM. Our complimentary transportation courtesy of the hotel was already outside waiting. Dexter and I carried our bags to the information desk where they confirmed that we were going to the Riu Tropical resort. We carried our bags onto the shuttle bus and went straight to the hotel in Negril to get settled in. We each had our own room, but Dexter upgraded his room to a suite after taking inventory of his accommodations. Dexter had become the diva he'd always wanted to be. It made no difference to me because I had a king size bed and a big room all to myself. Dexter pointed out the fact that I could afford to book the whole hotel for a week if I wanted to and he couldn't understand why I didn't upgrade to a suite like him. I hadn't completely grown out of my frugal ways and spending a couple of thousand dollars a night on a hotel suite wasn't my idea of splurging. We both went to our rooms and changed into our bathing shorts, t-shirt and sandals.

I knew I had to keep track of time because Jessie's flight was due to land at 4:00PM and I told her that I'd meet her at the airport when she arrived. Meanwhile, Dexter and I walked around the hotel to check out the scene and some of what Negril had to offer. Dexter was never too shy to meet anybody, so he got off to work very quickly after we arrived. We were downstairs in the bar playing pool and between shots he started flirting with the beautiful bartender who welcomed his every advance. She tried her best to tell us where to hang out and some of the hottest spots for the nightlife in Negril where we were staying, without losing herself completely in Dexter.

Dexter and I had been playing pool for close to an hour when I realized that I needed to catch a cab back to the airport to go meet Jessie. I asked the bartender to keep him entertained while I ran back to the airport to retrieve something that I had forgotten. I had to make up a lie to get back to the airport. Dexter didn't even question my lie because he was too busy flirting with the bartender. I took a cab from the hotel back to the airport and on the way to the airport, I had a lovely conversation with a cab driver who aspired to come to the states. A few people in Jamaica had been selling him a dream of America that seemed nonexistent. He had heard from some of the people who traveled to America from his country that the opportunities were endless; there was no homelessness, unemployment or poverty. He was shocked when I told him that someone had been lying to him. I told him that America was no different from the rest of the world and as a Black man the dream in America is not always so easy to attain and that he had to work twice as hard. The cab driver whose name was Ballo told me that his people are hardworking folks who don't mind the grind to earn an honest living.

Ballo had to be the craziest driver that I ever encountered. Maybe Jamaica as a whole has the craziest drivers that I have ever seen. The roads are so narrow; I was expecting to crash any minute. We arrived at the airport around 3:30pm, which was early enough for me to wait for Jessie. The cab driver was very nice so I gave him $50.00 US for taking me to the airport. He offered to wait for Jessie and me but I told him that we were going to ride back the complimentary shuttle bus offered by the hotel. He gave me his cell phone number in case I might need a driver for sightseeing later during my trip.

Facing My Deception

Jessie's flight came in on time as scheduled. I waited outside the Customs section of the airport for her to come. It took so long for her to come out I was starting to lose my patience and wondered what was taking so long. After about thirty-five minutes of waiting, she emerged with more luggage than P. Diddy leaving for a world tour. All she needed was an entourage and she would have been mistaken for a superstar diva. I thought Dexter brought too much luggage, but Jessie had him beat ten fold.

The first words out of Jessie's mouth when she saw me were "How can you book me on a coach flight? I never fly coach." I forgot that I was dealing with the female version of Dexter. Jessie always wanted everything first class and that was something that I needed to get used to myself. I knew she was going to be even angrier when she found out that she had a regular room at the hotel. She finally dropped her bags on the floor to give me a big hug then said, "Are you ready to have some fun?" And just like that, she changed the mood. I was happy to see her mood change to positive so quickly. A couple of baggage handlers came over and directed us to the desk where we had to check in for our complimentary ride. They also offered to carry her luggage to the waiting van outside. I took the lightest bag and allowed the guys to carry the heavier suitcases. After boarding the van, I gave the guys $10.00 US each for their help.

As Jessie and I were riding back to the hotel in the van, I contemplated telling her about Dexter being in Jamaica with us, but I didn't want to spoil her good mood. I felt that a surprise would be better and her reaction could possibly be different in front of Dexter. I didn't want either of them to feel like a pawn in my game of deception. She was excited about the vacation and she couldn't wait to get to the hotel to put on her bathing suit to go lay out in the sun on the beach. We asked the van driver about the places that we could go to if we wanted to party. He suggested that we hang out at Rick's café, The Jungle and a few other local spots in Negril that offered live reggae. As far as sightseeing, the driver didn't know where to begin because there's so much to see in Jamaica. One of the hottest tourist attractions in Jamaica is Dunn's River Falls in Ocho Rios and the driver highly recommended that we experience it. He also suggested the Bob Marley Mausoleum in Alexandra and a few other interesting places.

Jessie took a mental note of all the places that the driver mentioned, but she needed a day or two to relax before she could do any sightseeing. I was game to relax for a couple of days by the beach sipping on margaritas. After about an hour of driving, we finally arrived back at the hotel in Negril and we had to tip the driver for getting our luggage out of the bus. Jessie went to the front desk to check in. The bellhop took all her bags, placed them in this carriage, and rolled it to the elevator where we went up to the fourth floor to her room. Her reaction to the room was the same as Dexter's. She wanted to upgrade to a suite just because she could afford it. She told the bellhop to hold on while she called the front desk to see if they could upgrade her room to a suite. Unfortunately, there were no more suites available so she had no other choice but to stay in her room. The bellhop unloaded her baggage and I handed the bellhop $10.00 for his services then he left. I gave more tips during my first few hours in Jamaica than I have ever done my whole life; everybody wanted a tip. I told Jessie that I'd be downstairs by the bar waiting for her after she got ready.

On my way to the bar, I was grinning because I couldn't wait to see Jessie and Dexter's faces when they saw each other for the first time in Jamaica. I knew that I was in for it, but they'd get over it in due time. They're both close to me and I wanted them to get along if we were to remain friends. When I reached the bar downstairs Dexter was still sitting at the bar trying to undress the bartender with his eyes. His conversation must have been flowing because I was standing behind him for five minutes listening to him trying to bullshit his way through her panties and she was falling for it. I didn't know how many drinks Dexter had or what he told her, but the bartender was giggling and laughing like she had just met her prince charming. But from where I stood, all I heard was the same bullshit that Dexter always dished out to the women in the States. He was becoming an international player now.

I had heard enough of his crap so I asked the bartender for a beer and he immediately recognized my voice and turned around to ask what took me so long and if I found what I went looking for. I told him I found her and she'd be down in a few minutes. Dexter was a bit tipsy, so he didn't fully grasp what I said. Dexter had never gotten drunk, but he likes to feel a buzz and when he gets that buzz, he's very talkative. After sipping a couple of beers and kicking Dexter's butt in a few games of pool, Jessie finally showed up at the bar. The look on Jessie's face when she saw Dexter and me playing pool was enough to disarm a whole army battalion. She looked like she had been crossed by her best friend and she was. Jessie didn't even say anything to Dexter as she walked up to me and shoved me in my chest.

Dexter turned to me and said, "I know you didn't bring Ms. High and Mighty down here to ruin our fun?" I turned to both of them and said, "Guess what? I'm not even going to get in the middle of this because both of you guys are my friends. I wanted to spend time with both of you and you better figure out a way to get along while we're down here because we're going to be spending a whole week together." Jessie cut her eyes at me, while Dexter threw the pool stick on the table and walked back to the bar to settle his tab with the bartender. Our drinks were on the house because we had all-inclusive package deals. He left her a generous tip and told her that he would see her later. I also left a few dollars for the bartender as I made my way out of the bar after Dexter.

I knew that Jessie and Dexter couldn't avoid me for a week, but I didn't know how long their childish, adolescent behavior was going to last. I told them both that I was headed down to the beach and if they wanted to join me, they were welcomed to. The hotel where we stayed was right on the beach. I asked the clerk at the front desk for a beach towel and I didn't have to walk too far for my feet to hit the hot sands of Jamaica. It was still hot outside and the Jamaican sun was beaming on my skin. I needed to cool down, so I got one of the guys working on the beach to bring me a chair and I set my towel on it. I handed the guy five bucks for the chair and placed the rest of my money back in my pocket.

I ran in the water and dove in head first. The water was clear, clean and refreshing. That's all I needed, a quick swim to ease my mind. I was not in the water too long when I noticed Jessie and Dexter walking towards the water with beach towels over their shoulders. I walked out the water and pointed my chair out to them. They asked the same guy to bring two beach chairs and set their towels on them. Dexter came out to the water right away, but Jessie wanted to lie out in the sun to work on her a tan.

Forgive and Forget

I was happy to see that Dexter and Jessie had settled their differences and decided to join me at the beach. However, I wondered how and why they came to their senses. Dexter had swum out to about a hundred yards away from shore and came back to where I was a few minutes later. When he got up from under the water I asked him what prompted him to come to the beach to join me, he told me that a little birdie helped them come to their senses. I asked "Who?" He told me the bartender who had witnessed the whole episode when it took place thought he and Jessie were being unfair to me and told them that I only brought them together because I cared about them both. I thought it was very kind of the bartender to intervene and bring those two knuckleheads to their senses. I knew that I had to be especially nice to the bartender the next time she was on duty. Jessie and Dexter probably felt ashamed for lashing out at me in public and I knew that they would both soon apologize; they always apologized after one of their episodes. I just wished they would stop having these episodes.

While Dexter and I were in the water, this guy came by and asked us if we wanted to rent a couple of jet skis. Dexter jumped up and said, "How much?" the guy told us it was seventy-five US dollars for an hour for both us of to ride one and seventy dollars if we each wanted our own. Dexter took one look at the guy and almost lashed out at him for even suggesting that we would share a jet ski. He asked the guy if he had two jet skis available and the guy shook his head yes. I told the guy to wait because I wanted to find out if Jessie wanted to ride one as well. I ran out the water, went to her, and asked her if she wanted a jet ski, she said no, but she would be happy to ride with one of us. I went back and told the guy to bring two jet skis. I didn't have enough money on me to cover the jet skis, but Dexter had brought enough money. We paid the guy and he showed us how to operate the jet skis and handed us two life vests to put on. We strapped on the life vests and Dexter and I were off to the races. Before we left, the guy pointed out how far we could go and what was beyond our limit.

Dexter and I started racing and acting like fools from the time we got on the jet skis. He was trying to put on a show for all the onlookers on the beach and he always loved to Jet Ski. He mastered the art through our travels to the Caribbean. We had been on the jet skis for about a half hour when Jessie waved us in because she wanted to ride. Dexter and I both rushed to offer her rides, but to my surprise, she opted to go with Dexter instead of me. I was thinking that she probably enjoyed the fact that everyone at the beach was fascinated with Dexter's crazy ass on the Jet Ski. Dexter helped her onto the Jet Ski and told her to hold on. Before they could take off, the guy who owned the Jet Skis came by and gave Jessie a life vest to put on. Jessie was holding on for dear life as Dexter took off and started doing stunts on the Jet Ski showing off his devilish skills. Jessie was enjoying every minute of it and she looked like a junkie enjoying the rush. Meanwhile, I was just riding the waves trying to stay on the Jet Ski. I didn't have any tricks to perform, I was just happy to ride the waves.

It was getting close to an hour and I was tired of riding the Jet Ski. Honestly, the damn thing hurt my hands after a while. I pulled in to shore a few minutes early to turn in the Jet Ski and lay out in the sun. Jessie and Dexter came back a few minutes later smiling like two kids who just got off a roller coaster at Six Flags. Personally, I hate roller coasters and I would never ride one, but to each his own. I had an embarrassing moment on a roller coaster when I was a kid and I vowed never to ride one again. The tension between Jessie and Dexter seemed to have subsided quite a bit and I was happy to see that they could actually get along.

Jessie and Dexter got off the Jet Ski and decided to stay in the water. I had no idea what they were talking about or if they were plotting against me for what I had done to them, but I was suspicious. Dexter was a prankster and Jessie was cunning, but whatever it was they were planning I wasn't going to be caught off guard. They became a little bit too chummy for me all of a sudden. They went from bitter enemies to best friends and that was just too weird and difficult to fathom.

I was out relaxing for about thirty minutes on the chair and was getting bored of sitting there by myself. I decided to join Dexter and Jessie in the water. We were having a great time in the water as we pretended to be Olympians swimming for gold medals. I won all the races each time. I was a better swimmer than Dexter and Jessie and I enjoyed beating them. We had spent close to two hours at the beach and we were getting hungry. We decided that we were going to go take our showers and head out to dinner. We made plans to meet at the bar at seven o'clock.

A Quickie at The Bar

Dexter wouldn't be himself if he didn't try to test his limits with a woman within a few hours of his arrival in Jamaica. While Jessie and I went to our rooms to get ready for dinner, Dexter made his way back to the bar to take care of some unfinished business with the bartender. The place was relatively quiet and she looked quite bored when Dexter showed up. He flirtatiously asked her how to make a "Sex on the Beach" drink and asked if he could come around the counter to mix it with her. She told him she could get in trouble if she brought him behind the bar, but at Dexter's urging she went against her better judgment and told him that he could come around for only a few minutes.

While the bartender was standing there showing Dexter how to mix a Sex on the Beach, he was lost in her ass. By the time she felt his hands going up her thighs, her underwear was uncontrollably wet and she couldn't wait for Dexter to penetrate her. She mixed the drink for all but ten seconds until she found herself bending over by the ice machine with Dexter inside of her banging her as hard as he could. She didn't even notice when he slipped on the condom. She wanted to close her eyes to enjoy the pleasure that she was getting from Dexter, but she also had to be on the lookout for patrons coming into the bar.

Dexter soon pulled out of her and went down on her while she stood at the bar rolling her eyes in her head as he ate her. She was trembling from the waist down as she grabbed Dexter's head between her legs and started winding on his face. Dexter ate her until she came repeatedly. They went to the stock room in the back where Dexter sat her on a pile of cases of beer and fucked the hell out her until he splattered semen all over her back after pulling off his condom. She was very satisfied for the whole fifteen minutes, but Dexter would avoid going to the bar for the rest of the trip while she was on duty.

Conning the Con Man

I was the first person to arrive at the bar at seven o'clock as scheduled. I had to wait an extra fifteen minutes for Dexter and Jessie to show up. Because of Dexter's little escapade with the bartender, we had to wait an extra fifteen minutes. The most surprising thing about their arrival was not their tardiness, but the fact that they were so chummy with each other. They arrived hand in hand like two lovebirds. I couldn't understand where they were going with their prank or how far they were willing to take it. I played along as if their nature and characters hadn't changed. I acted as normal as possible to discredit their prank. After I was dressed, I had placed a call to Ballo to pick us up for the restaurant. He showed up on time as promised and took us to this local restaurant in Negril across from the Samsara Hotel. Ballo swore it was the best local food in town and was willing to bet his cab fare on it. We invited Ballo to have dinner with us, but he declined because he had already eaten before he left his house. We arranged for him to pick us up an hour later.

When we got to the place, we were surprised because it didn't look much like anything. At first glance, it could easily be mistaken for a tent with a tin roof. It was as outdoorsy as it could be with hardly any enclosure whatsoever. There was a small-enclosed lounge where no more than eight people could fit comfortably. The restaurant itself was like my back porch in the states. It felt weird at first; but we were troopers and gave it try. There were only four tables set and we were the only patrons. The server came around to greet us and asked us if we were having dinner and we told her yes. She told us that we could sit anywhere we wanted and we chose the table in the middle of the tent. We went to sit down and out of the blue Dexter crossed over to Jessie and pulled out her chair for her. Dexter as a well-mannered gentleman was an oxymoron if I ever knew one. The waitress came back with the menus and she asked if we wanted anything to drink. From the way she looked and spoke, I knew we were in for an authentic Jamaican experience. We each ordered a Red Stripe beer and spring water.

Meanwhile, we started to look over the menu to see what looked appetizing. Dexter was overly attentive to Jessie's needs and kept referring to her as "honey" and she was calling him "sweetheart." I told them both that with all the sweetness going on between them, they might become diabetic if they didn't slow it down. It was obvious that they were trying their best to get to me. The waitress came back moments later with our beers and water and asked us if we were ready to order. Jessie was getting ready to order when Dexter interrupted and said, "Allow me, honey. What would you like?" Jessie told Dexter what she'd like and he ordered the fish fillet with potatoes for her. I jumped in after him and ordered the fish fillet with rice and peas, and Dexter finally ordered the jerk chicken with rice and peas for himself. I could see the smirk on their faces in the corner of my eyes every time I turned my head. They were having their fun with me in the worst way.

When the food arrived, it looked delightful and smelled delicious I wanted to dive right in, but Jessie stopped me in my tracks to say grace. She was efficient and brief as she was probably hungrier than I was. As we were eating and voicing our opinion of the food, Dexter and Jessie started feeding each other and flirting. I was not ready for that kind of metamorphosis from them and realized they were willing to take their stunt all the way. I had seen enough and I needed to say something. I said to them "You better be careful what you wish for." They both looked at me as if they wanted to say, "What are you talking about?" I told them that love had no boundaries and did not always recognize playful games. They both had this innocent grin on their faces because they knew they had gotten to me.

Throughout the whole dinner, they continued to flirt with each other and complimented each other like I wasn't there. Overall, we had a very good meal and the waitress was very attentive to our needs. After we finished our meal, we sat there and had a couple of beers before Ballo showed up to take us back to the hotel. The meal was very reasonable. With the total cost being twenty eight hundred Jamaican dollars, it turned out to be just a little over fifty US dollars for a very good meal. That night, we figured the money conversion while we were at the restaurant. At first, when the lady told us the bill came to twenty eight hundred dollars, Dexter was getting ready to tell her off about how the food was good, but it wasn't that good to be worth twenty eight hundred dollars. He didn't understand anything about the currency. However, after she explained to us that each US dollar was equivalent to fifty Jamaican dollars it made more sense to us. Before Dexter could make an ass of himself, I intervened and allowed the waitress to give us a break down of the money. We didn't have any Jamaican money, so we paid the bill with the US currency that we had and left a twenty-dollar tip for the waitress for her troubles. I caught Dexter slipping her an extra twenty and apologizing as we left.

When we were in the restaurant, Jessie sat back and observed the whole situation without saying a word. I was wondering what she was thinking when we were dealing with the waitress. In the car however, she explained to us that we both jumped to conclusions before asking any questions and that's why the situation went down the way it did. She also said she didn't want to meddle and add to the confusion that was already going on. Jessie made us feel rather small when she gave us her perspective on the situation. Because she was the only woman there with us, we took it as a woman's perspective and started to observe her analytical skills.

Tickle Me Blue

By the time we got back to the hotel, the sun was still setting at nine o'clock at night. We walked over to the cliff to watch one of the most beautiful sunsets that we had ever seen. Some thing about that scene made Dexter and Jessie want to get romantic and I felt left out. Jessie walked over to Dexter and gave him a hug and kiss. He held her in his arms as if to confirm that was just what he needed. At this point, I had no idea what was going on. I knew that Dexter and Jessie wanted to get back at me for bringing them to Jamaica, but that hug and kiss was a little bit too serious to be a game. The twinkle in their eyes also confirmed that something special was about to happen between them. For a minute, I felt like Dexter had double-crossed me. I wanted to get mad at Dexter for crossing me that way, but I had no right to. I never told Dexter how I felt about Jessie and Jessie never knew that I had special feelings for her because I always acted like I wasn't serious when she didn't respond positively to my subtle advances. We played around so much through the course of our friendship; she figured I was just clowning around with her all the time.

My blood was boiling, but I didn't want Jessie and Dexter to know. Dexter was about to steal my girl right from under my eyes. I didn't know what to make of it and I didn't want them to know that they were getting to me. Dexter was my best friend and I knew he wouldn't purposely do that to me. I could always tell when he was playing and when he was serious and he definitely seemed like he was serious about her. Jessie on the other hand, was a little harder to read because we didn't see each other too often after we graduated from college. The fact that Jessie had told me that she was seeing the psychologist also factored into my passive attitude.

Nightfall had come and it was time for us to hit the town. Dexter, Jessie and I were at the bar playing pool for close to two hours and guzzling down margaritas. I kicked their asses in pool and I felt good about it because Dexter is so competitive, he hates to lose in anything. Jessie also has a competitive spirit, but it was just a game to her. We walked away from the pool table after Dexter figured out that he couldn't beat me. We went to the Jungle nightclub to listen to some of the best reggae, hip-hop and R&B. Since the club wasn't too far from the hotel, we settled on a stroll down to the club and do a little sightseeing in the process.

We couldn't even take a leisure walk for a couple of blocks without every cab driver stopping to ask us if we needed a cab. In Jamaica, we never needed to hail a cab because every cab driver was always looking for a fare. We got so tired of waving the cabs off after a while we started ignoring them all together. The Jamaican government needs to establish a local bus system in Negril. Of course, the cab drivers weren't our only problems. We couldn't take a step without one of the local townies asking us if we needed weed as well. When we told them we didn't smoke, they were overly surprised. Honestly, I couldn't blame them because most of the tourists down there were either drunk or high. We smelled weed everywhere we went and that stuff was strong. Our little walk turned out to be not so peaceful after all. We were annoyed from the time we left the hotel to the time we got to the club.

Casing the Joint

We paid the $1000.00 Jamaican (about $10.00 US) cover charge each, and then we walked through the parking lot to the nightclub. The club had an interesting setting. On the left side at the entrance of the club, the wall was lined up with slot machines like a mini casino and to the right there was a bar about ten feet away from the door and down the narrow hallway, there was a lounge area on the right and another bar right across. There was an additional bar right in front of the dance floor making it very convenient for patrons to get drinks. I liked the way the first floor was set up. The dance floor was reminiscent of most dance floors in the States and was small.

Dexter and I wanted to walk around to check out the whole place while the traffic was still light. We were one of the few people in the club early. Jessie's feet couldn't take anymore walking and she wanted to save them for dancing later on. So, she took a seat in front of the dance floor while we walked around the club. As we made our way around, we noticed there were a lot more women coming in wearing the skimpiest of outfits. Some of them were fine, but many more were butt ugly. It was like any club in any city, the ratio for every fine woman to ugly women is one to four. Out of a group of five, there's one slight possibility for a fine girl, two all right looking girls, a big girl and a cock-blocking monster.

The eyes of the big girls and the monsters always seem to follow me for some reason. I must have a big sign on my forehead saying "Welcome Big Girls and Monsters." They gravitated towards me like flies to feces. I swear on my life, I will remain a virgin before I sleep with one of these big girls whose thighs have to apologize to each other every time they take a step. It's almost as if you can hear the thighs talking when they rub against each other talking about "Excuse me, can I get by? Sure, you can. Can I get by? Sure you can." I'm sure you get my drift. I don't have anything against big women, but they all seem to think that I want them.

I think the good-looking women who walk around in groups are insecure. Only insecure people surround themselves with a bunch of people who can potentially hinder their chances of meeting a mate. Insecurity comes in different forms. Sometimes it's physical, other times it's emotional. It can be physical in the sense that a big girl's presence within the group shows strength. Emotionally it can be that the best-looking girl in the group doesn't feel beautiful unless she has the head-turning monster within the group to draw the attention to her. Most women think that men are drawn to the most attractive one in a group, but that's not necessarily the case all the time. Sometimes, we work our way down from monster to scary to cute to fine. And occasionally, we settle for the monster depending on how horny we are or how many drinks we've had.

Many women have missed out on opportunities to meet the man of their dream because they walk around in a group all the time. No man in his right mind is going to approach a woman when she's in a group. Women need to leave all that high school crap behind if they want to meet a good man. Some women don't realize that the monster in the group is always going to hate on the men that approach the group because she's usually ignored by most men. Even the big girls get more play than the monster. The big girls get play because most of the time they have bubbly personalities. The monsters walk around mad at the world for all to see. Whatever reason they have for being mad, they should leave it at home when they go out.

The DJ was playing old school reggae and R&B mix. We were walking back towards the entrance when we noticed people coming from the second floor. We decided to take a look and see what was up there. They had another bar, a pool table and seventies music playing on the open balcony. The balcony added to the island atmosphere. The Jungle nightclub received our stamp of approval as a nice club. We couldn't wait to get our groove on with some of the finest Jamaican women.

We went back downstairs and found the club half packed with women. There was this white couple on the dance floor dancing to a song that was probably being played in their heads more than anything, because they were totally offbeat from the actual song that was being played. Dexter and I started to wonder if they were dancing to the lyrics or the beat. Either way, they were totally off. It was like a scene out of Saturday Night Live at the Roxbury. We found Jessie laughing her ass off at the couple and of course, we joined in with her. However, I liked the fact that the couple acted like the rest of the club was oblivious to them. They were there to have a good time and were obviously in love with one another. I started thinking that most couples, whether black or white let go of their inhibitions when they get older and don't mind letting it all hang out when they're on vacation.

Getting Groovy

Since we were close to being drunk from gulping down margaritas at the hotel, the last thing on our minds when we got to the club was to get more drinks. We all had a good enough buzz to let down our guards a little too. Dexter and I pulled up a chair next to Jessie so we could watch the crowd.

Dexter and I noticed one thing about Jamaican women; they go out like wolves in a pack. They formed circles all around the dance floor and they take turns going in the middle to show off their moves to each other. At one point, Dexter and I almost got dizzy from watching these women move their hips to the reggae beat. They were winding their bottoms like something out of this world. I also watched them perform the latest reggae dances before those dances made their way to the States. I have to admit that some of the men in Jamaica looked gay moving their hips the same way as the women.

After watching the crowd for close to an hour, the DJ decided to play Kevin Little's hottest song called "Turn Me On" and the crowd went crazy, including us. Even Jessie got up and ran to the dance floor with Dexter in tow. We got on the dance floor and Dexter was moving his hips like he was a native Jamaican. Unexpectedly, the crowd started cheering him and Jessie on for putting on such a good show. I must've been dancing like the old white couple that I mentioned earlier because some people were gazing and pointing at me while trying to contain themselves. I didn't give a damn. I knew I couldn't keep up with Jessie and Dexter, but I damn sure was trying in my mind. I've never been a good dancer and to be honest, I never tried to be. Contrary to the myth, not all of us are born with rhythm. I need to learn how to develop rhythm too.

We were having a great time when all of a sudden this goddess of a woman walked on the dance floor wearing the tightest little black dress and the sexiest walk that Dexter and I have ever seen. This woman was gorgeous and she was alone. She was about 5ft 6inches tall with legs like Tina Turner and booty like J-Lo. She was brown complexion, curly long hair, light brown eyes and the nicest smile on earth. From what I saw, she knocked the whole club off its feet. All eyes were on this woman and none of the men was gutsy enough to approach her. This girl was also fixated on Dexter for some reason. Dexter didn't want to be rude to Jessie, but he wanted to go over to dance with the goddess in the club. I noticed the look in Dexter's eyes and I immediately tried to cover for him by turning Jessie around towards me so he could get a better glimpse.

I didn't know what tune this girl was dancing to, but her moves were close to something that belonged in an exotic dance club. Nevertheless, all the men were enjoying it, including me. This girl was a goddess and a diva wrapped into one. Out of all the men in the club who were staring at this woman, I knew Dexter was probably the only one with enough balls to approach her. And my man has never proven me wrong before. As I stood there trying to put my best moves on Jessie, Dexter made his way to the goddess. It wasn't long before she was all over Dexter and him all over her. They were putting on a show for everybody to see. For a quick moment, I wanted to be Dexter's chest because that woman was running her hands so sensually over his chest that I got a hard on and Jessie could feel it. I was hoping that Jessie didn't think I was getting hard because of her as she backed away from me. Anyway, I had to back off Jessie too to let my little friend calm down and allow the blood to circulate back up to my brain.

I could see all the jealousy and envy in everyone's face as Dexter and the woman took over the dance floor turning it into a dirty dancing session. The men's eyes were filled with hate for Dexter and the women were just envious of the girl. However, neither Dexter nor the woman paid attention to the rest of the club. Even Jessie was a little angry with Dexter for deserting her. The jig was up and Dexter had to stay true to himself, however, from the look in Jessie's face I think she was starting to take the little game she and Dexter were playing too seriously. Somewhere along the way, her feelings had taken precedence over getting back at me for bringing them to Jamaica together.

I was trying my best to show Jessie a good time but her eyes were glued to Dexter and the woman. It was then that I realized that Jessie might have a thing for Dexter. She was getting jealous over Dexter knowing damn well he was a ladies man. It was as if she'd forgotten about the psychologist. I also wondered if Jessie was envious of the spotlight too. She started to come across as needy because she was ignored for the catch of the day. Just imagine how I felt, trying to keep her company on the dance floor, but enough was enough! I told her that I was tired and needed some water. We got off the dance floor leaving Dexter and the woman to continue with their little charade.

I went to the bar and got three bottles of water, and took them back to our table. I knew Jessie might be thirsty, but I definitely knew that Dexter was thirsty from all the sweat pouring down his forehead and chest. I didn't get a fourth bottle because I didn't want to upset Jessie further. She would get really upset if I bought a bottle of water for the woman, I thought. Jessie's face was filled with disgust as Dexter made his way around the dance floor through the crowd with the girl in tow headed towards our table. As he got closer to the table, I handed him the bottle of water and he immediately twist off the cap to gulp down half of it. My man was quenching his thirst. He politely asked the woman if she wanted some water and she reached for his bottle and gulped down the other half. It was as if I could read Jessie's mind; she must've been thinking that they just met and already they were sharing a bottle of water. The whole thing disgusted Jessie. Dexter had reverted to his old self.

After quenching their thirst, Dexter introduced the woman as Michelle from Chicago. Michelle was taking a mini vacation in Jamaica to clear her mind and she was only visiting for 4 days. According to Michelle's story, she was a television news reporter from Chicago who had just witnessed a tragedy while doing a story on location. Her station felt it was necessary for her to take a break for a few days. She was sent on all expenses paid vacation to Jamaica. She sounded intelligent and convincing enough for her story to be believable. After all, she was a storyteller, right?

I wondered why it is so easy for us to believe attractive people's tales. It seems like we always second-guess unattractive people's story and motives most of the time because of our own insecurities. Most of us tend to think that unattractive people are evil liars who'd make up anything to compensate for their lack of beauty. The fact that a lot of unattractive people seem to be angry most of the time may play a factor in people not liking them all together. Michelle was so beautiful, she could have told us that she was an astronaut and we would have believed her. At least, Dexter and I bought her story, anyway. Game recognized game and Jessie definitely recognized something fishy with the so-called reporter's story, but she kept hush about it for fear of being labeled a player hater.

Dexter and Ms. America as I started referring to her ended up dancing the whole night together on the dance floor leaving me to console Jessie and not get my mack on with any other girls that night. I could tell that Jessie didn't want to stay at the club anymore, but she also didn't want to spoil the night for us. She abhorred Dexter the same way she did back home. To tell you the truth, I was tired of being Jessie's doormat too. I left her sitting at the table in her sorrow as I took to the dance floor with this beautiful Jamaican sister.

It wasn't long while Dexter and I were having fun on the floor that we noticed Jessie and this Pretty Boy Floyd getting their groove on right next to Dexter. It was as if this guy glided into the club on a big cloud to rescue Jessie from her misery. I'm no homosexual by any means, but this guy was what most women refer to as fine. The brother was about 6 ft 3 inches tall with enough muscles to put Shemar Moore to shame. He was light-skinned with pretty, green eyes, which was a no-no in Jessie's book, according to what she used to tell me was her type. Jessie never liked the light-skinned pretty boys, but she needed him that night to make Dexter jealous. She liked dark skinned pretty boys. They had to be pretty, nevertheless.

The pretty boy was also more of a show-off than Dexter. He had his shirt opened so that his washboard stomach was exposed for everyone to see. However, he didn't have anything on Dexter as far as moves on the dance floor. He looked rather awkward trying to dance seductively with Jess. The dude looked like he had two left feet in a potato sack doing the bunny hop all night. He needed to just stand still and allow the women to enjoy his beauty. I'm no great dancer, but Barry Manilow could've done a better job on the floor than this guy. It was almost starting to become laughable watching this guy dance. Even Jess recognized that the guy had no moves and she tried as best she could to keep him close to her doing the two-step.

We all had a good time that night. While Jessie and Dexter were both able to leave the club and go home with their dance partners, I was left by my lonesome to hug the pillows that somebody else drooled over just a few days before I came to Jamaica. I know that the sheets were washed, but that didn't mean that somebody didn't drool on them. It really didn't bother me that much that those two were taking people home with them. It's never been my style to do it and honestly, I didn't know how. How was it going to look that a woman went home with a virgin? I didn't know what sexually experienced people did in the bedroom, but I was definitely a virgin who hadn't been with a woman and I knew it would show. I wasn't that good of an actor to be able to act like I knew what I was doing, anyway. I gotta tell it like it was.

The limited porn that I had watched in my lifetime was all the experience that I had with women. Sure, I watched how the hunks lay down their pipes on the cheesy films, but I always wondered if women had sex while still wearing high heel shoes. Also, if they just automatically go down on their knees to service men as easily as they did in porno flicks. I also imagined a woman slapping the hell out of me for thinking that I can just lift her dress up and start eating her like I haven't been fed in years. She would definitely know that I was hungry.

Mr. and Ms. Right Now

I didn't know what happened the previous night among Dexter, Jessie and their partners, but the following morning when we met for breakfast, there were five people at the table and two of them I didn't know. I got the feeling that Pretty Boy Floyd whose real name I never knew or didn't care to know and Ms. America enjoyed showing off what their mama gave them more than we could stand. We met at the restaurant at 10:30 AM and I saw more skin than most people did all day. Pretty Boy Floyd was wearing one of those tight ass bathing suits that the white boys used to wear back in the sixties leaving us to wonder how Jessie got any pleasure from him at all. It does not take a gay man to see that my man was not packing. Pretty Boy Floyd also kept running his hands over his washboard stomach to make sure it was still there. Maybe he was just too sexy for his body that he had to make sure that he felt it every second.

Ms. America was the most comfortable woman that I ever saw in a thong. She felt the need to keep getting up for no reason to show off her nice round ass with the string in the middle of her crack. If she didn't need water, it was a new fork, a spoon, or a towel, but after a while, she started to play herself. It got to the point where we all had enough of her crack. An ass is only good for as long as you can only peek at it for a few seconds. This woman might as well have thrown on some pumps and start shaking her ass and climbing the volleyball pole because she got up so much to show it off; it started to look like a strip show. Even Dexter was getting tired of watching her ass come and go and I'm sure he tapped that ass the night before. I never saw such vain people in my life. Dexter was nowhere near as vain as these two fools were. At one point, when Ms. America got up to go fetch a napkin like a dog in heat, Jessie sarcastically asked her if she needed anything else while her ass was still up in our faces. The whole situation was ridiculous.

I couldn't blame Dexter for sleeping with that woman, but anything beyond that I wouldn't understand. Jessie on the other hand, was not really working with anything to make Dexter jealous. Jessie's guy seemed to be as dumb as a doorknob. Well, other than looks, Ms. America didn't seem to have much to offer either. I sat at the table watching four beautiful people who had nothing in common make fools of themselves simply because of aesthetics. Overall, I thought Dexter and Jessie were gorgeous people compared to the other two idiots who felt the need to thrust their beauty upon people every chance they got. By the time we got through breakfast, I didn't know what to make of the situation. In the end, I was the odd and sane man out. Sometimes being odd can be a great thing.

After breakfast, we all walked down to the beach to lie in the sun and relax. Pretty Boy Floyd felt the need to do a few push-ups on the sand looking more ridiculous than ever. All this time, Dexter hadn't taken off his shirt yet. I knew that the minute Dexter took off his oversized t-shirt this clown would find his rightful place. He may have had a nice body, but Dexter was more cut and defined than him, and I wanted my boy to show him out. Meanwhile, Ms. America felt the need to expose the crack of her ass even more by lying on her stomach while Dexter rubbed sun block lotion all over her body. I didn't think she was anymore beautiful than Jess, she just seemed like she frequented more strip clubs than Jess. Her every movement was reminiscent of a stripper.

I have always adored Jess as a person and a friend and I wasn't going to start giving more props to some Lisa Raye wannabe that I just met than I give to Jess. Jess is not an in your face person like Michelle, but she also had a killer body that she rarely exposed. Jess was wearing a bikini bottom that matched the top of her two-piece bathing suit and when she took off her shorts; all the men on the beach were lost in her ass, including me. She wasn't wearing a thong, but her booty made the bathing suit look close enough to a thong. Jess had an onion booty like Beyonce. If you got close enough to her booty, it would make a grown man cry.

It was a nice showdown between my two friends and the two idiots who thought they were God's gift to the Earth. While Jessie and Michelle laid out in the sun to work on their tans, Dexter and I walked over to the Jet Ski rental guy and rented two jet skis for an hour. Pretty Boy Floyd was a couple of feet away from the girls doing pull ups on some bar that only he could have discovered. Jessie wasn't paying much attention to them, but Michelle was wallowing in the pleasure of watching a male version of herself show off his workout routine on the beach. He looked laughable at best.

As Dexter and I made circles around the water on the jet skis, I noticed Jessie's hands waving us to shore. I sped up towards the shore to see what she wanted. She told me she wanted me to take her for a ride. The Jet Ski rental guy walked over and handed her a life vest. She strapped it on then hopped on the Jet Ski behind me. I didn't want to be too adventurous on the Jet Ski with Jessie behind me, so I took off slowly. Do you know that homegirl yelled at the top of her lungs for me to go faster? I put the pedal to the metal or more like my hand to the accelerator and took off on the endless sea. However, I had a limit to how fast I would go. Jessie was not going to turn Mr. Careful to Mr. Adventurous all of a sudden just because she was yelling at the top of her lungs. If she wanted more speed, she should've asked Dexter to take her for a ride. I'm conservative when it comes to certain things and nobody will ever be able to change that no matter how fine or close to me they are.

Soon after we took off, Dexter flew by us doing more stunts than Evil Knievel on water. He knew that Jessie was enjoying all his fearless stunts and she wanted to be on his Jet Ski with him. But, she settled for a boring ride with me because she was angry with him. As we were riding around on the calm waters of Jamaica, I noticed from afar that Pretty Boy Floyd was rubbing Michelle down with sun block. I drew Jessie's attention to them and she whispered in my ears that all men are dogs. It didn't take long for Dexter to also notice the rub down, but he wasn't sweating it. Dexter knew that Michelle was Ms. Right Now and Jessie had to realize that pretty boy Floyd was also Mr. Right Now.

Dexter had dated enough women to know that he couldn't let Michelle get to him, but he wanted to make sure that Jessie knew how to react to the situation. He pulled alongside of us and told Jessie not to say anything to them and when we got back to shore, he had a plan. Jessie was upset and said she wasn't going to let a pretty boy disrespect her like that. Dexter pointed out to her that he was only disrespecting himself and if she made a big deal of it, she would look foolish. Dexter was making a lot of sense to me, but I knew no better. I wasn't a player extraordinaire like Dexter, but his game was tight.

It was getting close to our allotted time for the skis and we had to return them. As we rode towards the shore, Pretty Boy Floyd and Michelle decided to go into the water for a dip. They were under water fooling around as we made our way to the rental guy. Dexter nonchalantly walked over to where they were sitting and took her sunglasses and buried them deep in the sand along with Pretty Boy Floyd's wallet and hers that they'd hidden under her towel. Dexter made it look like they were robbed. That would teach them not to disrespect my friends.

When Michelle and Pretty Boy Floyd finally made their way out of the water, we all acted like we had been robbed. The two fools thought we were all victims and we knew they carried all their money and credit cards in their wallet from the stash that was in there. They were stuck in Jamaica for however long with no money and identification. We could only imagine how miserable of a time they had after we left them. Later, Dexter went back, took the wallets along with the money, and mailed them back to their home addresses. That was the end of Dexter and Jessie's love escapade in Jamaica with those two strangers.

We later found out on CNN that Michelle was actually a stripper from Magic City in Atlanta. She was in Jamaica hiding from her boyfriend because he had threatened to kill her after he caught her cheating on him with one of her customers. The story made headlines after the boyfriend was caught trying to board a plane to Jamaica with a loaded revolver. Pretty Boy Floyd was just dumb and nothing more. His family was apparently wealthy and he was in Jamaica for a week having a good time, so he told Jessie.

One last Day of Adventure

We had been in Jamaica for close to a week and time was winding down before we would head back to the States. We wanted to see as much of Jamaica as we could in one day, so we called Ballo, who officially became our driver, to take us to the Bob Marley Mausoleum and Dunn's River Falls in Ocho Rios early in the morning. Ballo told us that the whole trip would cost us about one hundred and fifty dollars US and it wouldn't take more than a couple of hours. We found out that day; Ballo was a big ass liar. It took us close to two hours to get to Dunn's River Fall from Negril and another three hours to get to the mausoleum in Alexandra. From the mausoleum, it took us an additional four hours to get back to the hotel. Mind you, Ballo was one of the craziest drivers we had ever seen.

Before we got in the car, Ballo took one long look at us and asked if we were still going to Dunn's River Fall. We told him yes and he responded "not with those clothes you ain't."
Ballo told us we weren't appropriately dressed to go to Dunn's River Fall and that the whole purpose and fun of visiting The Fall is the climb. He told us we needed to wear our bathing suits and bring a few towels to dry up afterwards. We all ran back to our rooms and changed within a few minutes. Jess took a little longer than the rest of us, but it wasn't too long. We were finally ready to go and Ballo lit up a spliff before we took off. He attempted to share his spliff, but none of us smoked. I couldn't believe that Ballo was smoking that early in the morning. He told us he drove better when he was high and who were we to argue with a man who had been smoking weed all his life.

On our way to The Fall, Ballo tried his best to show us the landmarks in Jamaica and give us a brief history of the Rastafarian religion. For some reason, I always thought that Selasie was a big ganja smoker, but according to Ballo who didn't seem certain of the man, he was not a weed smoker at all. I think Ballo was a little bit too high to give us a detailed history of his religion. We also figured that one of the benefits of being a Rastafarian was the fact that they get to smoke weed all day and feel that Jah wants them to do so. It was an adventure watching Ballo overtake cars and driving as if he owned the roads in Jamaica.

When we arrived at Dunn's River Fall, we could see there were many people in line waiting to enter the park. Ballo told us to wait in the car while he went to get our tickets. The twenty-dollar cover was minimal compared to the fun that we would have. Mr. Dexter "Macho Man" Little wanted to wear his sunglasses inside the park even though Ballo told him that he would end up losing them. We offered to pay the admission for Ballo to get in the park, but he declined. He told us that the waterfall wasn't going anywhere and that he could always visit it at anytime and he had been there many times before. He wanted us to just enjoy the experience as friends. He told us he would sit in the car outside and wait for us. I honestly believed that Ballo wanted to take the opportunity to enjoy smoking a few more joints while we were at the park.

As we entered the park, we noticed that there were vendors selling these special slippers with special soles with tiny grips that kept people from slipping when climbing the waterfall. Jessie and I immediately bought slippers for ten dollars each, but my man "Macho Man" Dexter insisted that he could climb The Fall wearing his beach sandals. When we first got near The Fall, we were at the top and Dexter was asking, "What the hell are people making a big deal of?" He didn't know that The Fall had to be climbed from the very bottom. One of the employees of the park directed us to the bottom of it near the ocean, which was about one hundred feet from the top. It was a breathtaking view. We took a bunch of pictures with our disposable waterproof cameras from the bottom of The Fall.

From looking at The Fall, it seemed like it was going to be an obstacle course. As we made our way to the top of it, Dexter wanted to show off his athletic prowess by climbing right into the forceful waters in the middle. And not a moment too soon, he was on his back gulping water like a thirsty mule. He kept slipping and falling and Jessie and I kept taking pictures of him from the safer and less rigorous side. We climbed the easiest way possible as we watched Mr. Macho Man try to make it hard on himself. Dexter always pushed himself physically and although he fell many times, he looked like he was having a better time climbing The Fall than we did. It didn't take us too long to make it to the top of the waterfall. Dexter lost his sandals on the way up as well as his two hundred dollar glasses. The whole experience was fun and we all wished that we had done it earlier in the week because we would have had more time to enjoy it.

After we were done climbing The Fall, we were a little fatigue, so Jess and I wanted to take a short break to catch our breath. However, Mr. Macho Man Dexter wanted to climb it once more. The second time around was no better for him as he tripped and fell at exactly the same spots. Jess and I took even more pictures as we were on the sideline as spectators. I knew that when I got back home I would have the proof that Dexter was not as invincible as he thought.

The funniest moment was yet to come. When we got to the car, Ballo was sitting on the hood and started cracking on Dexter in his patois accent. He said, "Mr. Superman, wa m' to ya shoes and glasses? It's a good ting you didn't carry ya passport too cause you'd be living here as a Jamaican citizen while your passport made its way down the ocean along with the rest of your stuff." He went on "Ya lucky ya didn't lose ya shorts as well. Me seen tourists come back to their cars butt naked afta climbing The Fall." I had to agree with him on that because my shorts came down a couple of times as I was climbing up and Dexter showed a little bit of crack more than a few times when he was climbing and we had it on camera. The water was fierce and it could literally strip someone of his or her shorts. We found out that day that Ballo was down to earth and had a sense of humor.

We left Dunn's River Fall in Ocho Rios and headed to Bob Marley's Mausoleum in Alexandra up in the mountains. Ballo was driving crazier than ever because he knew he had lied to us about the amount of time it would take to make it there from Dunn's River Fall. It took us close to three hours to make it to the mausoleum and each moment passed Ballo kept telling us how close we were. We also witnessed the funniest thing that day. Half way to the mausoleum, Ballo told us he couldn't go anymore and when we asked "why?" he told us that either one of us had to get behind the wheel or he had to pull over to get high. We couldn't believe how much of a fiend he was. The best solution was for us to pull over and allow Ballo a few minutes to smoke a joint. There was no way any of us was gonna take the wheel to drive on those narrow roads with the crazy ass Jamaican drivers anyway.

All day we didn't see Ballo eat anything and we wondered how he was able to function on just weed. What happened to the munchies? Is it a myth? We had stopped earlier in the day to get food from a local eatery, but he didn't have anything to eat then. One of the reasons why Ballo had to pull over to smoke was because we didn't enjoy the smell of weed in the car and he wanted to show us the respect. While he was outside smoking, we were in the car cracking up. This dude was about as skinny as a toothpick with dreads coming all the way down to his back and was missing a couple of teeth to top it off.

All we could think about while he was huffing and puffing was a scene out of a scary movie where a mop is miraculously smoking. He literally looked like a mop standing there smoking. What was even funnier was the fact that Ballo was as toned as a bodybuilder. He was like Popeye after he'd just eaten a can of spinach, only Ballo was the size of Olive Oyle and he smoked weed instead of eating spinach. He was energetic and more focused than ever after he got high. I don't know what kind of effect Jamaican weed has, but Ballo was more than relaxed. He told us he could go another eight hours without eating anything as long as he had enough weed to smoke.

We finally made it to the mausoleum after a couple of hours of driving. We had no idea what a mausoleum was, and we didn't have any expectations. At first, we thought the place was closed, but after beeping the horn a couple of times in front of this big gate, this guy opened the gate to greet Ballo. It seemed like business as usual. There were a couple of tour guides with huge joints in their mouths waiting around for the tourists to arrive. We must've been the last group to get there that day as nightfall was starting to approach. We walked to the front counter in what appeared to be a store and we paid twelve US dollars each to go on this tour. Our tour guide was a short guy who was very dark skinned with the reddest eyes that I have ever seen. He was smoking a joint the size of a Cuban cigar. The smell of his weed was giving us all a headache. Jamaican weed is the strongest weed that we have ever smelled. The weed that people smoked in the States is watered down compared to what they smoked in Jamaica.

It must have been a customary thing, because the tour guide offered us a puff from his joint. We politely declined. The mausoleum tour was the briefest tour in the history of tours. This tour guide who was dressed in khaki pants and a shirt with the famous Zion lion emblem on his shirt must've thought it was amusing for him to try to sing all of Bob Marley's songs. We made our way from the bottom of the hill to the sycamore tree in Bob Marley's childhood backyard, to his one bedroom shack that he shared with his mother, to the rock where he sat and wrote many songs, to his tomb and that was the tour. Did I mention how quick the tour was?

First of all, the tour guide was not the best singer in Jamaica, but his confidence was up there like he was Shabba Ranks performing in front of thousands of people at Sun Splash. He was trying his best to prolong the time by trying to serenade us with his raspy voice. Five minutes after the tour was over, we felt like we were robbed. We tipped the tour guide a couple of hundred Jamaican dollars and he looked at us like we were crazy. We looked back at him like he robbed us and we spent almost three hours driving there to get robbed. Ballo could've just pulled out his penis and stick it up our asses and it would've felt better than that quick tour we took. We got screwed. The money for the tour didn't matter much to us, but the amount of time that it took us to get there made us feel worse than the tour itself. That tour was quicker than a man who suffers from premature ejaculation.

We were so disappointed on the way back to the hotel, we all fell asleep and allowed Ballo to drive the whole way back without any conversation. He must've been flying on the way to the hotel because our heads hit the roof of the car on more than a few occasions. We finally arrived at the hotel around 8:00 pm without much time to rest. We all headed to our room for catnaps and told Ballo to pick us up in a couple of hours. We weren't sure what we wanted to do, but the concierge at the hotel had been telling us about Rick's Café all week. So, we decided we were going to go see what the big fuss was all about. When I got to my room, I realized I couldn't really nap because I had fallen asleep in the car on our way back to the hotel however uncomfortable it was. I called Dexter and Jess to see if they were napping, but they couldn't close their eyes either. I told them to be ready by 9:30PM because I knew how long they would take to get dressed.

Jess and Dexter operate on colored people time when it comes to getting dressed. They both would go through many outfits before settling on one. It might be normal for a woman to wear a few different outfits before deciding which one is better for her, but I found it appalling for a man to do that. It's okay to lay out a few different outfits on the bed, but to try all of them on is a different story.

One Last Night of Fun

Before I took my shower, I laid out some of my best clothes on the bed. I took the longest shower that day. Everybody in the hotel must've been pissed because I knew I used all the hot water. I came out the shower feeling clean as a whistle. I threw on my Nicole Miller underwear, some deodorant under my arms and I was ready to get dressed. That was until I realized how ashy my elbows and feet were. So, I pulled out my big ass bottle of Kerry lotion and I rubbed that lotion all over my crusty feet and ashy elbows before I got dressed.

I picked up a nice pair of sky blue linen pants from the many pants that I lay down on the bed before I went in the shower. I held it up against my body with this white linen shirt the same way a woman who's pressed for time would before she got dressed. I had watched my mother go through that routine many times when I was a child. The combination looked good enough to me. I threw on the linen pants, white undershirt and the short-sleeved white linen shirt. I wore my favorite light brown sandals and I lightly sprayed my favorite Aqua Di Gio cologne around my neck and wrist. Overall, I felt good and clean and was ready to take over the town. Before I left the room, I called Jess and Dexter and told them to meet me by the bar in a few minutes.

I was tired of being in my room and I didn't want to wait there any longer. I went downstairs to play a game of pool while I waited for Jess and Dexter. I ended up playing more than one game as they took forever to get downstairs. While I was playing pool, I ordered a virgin pina colada to quench my thirst. As I shot the third ball in the corner pocket, I heard this sweet sexy female voice ask if she could join me. Without hesitation and looking to see who it was, I said, "Sure." Amused by the seductive voice, when I turned around to see who it was, I was shocked to see this giant of a white woman who was about 6ft 3 inches tall, 240 pounds who looked like a wrestler from the WWF. At first, I wanted to tell her that I didn't want to play anymore because I had somewhere to go, but the look on her face scared the living daylights out of me and the additional fear that she might actually be able to physically whoop my ass forced me to say "sure we can play."

This woman got on the pool table and started kicking my ass like she was on some professional pool tournament on ESPN or something. Her long ass body was leaning all across the table making impossible shots that I had only seen on television. I was hoping and praying that Dexter and Jess would get down to the poolroom soon, because I was so embarrassed. I could see the bartender smirking every time I took the rack to set the balls after I lost a game. I couldn't beat this woman not even once. Finally, Dexter and Jess emerged and before they could set foot in the game room, I threw down my stick and told the woman that I had to go because my friends were here. I couldn't let Dexter and Jess watch this woman kick my ass the way she was doing. I rushed out of the game room as if my life depended on it. I was bragging earlier about being the best in pool and I didn't want that to change. What Dexter and Jess didn't know wouldn't hurt.

It was a Saturday night and our last night in town and we wanted to have a grand ole time before we left. Jess, Dexter and I wanted to have dinner at Rick's Café. I had called Ballo earlier to ask him if he knew where Rick's Café was and he told me it wasn't too far from the hotel. He was at the hotel at 9:30 PM to pick us up, but Dexter and Jess didn't come down until 9:45PM. They allowed me to get my ass whoop for fifteen minutes too long by a giant of a woman. When we got outside, we found Ballo leaning on his car smoking a big joint. As we made our way into the car, he took one last long puff from his joint that almost choked the hell out of him. He put the rest of the joint out and placed it in his pocket for later. We were sure he was gonna smoke the rest of that joint while he waited for us at the restaurant.

His Speedy Gonzalez ass made it to Rick's Cafe in no time. Ballo dropped us off in front of the restaurant and waited in the parking lot for us. We were seated by a nice-looking waitress and ordered a few rounds of drinks before our food came. We ordered the "authentic Jamaican dishes" like curry goat with rice and peas, curry chicken and jerk chicken. To our surprise, the food was great and we had a good time watching the crazy white tourists jump off the seventy-foot cliff like they were children. They couldn't pay my chicken ass a million dollars to jump off that cliff. I always had a fear of heights. It was fun watching those fearless, crazy people jump. There were a few Rastafarians jumping too, but they were a little smarter than the white folks. They wanted to be paid to jump. After watching people pay them to jump off the cliff, it basically confirmed my belief that nothing in Jamaica was free. What fun do people get out of watching someone jump off a cliff other than the stupidity of the act itself? I wouldn't pay just to watch it. I enjoyed the experience because it was free. Why would I pay to watch someone get his thrill off a cliff?

We must've spent two and a half hours at Rick's Café eating, drinking and talking. We had overstayed our welcome and it was time to go. There was a long line of people waiting to be seated and we carelessly took longer than we should have in the restaurant. We had to hit the club one last time before we left anyway. We paid our tab with a huge tip and walked outside and found Ballo looking as high as a kite. I was looking at Ballo and thinking to myself how simple his life was. I never bothered to ask him what type of house he lived in or how he grew up, but from his demeanor and his character, I could tell he lived a stress free life and had grown accustomed to the poverty that was prevalent all over his country. Ballo seemed to have accepted his situation.

Though Ballo accepted the poverty-stricken life and tried hard to make the best of it with the little hustle he was able to get with the tourists, a part of him also resented some of the tourists for looking down on the Jamaican people in their own country, sometimes. What I saw in Jamaica was no different from what I saw when I visited the other Caribbean islands. I can blindly choose any island in the Caribbean on the map and they're sure to share the same issues that plagued Jamaica. In Haiti, Barbados or the Dominican Republic, the white people seem to own all the wealth and they act like they're better than the natives. I think the Caribbean folks contribute to their feelings of inferiority because they treat them with more respect than they do their own compatriots.

The colonial state of mind is still prevalent all over the Caribbean and the white folks who live in the Caribbean make sure that their houses are up in the hill above all the Negroes as a sign to reinforce their status in society. The fact that they have the money to buy justice also earns them great respect all over the islands. Don't get me wrong, there are also prominent black people as well on these islands, but some of them seem to disassociate themselves with the masses once they "make it."

What I noticed in the Caribbean was really no different than what some of our brothers and sisters are doing to themselves in the States. Some black people would give any white person on any given day more respect. They won't think twice about stabbing or shooting another brother. However, they know that if they were to stab or shoot a white person that the investigation by the police department would be twice as rigorous and the police wouldn't rest until the killer is caught. I guess we have society to thank for helping to condition us to be that way. The torment that our community suffers when a crime is committed against a white person is enough to keep us in line. The lackluster effort that is put forth when a brother is killed by another brother just continues to reinforce the lack of respect shown to us and we show for each other.

Violence should never be an option to get out of any situation, but any violent act should receive the same type of investigation whether it's black on black, white on black, yellow on white or black on red violence. I yearn for the day when people are looked upon as people. It just seems through my travels around the world that my brothers and sisters seem to be suffering everywhere and the injustice is worldwide. Sometimes, I wonder if there's truly a God to allow all this suffering to linger around the world.

Ballo's big dream is to make it to America one day to live in a society where the streets are supposedly paved with gold. Somehow, America has managed to sell itself to the rest of the world as the land of opportunity concealing the fact that the problems people in other parts of the world face exist here as well. American tourists are cherished in Jamaica and who can blame them. Some of the questions Ballo asked while we were in the car raise my suspicion to something that seemed to be very common among immigrants. Some of these immigrants go back home and paint an inaccurate picture of America to their fellow countrymen either to make themselves seem better or to belittle their fellow countrymen. They're creating this sense of false hope about America. Of course, we have opportunities here in America, but at what cost have we been able to create these opportunities. Who has been subjected to the suffering?

I've always been grateful for having been born American, but at the same time, I can also resent being an American sometimes because of what my government has done to the rest of the world. Whenever, I meet people like Ballo, it forces me to think about my responsibilities in this world. I try my best to change the world as a teacher locally, but we need more of a global effort to help the rest of the people who are suffering around the world.

As we drove down to the Jungle Club, I quickly reflected on my good fortune and wondered how I could help make more of a positive change in the world when I got back home. I was lost in thoughts until we got to the club and Ballo had to wake me out of my daydream. I hate myself for saying this, but all my thoughts about the world's problem instantly went away when I looked at the line of gorgeous women in short skirts and tight jeans waiting in front of the club to get in. I went from a man with a conscience to a greedy bastard who wanted nothing more than a nice piece of ass to help me deal with the problem of the world better the next day.

We got out of the car and walked up to the line so we could make our way to the ticket booth to pay the cover charge and get our admission ticket for the club. Ballo told us he'd come back around 3:30am to pick us up or we could call him if we decided to leave the club early. The club was a short enough distance from our hotel and if we wanted to walk back, we could anyway. While we were waiting in line, Dexter was trying to get his mack on with this beautiful young lady named Darlene who looked to be no older than twenty-one years old. She had legs long enough for a brother to get lost in them.

She was wearing a short white mini-skirt that rested on her round booty just enough keep her privates from showing. She had on an halter-top that exposed her naval, she could've easily been a C-cup because she was braless and her breasts were as perky as a teenager's, and she knew that all eyes were on her. It was only appropriate for her to kick it to Dexter because a lot of the women seemed to have been lost in his beauty as well. Darlene and her friends were all from Atlanta and were down in Jamaica for a week vacationing.

Dexter may have thought that he was macking the girl, but by the time we got to the ticket booth, she had him paying for her and three of her girlfriends. By then, I was thinking to myself "whose macking whom here?" It wasn't a big deal for Dexter to dish out less than a hundred dollars to cover the admission for the girls, but it was the way she went about it. As far as I was concerned, she had more game than Dexter had ever seen and he was being played. Dexter also paid Jessie's and my way into the club to further demonstrate his baller status. I was looking at Jessie's face and I could tell that she was fuming at the fact that Dexter was trying so hard to impress this girl.

I took a look at the herd of women who accompanied Dexter's new friend and I noticed that there was one other cutie in the group who wasn't as conspicuous as the one Dexter was talking with. I approached her and Dexter introduced me as his brother to the whole group. Dexter and I used to do that a lot. We would always introduce ourselves to people as brothers to make the assimilation process into the group easier. I didn't remember everybody's name in the group; I only remembered Melanie and Darlene. Melanie was the girl that I was salivating over and Darlene was the one that Dexter was kicking it with. The other two women were just there to cock block in case they didn't get any play by the end of the night.

What I've always liked about Dexter is the fact that he approaches every situation differently and knows how to deal with each situation as it comes. In the case of the would- be cock blockers, Dexter knew that in order to keep them from blocking like the linebackers they were, he had to pay their way into the club and supply the drinks all night. I was not a player and as far as I was concerned those two broke ass linebackers would have died of thirst if they were waiting for me to buy them drinks. However, in this situation, I was the student and I wanted to observe the master at his best. Dexter had a plan. He always has a plan.

The terms cock blockers and linebackers were interchangeable as it related to Melanie and Darlene's friends because I could care less about their names. It seemed to me that they had one purpose and that purpose was either to block or sack one of us causing a big fumble with their fine ass friends. I had my guard up right away and I may have prejudged their true intentions. The cock blockers liked Dexter right away and that eased the door for me to get with the other dime in the pack. The worst thing that could've happened was for Dexter and me to get tag teamed by two cock-blocking linebackers. Dexter was always one step ahead in the game. Since he took the baller status initiative, I decided to allow him to shine like the baller he was all night.

Jess was the odd girl out this time. While we were vibing with these women, poor Jess was all by herself waiting for a stud to come by and rescue her. Unfortunately, that night, most of the studs stayed home. There were a few okay brothers in line but Jess was deterred by the unclean looks of their dreads. Jess was never into guys with dreadlocks. She's always been attracted to the clean-cut guys and she just didn't believe that people with dreads wash their hair regularly. Jess has always been particular about hygiene and I can't blame her for being like that. Who knows what's out there creeping out of people's bodies, right?

We finally made our way into the club with the ladies after a few minutes of waiting in line. When we got in the club, to our surprise, there were three times as many gems inside the club. My boy Dexter was not one to be held down by any woman, so he quickly ushered Darlene to a corner table and waved to one of the waitresses to get drinks for Darlene and Melanie's friends. Dexter walked a few feet away from the table to catch a bird's eye view of the whole place. He also knew that the blockers were going be watching us all night because the place was crawling with fine women, so he made sure that they were sitting in a corner where their view would be obscured all night. He bought each of the girls two rounds of drinks; forcing them to be stationery while we cased the joint. No woman wants to be walking around a club with two drinks in her hands. We knew that the women were going to be standing in that spot until they finished their drinks. We each got a drink and told the ladies that we'd be back in a few minutes. Dexter also bought Jess her favorite apple martini. Jess stood apart from the group, as she did not feel like mingling with one of Dexter's possible hoochies.

We walked around the club and for the first time I felt like I was hanging with a god. Every woman in that club was trying to get a piece of Dexter. The women in Jamaica were a lot more aggressive and Dexter loved every minute of it. I had seen women fall over him before, but not like they did in Jamaica. After witnessing all the feeling, grabbing and pinching of Dexter's butt as we walked around the club, I turned to Dexter to give him dap and he gave me that look like he had been there before. I got a few pinches too, but none of the women were as fine as Melanie. I was more anxious to get back to Melanie than Dexter was to get back to Darlene. Darlene was fine, but there were women three times as fine as her all over the club. She just exposed a lot more skin than some of the other women. My heart was set on spending the whole evening with Melanie from the time we got in, I was trying to rush Dexter back to the girls, and he sensed my sense of urgency. He pulled me to the side and started to unleash his plan on me.

Dexter told me that it's always better to start talking to a woman outside of a club where it's less noisy and crowded because they can hear you better and see where you're coming from. Specifically, in the case of Darlene and Melanie, Dexter told me not to worry about a thing because they weren't going anywhere. "We paid for them to get in the club, we bought them drinks and they were sweating us and that basically meant that they're our fallback pieces for the night. What we'll do is go around and dance with them every now and then just to keep their interest while we look for better prospects. There's no guarantee that we're gonna get any ass from them anyway, so we need to line up as many prospects as possible without making it obvious that we're with any of them," said Dexter. I was watching a part of Dexter's game that I had never seen before. I knew he wouldn't have paid for four women to get in the club back when we were just regular working folks. He would only pay for the one he was interested in and maybe buy one drink for her friends. However, the more money a man has, the better his game.

My man's game was tight and I was amused by it all, but I still wanted to get back to Melanie. I knew nothing about setting up women for a piece of ass. I was trying to hold on to the piece of ass that I knew was secured. After about a half hour of walking around the club making eye contact with as many prospects as possible and buying a few drinks for some of his admirers, Dexter decided to go back to the table to ask the women to dance. When we got back to the table, we found Melanie and Darlene still sipping on their second drinks, which were still halfway full. The other four glasses stood empty on the table and the cock blockers were nowhere to be found. We asked

Darlene and Melanie where their friends were and they told us that they were on the dance floor. We were almost done with our drinks, so we guzzled down the final sip and took the girls to the dance floor for about fifteen minutes.

We were grooving on the dance floor, and I could tell by the big smile on Darlene's face she was very impressed with Dexter's moves. He wasn't trying to lay it on thick or anything, but he gave her just enough for her to look forward to more. Melanie seemed comfortable enough with my conservative moves on the dance floor, but every now and then, she'd grab my hand and put them around her hips as an invitation that she wanted me to get freaky with her. After about fifteen minutes of playing some of the best hip-hop, the DJ changed the music to reggae and that was Dexter's cue to leave the dance floor and go search for his other prospects. He walked Darlene back to her table and the cock blockers noticed that their drink supplier was heading back to the table, so they followed. Dexter bought everyone two more rounds of drinks. Once again, securing his spot for the night, he told Darlene that he had to go to the bathroom.

Part of me was hoping that Dexter didn't find another woman better than Darlene, because it would hinder my chances with Melanie. In a group of four women, chances are that two of them are going make it harder for any one of them to leave the group because of a man. However, with two women willing to leave, there was a fifty percent chance that it might actually happen. We were leaving the following day and if I knew Dexter, he would probably try to sleep with more than one woman in one night. He had done it before. I knew what Dexter was up to and I knew that I would find him in the back with another woman if I went to look for him.

Curiosity got the best of me and my nosey side won. I went to take a peak at the woman that Dexter was willing to risk losing

Darlene for.   To my surprise, she was fine as hell, but
everything about her said, "skank." She was practically
throwing her pussy at Dexter and he loved himself some skank,
especially when he was due to leave town the next day. She was
so eager to give Dexter some ass; she would have probably
waited up all night in her room for him to show up.

About a half hour had gone by when Dexter emerged from the
bathroom, supposedly! Dexter walked back to our table with a
big grin on his face and his fly wide open.   I was trying to
motion to him that his fly was open, but one of the loud ass
linebackers had to scream it out loud trying to embarrass my
boy. She was like "Why is your fly open in the middle of a
club?" Dexter quickly turned and zipped up his fly, but from the
smile on his face I knew he had just received special oral favors
from the girl who was jocking him from the other side of the
club with this big " I can't wait to eat you alive" look on her
face. Not a moment too soon, he told me that he was gonna
leave with that woman for a quickie. He used the girl's cell
phone to call Ballo to tell him to be in front of the club in ten
minutes. He told Darlene that he realized he left his wallet at the
hotel that he had to go back to retrieve it because he didn't trust
the maids there. That Negro knew that he didn't bring his wallet
because he was gonna try to run game on these women.

I pulled Dexter to the side and asked him what happened to
teamwork in a tone filled with hate. Dexter was the person who
got me used to the word knucklehead because he was always
acting like one. He promised that it wouldn't take long and that
he would come back for Darlene later because he wanted to
wake up next to her in the morning. Whatever the tramp did to
Dexter, he wanted more of it. I knew he was going back to the
hotel to have sex with her. I told him not to let me down
because I really wanted to get with Melanie. He assured me that
he was just as anxious to get a taste of Darlene. After he told me

that, I took one look at Darlene and I knew that Dexter couldn't pass up that opportunity. Something about Darlene said "freak" in a way that words couldn't describe. She just looked like she could swallow a man whole in her own way.

The whole time we were in the club doing our thing, Jess was on the dance floor with this guy with dreadlocks. He was one of those Eric Benet types that she just couldn't resist. All that bullshit she was talking about; not liking guys with dreadlocks went out the window after she met the guy I called "Mr. Fine." I could always count on Jessie to be a sucker for a fine looking guy. She suffered from Halle Berry Syndrome. In order for her to get with a guy, he had to be fine. She had a weakness for good-looking guys. Maybe, she enjoyed sharing a mirror with a guy who was just as pretty as she was. She looked like she was having a good time with Mr. Fine, so I didn't bother checking up on her.

I kept Darlene, Melanie and the linebackers entertained for about an hour before Dexter finally showed up. And I had to buy a few round of drinks in the process. Those linebackers could guzzle down a whole keg by themselves. Dexter told me that instead, he went back to the girl's hotel, which was located across the street from the club. He had to tell Ballo to come back later for us promising that he would hook him up with a few dollars for making him come down to the club in the first place. He said he and Lady Tramp couldn't wait to tear off each other's clothes, so he decided to go to the closest room. Before he left the club, he guzzled down a Red Bull for energy sake.

According to Dexter, Lady Tramp didn't wait for them to get through the door to tear off her panties and rubbed it all over his face. She had started to blow him in a dark corner in the club and she wanted to finish the job. After closing the door behind them in her room at the hotel, she pulled out Dexter's eight inches and deep throat it like Vanessa Del Rio herself had taught her how to deep throat Dexter's long snake. She was doing tricks with her throat that Dexter had never experienced before. She used her tonsil to perform tricks that doctors and research scientists would think impossible. She gagged on the tip of his eight-inch dick creating a tingling sensation that he could only describe as heavenly. She spent about fifteen minutes giving him the oral royal treatment that was suited for a king. She also juggled his nuts in her mouth like she was a professional circus juggler. Dexter claimed that his nuts had never been soothed and stimulated in such a manner.

He slowly pulled up the body fitted rubber material mini dress she was wearing up her thighs and proceeded to rub her clit until she could no longer stand it. She was hot and she was screaming for him to take her from behind. Instead, he stuck his index finger inside of her while he rubbed her clit with his thumb. She was screaming so much in pleasure; the people in the room next door asked if they could have some of what they were having. Disregarding the remarks of their next-door neighbor, Dexter pulled out a magnum condom and slipped it on and without warning, he slid all his eight inches inside her while still rubbing her clit.

Dexter knew that time was of the essence and he wanted her to submit to his prowess quicker than he would have liked. While stroking her as hard as he could and rubbing her clit with his right hand, he stuck his thumb in her ass and she started screaming that she was cumming. The harder she screamed, the harder he stroked her. She came over and over again and then asked Dexter to give it to her in her ass. He politely obliged by putting on a new condom and slowly penetrated her from the back. He started banging her slowly, but she kept pushing her ass up against him, forcing all of his eight inches inside of her. He didn't know that she was a pro at first, but after realizing that her ass had seen just as much action as her pussy, he started banging her hard from behind until she let out a louder scream that she was coming again. He was about to come himself, so he pulled back, allowing the sensation to settle down. Her goods were just too tasty for Dexter to come so quickly. Besides, he really wanted to come in her mouth. He pulled his dick out of her ass, took off the condom, and stuck it in her mouth. She twirled her tongue around it and took it in her mouth like it was a banana split. With every lick, Dexter succumbed to her prowess. She added a little suction on the tip of his dick that sent him exploding all over her mouth. She took it down her throat like a pro.

Dexter went in the bathroom to freshen up before heading back to the club. He used one of the washcloths to wipe off her scent and juice. His pants never came off while he banged her on the edge of the bed. They were down his ankles the whole time. He checked himself in the mirror then flushed the two used condoms down the toilet. By the time he came out of the bathroom, Lady Tramp had fallen deep asleep. He pulled the covers on top of her and pulled the door close behind him and left.

Hearing all that heated shit from Dexter, gave me a hard on for Melanie and I was hoping that maybe I might be able to score with her. But first, I was happy to see that Dexter came back as promised. We stayed at the club for another hour and Dexter spent most of it with Darlene. Occasionally, he would walk away for five minutes just to collect a few numbers from the other women who were visiting from the States. Dexter's insatiable sexual appetite just couldn't be tamed. He was setting up future ass for when we got back to the State while he still had potential ass waiting in the club. Jess may have been suffering from Halle Berry Syndrome, but Dexter definitely needed to see Eric Benet's sex therapist.

It was three o'clock in the morning when we decided to leave the club. The linebackers were on the dance floor getting their groove on and we wanted to sneak out with their friends before they could line up for a sack. Unfortunately, the girls didn't want to leave without telling the linebackers that they were leaving. Darlene walked over to the dance floor and told one of the linebackers that she was going to leave with Dexter and that she would see them the next day. As Darlene was making her way back to us, the two linebackers must have exchanged words when one of them screamed, "we came together, we're leaving together." Despite all our efforts to get these cock blockers drunk, they were still sober enough to interfere with our game.

One of the cock blockers seemed like she was all too familiar with the game. She didn't want to let up. I noticed that she was as belligerent as a bull, so I went to one of the skinny Jamaican dudes with dreadlocks and offered him and his friend twenty dollars each to keep the cock blockers on the dance floor for the rest of the night. I had to pull out a trick of my own because I was horny as hell. Dexter and I made our way out of the club with the girls leaving the two Jamaican dudes to entertain the cock blockers.

I was the happiest man that night when I left the club with Melanie. In all my attempts to leave a club with a woman in the past, this was the first time I was successful with a positive outlook. I was imagining all kinds of crazy sexual things that I wanted to do to Melanie. I'm talking about things that I had only seen on television and while watching porno flicks. With all of Darlene's thirty-two pearly whites exposed half the night, I knew that she was down for whatever with Dexter. I couldn't really read Melanie's face because I had never been down that road before. I just assumed that I was gonna get some ass based on the fact that she was willing to leave the club with me smiling. What's that old saying again, "when you assume you make an ass out of you and me" right? Well, I hate that saying.

When we got outside as expected, Ballo was leaning on his cab waiting for us. We came out and got in the cab with the girls and Ballo noticed that Jess was not with us. He asked if she was coming, but Dexter and I had completely forgotten about Jess. We allowed pussy to make us lose our senses and we were about to leave the club without telling Jess a thing. After Ballo asked about her, I quickly ran back inside the club to tell Jess that Dexter and I were leaving with the women. Jess was a little mad that we were leaving without her, but she was comforted and wrapped in the arms of her Eric Benet look-alike. I told her to call us when she got to the hotel and that Ballo would come back in ten minutes to pick her up. I didn't want to get nosey about the guy she was dancing with because I was too anxious to find out if I was finally going to score.

Whether Jess was going to take the pretty boy home with her didn't really matter to me. She was a big girl and I knew she could handle herself. However, just in case the pretty boy acted up, I pulled a few strands from his locks for DNA purposes after getting his name in case the cops needed them. He was all too happy for me to tell him how nice his dreadlocks were as I pulled off a few strands. These pretty bastards usually don't care who a compliment is coming from as long as they're getting one. I acted like I was giving him props and he was more than willing to let me see how together and clean his dreads were motioning his head back and forth like a little bitch. He didn't even realize that when I tugged on his hair and ask if they ever fall out that I was actually collecting evidence from his dumb, pretty ass. I must've pulled at least five strands and I placed them in my pocket before shaking his hand and giving Jess a hug and a kiss on the cheek.

After making sure that Jess was going to be all right, I dashed out of the club like a runaway slave. I didn't want Melanie to change her mind about leaving with me. I got in the cab and told Ballo to come back for Jess after he dropped us off. It almost seemed like Ballo could sense the urgency in me, so he put the pedal to the metal like he had never done before. We were at the hotel in less than a minute. As we exited the cab, I pulled out a crisp twenty-dollar bill and handed it to Ballo for his kind consideration. Desperado must've been written all over my face because I was so easy to read when it came to women. I couldn't even hide it from Ballo. And I was sure even Ballo thought he could get more pussy than me. That's fucked up because Ballo had no front teeth.

When we got to the hotel, Dexter wanted to get cute, so he decided to give Darlene a piggyback ride to his room. I always felt like Dexter was outdoing me when it came to romance, but he always kept it real with the way he treated women and the little things he did for them drove them wild. That piggyback suggestion pretty much sealed the deal for him with Darlene. I was standing there with this dumbfounded look on my face because I didn't have any romantic suggestions for Melanie on our way to my room. I simply held her hand as we walked towards the elevator. I didn't want to be corny by having her jump on my back like Dexter and Darlene. I was confident that Dexter was going to get a chance to taste Darlene's sweet ass, but what were my chances now?

Melanie was not as extroverted as Darlene was and I knew that I had heard enough from Dexter and other men that the quiet chicks were the biggest freaks. So, I was trying to anticipate this freaky experience with Melanie, but the problem was that I didn't know how to get it started. When we got upstairs to my room, I wanted to set the mood, so I asked Melanie if she wanted a glass of wine forgetting that she had just gulped down four drinks back at the club. And to make the situation worse, I was offering her something that I didn't even have in my room. At three thirty in the morning, there was no room service available and no concierge to bring me a bottle of wine. The front desk clerk almost laughed at me when I asked if they could send a bottle of wine to my room. I could pick up the smirk in his voice through the phone. It almost seemed like the whole world was laughing at me whenever I was trying to get some ass. It was no laughing matter to me.

Melanie and I sat on the edge of the king size bed in my room and in my own head, I was imagining us rolling around in the bed butt naked holding on to each other like two lovers who didn't know how to let go. For a moment, I had created the best possible scenario that could've happened. After I finally woke out of my dream state, I found Melanie leaning on me with her head over my shoulder. She was sitting there so innocently not knowing that I wanted to take advantage of her sexually. I also realized that Melanie and I were two awkward people in an awkward situation and we didn't know what to do.

After about fifteen minutes of sitting there silently holding on to each other, Melanie asked me what were my goals, dreams, and what I aspired to be. I don't know if that was her way of lightening the mood, but she threw me for a loop and I couldn't see myself trying to take advantage of her anymore. I realized that Melanie was a nice woman who thought that she had met a nice man and she wanted to spend time with me. In a way, I sort of appreciated her innocence and it gave me a sense that I was not the only person in this world who didn't think that sex defined who I was.

Melanie and I ended up talking for close to two hours about our upbringing and we found out that we both came from single parent households and our mothers were tough as nails. Melanie was 24 years old and she had just graduated from University of Chicago with a degree in accounting. She was offered a job by a big accounting firm that she was starting in two weeks and her mother wanted to do something special for her to celebrate her accomplishments. Her friends had a trip planned to Jamaica and she decided that she wanted to join them before permanently joining the workforce.

Around four-thirty that morning after chatting with Melanie, she decided to go to her hotel so her friends wouldn't worry about her in the morning. I called Ballo on his cell phone and asked him if he could take her home. As I was walking Melanie downstairs to the cab, I was trying to sneak a peak at her beautiful body and her sexy walk. A part of me wished that I had slept with her, but the other part of me was just grateful that she felt comfortable enough to leave the club with me and stayed in my room and talked to me.

I kissed Melanie for the first time when she was about to get in the cab, and at that moment I knew that she was a very special woman. We exchanged numbers and promised to stay in touch with each other when we got back home. Melanie still had a few more days left on her vacation and I was on my way home the next morning.

After Melanie left, I thought about the possibility of pursuing a relationship with her and the distance between us. Of course, I was in Boston, she was in Atlanta starting a new career, and that would just be too demanding for either of us. Melanie in a way restored my faith in women because she didn't care about my money, the way I looked or what I did for a living. She only cared about Malcolm the person and for that, I was grateful. Why is it that you can never be with the one you want?

The Morning After

The next day I got up very early because our flight was scheduled to leave out of Montego Bay's Sangster's International Airport at 9:00 am. I must've gotten no more than two hours of sleep. I called Jess and Dexter around 6:30 am to make sure that they were up and ready to go. Jess told me that she was already up packing her stuff and that she would meet me downstairs in the lounge at seven o'clock. Because Jess was up so early in the morning, I figured she must've sent the pretty boy home alone. It was too early to get into it, so I told her I'd meet her downstairs at seven o'clock. It was a little harder for Dexter to get out of bed because Darlene was still in his bed with him. Dexter picked up the phone when I called and sounded like a man who had been out of commission for a few days. There was no strength left in his voice and he sounded like he was overly exhausted. I told him he had to get up or we were going to leave Jamaica without him.

Dexter knew that he didn't want to stay in Jamaica by himself, so he got up and jumped in the shower to force himself to wake up. As neat as Dexter is, he didn't have too much time to pack, so he threw most of his clothes in his luggage without folding them and that bothered him. I guess that's the sacrifice one has to make for a piece of ass, sometimes. It was harder for Dexter to get Darlene to wake up because he must've fucked her so hard that she fell in a deeper sleep than the Lady Tramp.

We had planned to catch the complimentary shuttle back to the airport, but because we had to drop Darlene off at her hotel, we decided to call Ballo. Everyone showed up at the lobby at seven o'clock as planned. When I saw Darlene in the morning, it seemed like a metamorphosis had taken place. Her weave was all out of place, all the cake make up she wore to hide the blemishes on her ugly skin had been wiped off on the pillow in the room and she looked like a street walker that Dexter had picked with a two dollar bill. Jess and I were laughing our asses off at how bad Darlene looked. She went from beauty queen to Frankenstein's wife in a span of three hours. She just didn't have any natural beauty at all. I realized that day if I were ever to meet a woman, I wanted to meet her during the day in the sunlight so I can get a good look at her natural beauty. Nightfall made everything look good and the lights in the clubs just confirmed all of it. Darlene was fine as hell the night before, but somehow her beauty faded away; along with her make up like she was a vampire.

It took Ballo less than ten minutes to show up at the hotel to pick us up. I didn't know what kind of energy drink Ballo had been drinking or what type of weed he had been smoking, but he was always energetic and alert whenever we saw him. I wanted to ask him where he got his weed because he had the kind of energy that a woman would appreciate in a man. For a moment there, I considered becoming a weed head. Ballo was wide-awake as he came out of the car to open the trunk to place our luggage inside. I was glad that he was taking us to the airport because I wanted to justly compensate him for being a good guide and driver to us while we were in Jamaica.

It took us less than five minutes to reach Darlene's hotel. As she was getting out of the car, she wanted to exchange phone numbers with Dexter. He took one long look at her scary looking ass, told her that we were in a hurry, and had to go and she could look him up in the phone book under the last name Johnson. That Negro knew he was lying because there was not a Johnson in that car. We just shook our heads as Dexter buried his face in his lap shaking his head as if to ask why the hell he slept with her.

Dexter knew he had it coming from Jess and I, and not a moment too soon after Ballo pealed off, Jess started to let him have it. "I hope her pussy was better than she looks," she said. Even Ballo who had no front teeth, was grinning from side to side. I bust out laughing then she followed with "Were you so horny that you couldn't even turn on the lights first?" Ballo smirked then followed with his own comment "Sometimes when a man let his dick take the lead, he don't know what's left or right, what's good or bad or in Dexter's case, what's ugly or pretty." We all busted out laughing, but Dexter came back at Ballo with "That's why I ain't gonna give you enough tip to get your front teeth put in." Ballo answered with "That's okay, I'm used to not having any teeth, but even Stevie Wonder could've seen that woman was ugly." That crap went on for a few minutes and in the end, we all just laughed our asses off because it was a funny thing that happened.

The car was silent for a few minutes during the ride to the airport. We had been driving for close to a half hour and everybody had dozed off. By the time we were awakened by Ballo, we were at the airport and we only had thirty minutes to check in. We rushed out of the car and told Jess to go wait in line while we gathered our luggage. Ballo helped Dexter and I carry the luggage inside the airport to where Jess was waiting in line. There were a lot of screw faces as we made our way up the line next to Jess cutting about ten people who were waiting. We all thanked Ballo for his services and we each gave him a hug and four crisp US hundred dollar bills. Ballo gave us his number and told us to look him up next time we were in town.

We finally made it to the front of the line after waiting for fifteen minutes, just a few minutes before our flight departure. We were trying our best to rush the process, but it seemed like everyone in Jamaica was always at a stand still. We barely made it to the plane after that long check-in with the ticket agent. We were all seated in the same row in first class. Jess upgraded to first class and had the window seat, I was in the center and Dexter had the aisle seat. We were all tired and couldn't wait to lean our seats back to catch some zz's. The plane sat still for about a half hour before the pilot finally announced that we were ready for take-off. The beautiful flight attendant demonstrated the emergency procedures as best as she could while Dexter tried his best to flirt with her. She was trying her best not to respond to Dexter's flirtatious stares, but in the end, she couldn't resist him.

After watching Dexter and the flight attendant flirt with each for a while, I realized that Dexter was always testing his limits and was hoping to be challenged by a woman some day. He knew damn well that he didn't really want anything to do with the flight attendant, but for his own selfish, egotistical reasons, he wanted to see if she would respond to his advances. By the look on Dexter's face, I could tell that he was getting tired of playing these games.

The plane was airborne around 9:40 am and when the captain announced that the seatbelt sign was turned off we all leaned our seats back simultaneously as if to say good night. We were hoping to sleep the whole flight home, but after about two hours of flying, we hit turbulence and that woke us all up. Jess was a little shaken, so she grabbed my hand for comfort. Dexter just looked angry like his sleep had been interrupted. While we were up they were serving breakfast and we took advantage. We filled our stomachs as if we were little wanderers from Somalia who hadn't seen food in years.

That Empty Feeling

As we were sitting on the plane with nothing to read or do except watching the crappy movie that was being shown, I turned to Dexter to ask him a question, but he was deep in thought. I could tell that there was something on his mind because I knew him like that. Something was bothering him and he didn't know how to talk about it. I took the initiative to ask him what was wrong. Before he turned to me to say anything, he looked over to Jess to see if she was listening. But, Jess had her face buried in the pillow that the flight attendant provided for her. Just like a Negro, she ate and went back to sleep. I didn't know how personal Dexter was going to get, so I didn't push the issue. I checked to make sure that Jess was asleep and after confirming, I nodded to Dexter that she was out.

Feeling confident that Jess was asleep, Dexter turned to me and said, "Can I tell you something, man?" I responded "sure." I didn't know what to expect out of Dexter's mouth, but the serious tone in his voice and the look on his face were very new and foreign to me. I was hoping that Dexter wasn't going to tell me that he had some venereal disease or something. I knew that he easily bedded at least three hundred women since I've known him and he could've slipped and caught something along the way. Call me a drama king, but I always imagine the worst that could happen so that I'm not surprised when I hear it. I must've lost myself in thought after my response to Dexter, so he shook me and asked, "Are you listening, man." I jumped out of my imaginary world and said, "Sure, I'm with you, man." "Have you ever had that empty feeling?" asked Dexter. I said, "What are you talking about? What kind of empty feeling?" He said, "Have you ever felt like your life is not going anywhere even though you have a lot going on?" I still didn't get what Dexter was trying to get at, so I said, "no, I haven't." He turned to me and said, "Maybe you won't understand, 'cause you haven't been there."

I was trying my best to decipher what Dexter was trying to tell me, but I couldn't get it. I'm sure he noticed the confusion on my face when he turned to me and said, "I'm talking about women, man." I said, "oh, that problem. I wish!" However, I still wanted to know what Dexter meant by feeling empty. Therefore, I asked him straight up what the hell he was trying to say to me. We were trying our best to keep our voices low so the nosey people sitting behind us wouldn't be able to eavesdrop on our conversation. I know a lot of people would try to deny that they ever try to listen in on people's conversation on the plane and to that I say, "Bullshit!" We're all humans and we all have enquiring minds, especially when it involves juicy gossip.

By the low tone in Dexter's voice, I knew it was going to be something personal and dear to him. So I leaned in closer to him, so we could keep it as quiet as possible because the plane was silent as everybody was trying to catch up on their sleep. It felt like everybody on the plane stayed up late the night before. There was no explanation for people being as tired as they were from vacation. Every frigging body was tired, but we didn't want to chance it. Just because somebody's eyes are closed, it doesn't mean that they're asleep. That's how white people become material witnesses in court. They're always listening to some shit that they shouldn't be listening to. And the white people in the row behind us looked like they didn't need a subpoena to show up in court to divulge somebody's shit that they heard on a plane. They had that suspicious look. You know the motherfuckers who have nothing but fucking time on their hands? Yeah, you know that look. I know I sound paranoid, but

I didn't know if Dexter was about to unload some kind of incriminating shit on me.

As quietly as possible, Dexter whispered to me that despite the fact that he had slept with two different women in one night and the fact that he did the same shit day in and day out most of his adult life, he was starting to feel empty inside. I was shocked as hell when I heard those words come out of Dexter's mouth. I was looking around for a heart defibrillator to make sure that I could be saved if I got a heart attack. I couldn't believe that my man was getting tired of pussy. "Damn! Introduce me to some then" I said. Dexter shook his head after my statement as if to say to himself "you wouldn't understand anyway, you virgin bastard." Sometimes words don't have to be spoken, they're implied by certain gestures and I knew Dexter's gestures.

As much as I would have liked to believe that Dexter was getting tired of sleeping with different women, I knew better. I knew it was a matter of time before he got all excited about some new pussy that he could get his claws on. I was shocked, but not convinced. I think it was one of those soul-cleansing moments that Dexter was going through. However, my black ass was not a priest. "Go tell it to the priest in church when we get back" was what I wanted to say to him. He continued, "I'm serious, man. I want to give up all these women. I want to find one woman that I can be with for the rest of my life." I turned to him and said, "What kind of woman would that be?" Dexter paused for a long moment looking over at Jess before he gave me an answer. "I want a woman who's smart, sexy, caring, spontaneous, intelligent, classy, educated beautiful and funny," said Dexter. I was looking at him and thinking to myself "this fool must be living in his own idealistic world to think that he could find all these qualities in one woman. Even my own mother doesn't possess all those qualities and I adore my mother."

I didn't reply to Dexter's comment, but I started thinking about the one woman who came close to having all those qualities and I didn't have to look too far because she was sitting right next to me with her head buried in a pillow and drooling like Niagara Falls was falling on her pillow. I wanted to tell Dexter that Jess would be the perfect woman for him, but a part of me also believed that she was too good for Dexter. Though Dexter was my best friend, he's always been a ladies' man in my eyes and I didn't know if he could appreciate a woman like Jess. She had her flaws too, but she deserved a man who would think the world of her. Maybe I was thinking about my own feelings for Jess, but she's always been a great friend and a wonderful person to me.

After a few minutes of relishing in my own thoughts and feelings for Jess, I felt someone bumping me. It was Dexter asking if I heard him. I turned to him and said, "Yeah, I hear you, man. Where are you going to find such a woman?" He turned back to me and said, "I don't know, and that's the problem. I don't want to have to sleep with half the world before I find the right woman for me." After that statement came out of Dexter's mouth, all I could think was, "Would I ever be so lucky?" At that point, I felt that for the most part Dexter's statements were true, but he was not truly ready to leave the game just yet.

I wanted to know how committed he was to leaving the game, so I asked him what he planned on doing about it when we got back home. Dexter was very honest with his answer, he said, "Like every other indulgence, I have to ease my way out of it slowly. I have to stop going to the bars and nightclubs where these women frequent. I have to commit myself to becoming more cultured. I can't keep staying around these hood rats because I'll never get them out of my system. I have to employ new ways to meet women and I can't expect to sleep with them on the first date." His statement sounded sincere enough to me, but I doubted if he could hold up to it.

We arrived at Logan Airport a half hour later than the flight was supposed to land, but there was no rush so we didn't sweat it. We went to retrieve our luggage and caught a cab home. I was the first to be dropped off in Jamaica Plain. As I exited the cab, I told Dexter that I would call him later and I gave Jess a hug and a kiss. Dexter and Jess lived closer to each other in Hyde Park and Norwood, so it only made sense that they rode the rest of the way together.

A Love Story

On the ride home to Hyde Park, Jess and Dexter were silent most of the way. The cab driver was trying to make small talk with them. He assumed that Jess and Dexter was a couple. He told them that they were the most beautiful couple that he had seen in a long time and was wondering if there was a disagreement of some sort between them. The cab driver was a man in his sixties who told us that he'd lost his wife to diabetes five years earlier and he wished that he had treasured every moment with her while she was alive.

The man's story was so sad and moving Jess and Dexter never even interrupted him to tell him that they were not a couple. The man went on about how life was too short and sometimes we take our time on earth and our loved ones for granted without realizing it. He also told them that in everyone's lifetime they only get one chance at true love. Not that it's impossible for someone to find love twice, but true love only happens once.

From Jamaica Plain to Hyde Park, the man told Jess and Dexter the most beautiful love story that they had ever heard and it sounded like something that they themselves had experienced not as a couple but as two stubborn people who might let an opportunity pass them by. The story was almost like a déjà vu for both of them. The cab driver was a retired auto mechanic who had decided to go back to work as a cab driver in order to maintain his sanity. After a long battle with diabetes, his wife succumbed to the disease and his two kids got married and moved out of the house. He was starting to get bored at home and his wife dominated his every thought. He figured driving a cab would give him the opportunity to meet a variety of different people and he would get the chance to interact with them instead of dying of boredom at home.

The cab driver was from Nigeria and his name was Hakeem. He had moved to the United States with his wife and two young kids about thirty years ago. The story about the way he and his wife met was very similar to what was going on with Dexter and Jess. Hakeem met his wife through his best friend, but at first, they couldn't stand each other. However, the friend loved them so much and he wanted them to get along, so he decided to invite them to a weekend retreat at a nearby village in Nigeria. It was there that Hakeem and his wife discovered that the two of them belonged together.

According to Hakeem, he was a ladies' man at the time and his wife was working as a nurse at the local hospital. Of course, we didn't want to doubt that the man was a ladies' man in his hey day and who were we to put a dent in his story. Most men think of themselves as ladies' men at one point in their lives, anyway. For some of them it's true and for others it's a figment of their imagination.

Hakeem's wife couldn't stand his ways with the ladies, but there was a strong attraction between them. The more they thought they hated each other, the stronger their attraction became. As much as they tried to fight their emotions, their love couldn't be denied. After leaving the retreat the following Monday, they ended up catching a bus together back home without their friend and it was then they discovered how much they had in common and decided to give their love a try. Soon after, they were married and spent the next thirty years of their lives together.

The look on Jess and Dexter's face confirmed that they didn't want their cab ride to end so abruptly. However, the cab driver was getting very close to Jess's house. Although, they wanted to hear more about the man's wife and his life, the story would soon end as the cab pulled in front of Jessie's house.

Dexter and Jess hadn't gotten a chance to tell the cab driver about their different destinations because they were captivated by his story. Jess had reached her destination first and she turned to Dexter and told him that she would take him home if he didn't mind getting dropped off at her house. Dexter didn't want to disappoint the cab driver after he told them such a beautiful love story, so he decided to get out the cab at Jess' house pretending that they were together. They both told the cab driver that they were sorry about the loss of his wife, to keep his head up and not to drown in his sorrows. Dexter paid the fare with a generous tip. The cab driver wished them luck with their love affair.

Dexter and Jess

It may have been fate or it could've been that it was meant to be, but that cab ride would change the nature of Jess and Dexter's relationship forever. Dexter had never been to Jess's house in Hyde Park. He was surprised when Jess walked towards this big white Victorian home with blue trimming after getting out the cab. The house was breath taking from the outside and the street it was located on was very quiet. When Jess opened her door the aroma of the lemon scented plug-ins smacked them both right in the face. Dexter was impressed right away because he was a meticulous guy who kept his place cleaner than clean and smelling fresh all the time. He placed his luggage down at the entrance and stood around looking over at everything that his eyes could see. It was like he was on a whirlwind when he entered her house.

As they made their way from the hardwood foyer into the kitchen, Dexter's eyes were glued to the sparkle on the shiny hardwood floor. Dexter asked if the house had hardwood floors throughout as he followed Jess to the kitchen and Jess confirmed with an excited "yes!" Jess was a little happy that Dexter found her place so amazing and she offered a tour. She placed her luggage down by the entrance of the kitchen and proceeded to show Dexter the rest of the house. Her kitchen was to die for. She had granite counter tops with oak cabinets and the latest stainless steel appliances. In the center of the kitchen, she had an island built which served as a breakfast table with four stools surrounding it. Her kitchen was spotless. Around the corner from the kitchen was the formal dining room. She had a nice antique dinette set with six regular chairs and two armchairs. On the corner in the dining room sat an antique china cabinet with beautiful hand made glass. And one cannot help being mesmerized by the beautiful antique chandelier hanging from the ceiling in the center of the room.

Located directly from the dining room was the formal living room. Her living room was a lot more modern than the rest of the house, which gave it an eclectic feel. She had a beautiful canary yellow suede living room set with a beautifully hand painted abstract glass table that reflected some of the colors of the living room and her two toned oriental rug. It was a wide-open space that looked like it could serve more as a socializing room. Of course, there was also a family room where she watched television, an office and a library. The house was spotless and very inviting. Dexter didn't want to cross the line, so he declined her offer to visit the four bedrooms upstairs. He was starting to get turned on by Jess after stepping into her house. He realized that they were both neat freaks, attractive and independent people who would probably sleep with each other very quickly if given the chance. Jess also enjoyed the fact that Dexter appreciated a clean home. She had been to my house and she knew that I was not a neat freak like them.

Too much may not have been said between Dexter and Jess that day, but they both realized that they had more in common than they wish they had. The attraction between them also was undeniable. I think deep down inside Dexter was smitten by Jess, and she also enjoyed his dark, chocolate skin, his bright smile and his confidence.

As Dexter waited in the living room for Jess to put away her luggage, he looked through her photo album and saw how skinny and awkward she looked as a youngster. He noticed that she took a lot of pictures with her family. Her parents appeared to have been happy at one point in time. Even through the pictures, he could sense that she was surrounded by love as a child. When Jess made her way around the foyer to the living room, her face became flushed when she noticed that Dexter was looking at her photo album, which sat conspicuously on the coffee table. It was almost as if she were embarrassed like a little girl because the boy she liked saw her embarrassing pictures. Dexter sensed her discomfort so he quickly complimented her on her cuteness as a child. She couldn't believe that he thought she was cute. She had pictures in that album when she first got her braces and wearing her bifocals. Jess knew that she had come a long way as far as beauty was concerned. She was happy that he wasn't malicious about it.

Jess had changed from wearing a loosely fitted linen dress because of the Jamaican heat to a nice pair of tight fitted jeans, open toed high-heeled sandals and a white halter-top. She had also washed up very quickly and emerged as the beautiful goddess that she was. She had her hair pulled back in a ponytail revealing her beautiful features. The look on Dexter's face when he took a long look at her confirmed that she was banging. She grabbed her car keys from the table and told Dexter that she was ready. Dexter followed behind her and grabbed his bag on the way out the door. She waited until Dexter stepped out and she pulled the door behind him securing the top lock with her key.

Jess went around to the side of the house to open her steel gate so she could back her black convertible BMW out of the garage. She pulled the automatic garage opener out of her purse and with one push of a button her garage door went up to reveal her spotless car. While she went inside the garage to pull her car out, Dexter decided to wait until after she pulled out of the driveway completely so he could close the gate behind her. After she backed out of her driveway and the gate closed, she playfully peeled out leaving Dexter standing in front of the gate with his luggage. She acted like she was going to leave him there and Dexter's whole demeanor changed. He didn't know if she was trying to play a cruel joke on him or not, but she had a sense of humor.

After driving down the street to about half of a block, she stopped and backed up to pick up Dexter. The first words out of her mouth were "I got you!" as she pressed the automatic button to pop the trunk open. Dexter smiled and placed his luggage in the trunk then jumped in the front seat of the car. However, before pulling off this time, she pressed the automatic button for the roof of the car to come down dropping the convertible top. She also went inside her glove compartment and pulled out a nice pair of Dolce &Gabana shades. She was looking like a diva.

Even though Dexter and Jess weren't a couple, they sure as hell looked like one, and a beautiful couple at that. Dexter was trying to be funny and sarcastic at the same time, so he asked Jess if she got all dolled up to go see her psychologist boyfriend. The look on her face revealed that he was not supposed to know that. Jess did not want me divulging her business to Dexter. I think Dexter just wanted to know how far along her relationship was with the shrink. At first, she didn't say anything, but as they continued to drive to Norwood, Dexter wouldn't let up about it. She finally screamed at the top of her lung and through the wind blowing in her face, "It's not that serious, if you must know!" Dexter took her answer as a sign that she was not happy with her man. He told her that he didn't mean to get her all riled up about it and didn't say anything else to her the rest of the way except when she needed the occasional directions to his house.

A fun drive had turned to something that neither of them wanted it to be. When Jess dropped Dexter off at his mansion, she told him she was sorry for yelling at him earlier and if there was anyway that she could make it up to him. He turned to her and with a big smile on his face, he asked her if she wanted to have dinner with him. "I supposed so," she said nonchalantly. "Great, I will call you when I'm ready," he said as he grabbed his luggage and headed towards his house leaving her to wonder what he meant by that. She looked dazed and confused by his comment as she took off shaking her head and waving good-bye to him.

A Joyous Train Ride

A couple of days after I came back from Jamaica I needed to go down to the school department for a meeting to straighten out some paperwork early that Tuesday morning. It was a nice sunny day, so I decided to park my car by the Ashmont train station so I could catch the Red Line train to the Orange Line to Malden. After I boarded the train, I took a seat right near the door to my right. Walking behind me on the train was the most beautiful chocolate-skinned woman that I had ever laid eyes on in my entire life. It had to happen on my way down to the Department of Education in Malden, I thought to myself. She sat right across from me on the train. There was something exotic about this woman when I saw her. She had an island glow about her and her defining cheekbones were striking. I said island glow because I was still thinking about all those beautiful sisters that I saw in Jamaica just a few days prior.

The way she strutted her stuff was enough for me to imagine a runway lit up in front of her. She was about 5ft 8inches tall, but her four inch heels gave her this bigger than life stature. She had the smoothest chocolate skin that I had ever seen. She walked with the confidence of a supermodel and the aura of an intellectual. She had big beautiful dark brown eyes, medium length hair and a beautiful curvaceous body. She had a tiny waist and a nice round butt. There was definitely something foreign and unusual about her. As she was sitting across from me on the half-empty train, I was trying to sneak a peek at her legs. And when she looked up and noticed that I was taking inventory of her legs, she just smiled at me then crossed her legs the opposite direction. I was trying my best to keep from getting a hard-on on the train. I didn't want to portray myself as a pervert, but it took a lot of squeezing my balls between my legs to keep my manhood from rising.

She was smiling at me and I took her smile as an invitation to walk over and sit next to her to start a conversation. Before I could walk over, I had to contain myself and make sure that the blood from my head didn't already start to circulate down south to my other head. I kept my walk almost as tight as a homosexual in skintight jeans, looking very corny. I sat down next to her and I asked her name. "Why?" she responded. I couldn't believe it. No one has ever responded why when I asked their name before, this was the first time. I told her if I were going to try to start a conversation with her, I at least needed to know her name in order to address her. "What makes you think that I want to have a conversation with you?" she said. This girl was starting to become too much of a challenge. And I was in no mood to be challenged.

When I got up to walk back across to my seat, she whispered, "Are you giving up so easily?" I didn't know what kind of game she was playing but I was willing to play along for a little while, but not long. I'd be lying if I say she was not worth all the patience in the world. She turned to me and said, "That's what I don't like about you American men, you expect everything to be so easy. What kind of girl would I be if I just gave you my name without talking to you first?" At first, I thought, "This girl is tripping. She must've sniffed some bad glue before she left her house or something." Then I realized that she was probably right. As fine as she was, there were probably tons of men who tried talking to her everyday. She had every right to hold out on me.

Some men just make it so hard for women to open up to the rest of us good guys. For every nice guy out there who's looking for a serious girlfriend, there are about twenty jerks or players who are just looking to get in these women's pants. Despite what the women say, the success rate for these jerks is still over fifty percent. Some women are generally attracted to jerks. For every open minded or receptive woman out there, there are about fifty women scorned.

On beauty alone, Marjorie was worth a nine on a scale of one to ten. The only reason why I would not give her a ten was because I wanted to hold something back to curve her intelligence either up or down just in case. To be honest, I've wasted my time on far worse jezebels before. The train ride wasn't going to be that long, so I wanted to get the important things out of the way before either of us had to exit the train as I was close to reaching my stop at Downtown Crossing.

One of the cutest things that I noticed about Marjorie was her accent. She was talking like the words were being formed slowly from her brain as they came out of her mouth. It was something similar to a French or African dialect. It was clearly evident that English was her second language. I didn't want to make an ass out of myself by assuming that I knew where she was from. So, I allowed her to tell me that she was from Haiti and moved to the States after she graduated from secondary school back in her homeland. Her posture was straight as if she attended etiquette school or something. I had never seen a woman of that magnitude in my life. I asked her where she was headed; she told me that she was headed to Tufts University to pick up a copy of her transcript. I asked if she was an alumnus of Tufts University she said, "Yes." She also told me that she was planning on attending Boston University's medical school the upcoming fall.

I was impressed to say the least. This woman was gorgeous and on her way to becoming a physician. Was I really going to be that lucky? I could tell that she sensed the angst in my demeanor as the train approached the Downtown Crossing station. I told her that I needed to switch to the Orange Line in order for me to get to Malden. Most of the time I would just drive to Malden, but I didn't want to get caught in that rush hour traffic on Interstate 93. Sometimes I just like to hop on the train to get a feel of the city as a resident. Many city residents never take the time to enjoy what their own cities offer them. Instead, they allow foreign tourists to take advantage of the beauty of their cities. Not that there's anything wrong with that, but as a resident, I have always been interested in learning what my city is all about.

As the train slowed down towards the Washington Street/Downtown Crossing station, I asked Marjorie if we could continue our conversation over dinner. She told me we'd have to see. I presumed that getting her number was out of the question, so I simply wrote mine down on a piece of paper and handed it to her as I made my exit out of the train.

My meeting with the school department went very well that day because I was in a good mood. Marjorie had brightened my day before it even began. I was lost in a world where only the idealists lived during the entire meeting. Everything about Marjorie was ideal. I had just met the girl and I had already imagined what our children would look like. I was consumed by her and I couldn't wait to get home later that evening to hear her voice through the receiver on my telephone. I felt like Alice in wonderland on my way home. I was skipping like a little girl. Although there was no guarantee that Marjorie would call, I had a gut feeling that she wanted to find out what I was all about. Marjorie didn't strike me as superficial. She seemed genuine and smart enough to know that what's inside is more important than the outside. Of course, I could be wrong.

I wonder sometimes why we allow a complete stranger to bring so much happiness into our lives. Is it really our nature to bond with the opposite sex in such a way that we can sometimes lose ourselves in them? I was lost in Marjorie even though I hadn't spent an hour with her yet. The feeling that I was experiencing was very different from anything that I ever experienced before. I had never been so anxious to talk to someone my whole life. Marjorie seemed like a fantasy to me and I just imagined the perfect relationship with her.

One Last Call

When I got home that evening, I spent a few hours in my office going over my monthly bills and paying whatever was due. I started to drift into daydreaming mode again when the phone rang all of a sudden. It was Dexter calling to see if I wanted to go down to Boston Bowl to shoot pool. I wanted to hang out with Dexter, but the call from Marjorie was more important even though I wasn't certain that she was actually going to call. When Dexter asked why I turned him down, I tried my best to come up with a quick excuse but it wasn't quick enough. He caught me lying and he knew almost instantly that it had to do with a woman. The first words out of his mouth after I tried lying to him were "Who is she?" At this point, I was thinking that Dexter might've known me a little too well. It wasn't like I was standing in front of him and he could read my facial expression, we were on the phone. I had to come clean, so I told him about Marjorie and the way we met. Dexter was a little excited for me, but he was also cautious to warn me about getting my hopes up too high.

Dexter wanted to break down his mack daddy approach about women to me again. He went on about how women are hard to read sometimes and we shouldn't get too excited about them all the time because we can set ourselves up for failure. Dexter told me that women meet men on the train all the time and sometimes people are just friendly on the train to rid themselves of a person. I was on the phone listening to every word that Dexter dished out to me. I was also thinking about how Mr. Player could either be full of it or he could be right.

I started to think, "Why should I stay home and wait by the phone for a girl to call me when I have voicemail?" We're not living in the 80's anymore. She could leave me a message and I'd call her back. Dexter also asked, "how come you didn't give her your cell phone number?" Being that I was not a player and didn't think on my feet as quickly as Dexter did, I didn't even remember that I had a cell phone. Another reason was that I only used my cell phone for emergencies in the past. So, I was not used to giving out the number. And that reminded me that I had to upgrade my cell phone and calling plan. I was still carrying the old phone that could light up a whole residential block when I turned it on. You know the kind that's almost as big as a cordless house phone.

It didn't take much for Dexter to convince me that I needed to go down to Boston Bowl and whip his ass in pool. I told Dexter to pick me up in a half hour. Surprisingly, this knucklehead was already in front of my building while we were on the phone. He called me from his cell phone. No! I didn't have caller ID either. It was one of his spontaneous ideas again. All that garbage he was talking on the phone was to really get me to see things his way. However, he was also right in a way too. I should not have had to submit myself to a telephone just because I was hoping for this woman to call me. Dexter told me to hurry down before the place got too crowded.

Dexter was always a smooth brother to begin with, but after we became rich, this fool always dressed like there was going to be a red carpet rolled out for him everywhere he went. I asked him what he was wearing and he told me that he wearing black linen pants, a yellow linen shirt over his pants and black suede sandals. I asked him why he was so dressed up and he said that he had a surprise waiting for me. I was hoping that he somehow was able to find Marjorie and he brought her to my house. Obviously, that was not the case.

Since Dexter bought his new Mercedes, I don't think he gave that car a chance to get dirty. It just seemed like he washed his car everyday. I guess you can't look clean driving a dirty car. I finally made it downstairs and as I approached the car, I noticed three figures were sitting in the car. Dexter was up to his old tricks again. There was a friend and he wanted me to keep her company. When I opened the passenger door and looked in the back, I saw the most beautiful woman that I ever laid eyes on. She was light skinned with long curly hair, I'm not sure if her hair was real, but I really didn't care either way. Her eyes were hazel and I could tell from her hips that she had the kind of booty that I couldn't wait to see. This woman was bad.

I didn't know what Dexter told her about me, but she was overly anxious to get to know me. For the first time in my life, I felt like a player way before I discovered what the game was about. This gorgeous woman was all over me and I couldn't understand why. She was feeling my chest, my arms and massaging my head as if we had known each other for years. It was definitely more affection than I could handle. She hadn't even asked what my name was, but her prints were all over me. The only thing I could think about at this time was that Dexter had gotten me a call girl or a high-class prostitute. She didn't look as trashy as the street prostitutes, though. Dexter looked in the rearview mirror and gave me the thumb up. I had no idea what that meant because he failed to leave the player handbook in my mailbox prior to picking me up. I was just trying to go along with the flow until we got to Boston Bowl so I could have a chat with him away from the girls.

This woman was doing a lot of touching and groping without saying a word. I wanted to find out if she was a mute or something. I asked what her name was and she told me it was Charlene. Her voice was a little deep for a woman, but I didn't think much of it because I remember how Isabel Sanford's voice from the Jefferson's sounded. By then I definitely preferred the silent treatment she gave me earlier. Her voice could kill the mood. She continued with the touching and I was trying to nonchalantly feel her neck for an Adam's apple or something. Dexter was a practical joker and I did not want to be a victim of his cruel jokes. I held her tight against my chest to see if her breasts were real and I wanted so much to feel her crotch to see if we had the same organs. But a gentleman would never touch a woman's crotch fifteen minutes after meeting her, would he? Well, he wouldn't unless she was reaching for his crotch. This woman started reaching for my crotch and I figured what the hell? I might as well find out if she was a woman too.

She was wearing a short skirt with no underwear. It was somewhat reminiscent of the role Grace Jones played in Boomerang. However, she was a lot more attractive than Grace Jones and she wasn't as ferocious. As I worked my way up her thigh to her crotch, she grabbed my hand and said in her deep Isabel Sanford voice "Do you want to see if it's real?" At that point, only two things came to mind, she was either a transsexual or people had mistaken her for a transsexual in the past because of her voice. There was no other reason for her to make that comment. The chicken in me came out and I backed off her. Whenever someone makes a comment like that, I've been told it's because the possibility of the unknown exists.

There was no way in the world I was gonna be caught up in some freaky transsexual sexcapade with this sheman. Dexter's woman had a light mustache that was suspect to me too. If she took her time to make sure she was all made up before she went out with him, damn it, she could've taken the time to wax or shave that mustache of hers. I didn't know where he met these women but they were just a little too easy and clingy for my taste. As we were driving down to the bowling alley, Dexter kept pointing down to his crotch and the woman who was sitting in the front passenger seat had her head motioning up and down like she was giving him a blowjob.

The she-man in the back seat took one look at what was going on in the front then she asked me if I wanted to have the same fun Dexter was having. It's one thing to be completely sure that a person is one hundred percent female, but it's a whole other thing when you have no idea and they're eager to get on their knees. I told her I was fine and I didn't need to be serviced. I've heard of people being blown away by a blowjob, but I definitely didn't want to be blown by the job of a man.

Dexter heard when I turned down her offer and said, "Man, if she's half as good as her friend here, you don't know what you're missing." I was thinking to myself "If she has a penis like we both do, you don't know what you're in for." Dexter's freaky ass just wanted to get his thrill with two gorgeous people who only appeared to be female as far as I was concerned. I didn't buy that whole female thing, and I was not willing to take that chance.

We were very close to the Boston Bowl bowling alley when I noticed Dexter's body jerking all over the place like he was in a trance or something. The lady blower had done a hell of a job of making sure Dexter reached his destination before we reached our destination. As tough as Dexter was, he acted like a little bitch when he was about to come. He had better hoped that was a woman who made him cum like that. She must've gulped down all of it because when her head came up she was licking her lips.

When we got to the bowling alley, the place was packed. All the bowling lanes were occupied, but we were there to play pool. While Dexter and I walked over to the counter to pick up the balls and the sticks from the clerk for the pool table, I decided to pull him to the side to ask him what the hell he was doing with these women. He told me that it was his final call for ass and he was hoping that I would join him in an orgy with these women. He said he wanted to sleep with two women for one last time before he went out on a date with Jess. I was like "What? You're going out on a date with Jess!" He turned to me and said, "Yes." Part of me was a little angry, but I knew deep down inside that Jess and Dexter made a better couple. I had to tell him that if he hurt her, I didn't care how bad he was that I would whip his ass. Dexter laughed at my comment and promised that he would never hurt or mistreat her.

The whole time I was with Dexter and the two she-males, I kept thinking about Marjorie. I was wondering if I had missed her call. Dexter could tell that my mind was somewhere else, so he asked if I wanted to go home, sit by the phone, and wait like a little bitch for a phone call. I manned up on him very quickly and told him that I was about to whip his ass on the pool table. I paired up with Barry White's twin sister and Dexter paired up with the blowjob queen.

It turned out that the girls were pretty good in pool and they decided to pair up to play against us and whipped both our asses. After a couple of hours of playing, we decided to leave the bowling alley and head home. Dexter was still trying to get me to partake in his little orgy, but I declined. He made sure he told me that he was gonna bust a nut for me. I guess Dexter needed one for the road before he closed that chapter in his life. He took the suspected ladies home with him and had the last ménage a trois of his life.

Dexter had always been the kind of guy who defied convention whenever he could. The fascinating thing about him was that he was also a disciplined person. When Dexter decides to quit doing something, he usually follows through with his decision.

When he told me that he was going to give up the game for Jess, I knew he was serious and I could only hope for the best for both of them. I still wanted them both in my life.

Catching up with Mom and the family

I hadn't seen my mother during the two days since I came back from Jamaica and I missed her. I didn't know if I missed her as much as I missed her cooking, though. I called her to see how she was doing and was hoping that she would invite me over for dinner so I could tell her all about my trip. My mother was tripping when she got on the phone. She was like "You've forgotten that you have a mother Mr. Rich Man?" I told her no, I did not forget about her. I just didn't get a chance to call her from Jamaica. My mother always worried about me for no reason and when I see her, she wants to pass the blame onto me for not reaching out to her. I told her that I was sorry that I didn't get a chance to call, but I would love to come over to have dinner with her later that evening. She asked me what I wanted for dinner and I told her all my favorite dishes that she has known since I was a kid. I had only come back from Jamaica the past Sunday and I was going to see her on Tuesday evening. Sometimes my mother acted like I didn't have a life of my own.

My mom makes the best macaroni and cheese, collard greens, rice and beans and the best rotisserie chicken that I have ever eaten. I believe that Boston Market stole her recipe. Occasionally, Dexter would come over for dinner, but for the most part, it was just she and I. She also made the best sweet potato pie and kool-aid. No dinner is complete without kool-aid. I didn't care how much money we had, I wanted some of my mother's kool-aid.

I ain't no mama's boy or anything, but my mom and I are all we've got. She's the love of my life until I meet my wife and then I'd have to split the love between the two of them. My mother worked too hard to raise me as a single parent to not show appreciation and acknowledge her hard work everyday for giving me a great life. She's one of my closest friends and confidants. The woman that I end up marrying must definitely get along with my mom. If I have to lock them up in a room together for a month, I will do that. I don't think a man should have to choose between his mother and his wife. After all, without the mother, there would be no man.

After napping for a few hours, I got up, took a shower, and threw on one of my Nikey sweat suits and sneakers before I left the house. There was so much that I needed to catch up on with her that I decided to go to her house earlier than she expected me. But not before stopping at the florist on Walk Hill to pick up a dozen roses for the woman I love. I picked out the best stems of white, red, pink and yellow roses for my mother and had them arranged in a beautiful vase.

I showed up at my mother's house early thinking that she would still be cooking, but surprisingly she was done. Before she could open her mouth to say anything, I handed her the flowers along with a card that said, "You're the best mother in the world." She took one look at it and pulled me towards her for a tight hug. It brought a smile to my face. I love seeing my mother happy.

My mother had the table set and she was ready to chow. We said our prayers and I went to work on her food. I couldn't wait to get my hand on that mouth-watering chicken with some rice and beans and collard greens. I felt like a diver diving head first into the chicken. As expected, the food was great. Through dinner, I hardly said a word to my mother. She was starting to wonder if I had been captured in Jamaica and was left without food for a few days. The food in Jamaica was good, but it wasn't better than my mom's cooking. I must've thrown down for a good fifteen minutes without ever raising my head. By the time I lifted my head up to breathe, half the chicken was gone and my mother was sitting across from me smirking. She always enjoyed watching the way I devoured her food. My stomach was full and I couldn't lift another finger. The only reason that I would get up from that table was if nature called. And I know that my mom did not want nature to call. She didn't have enough air freshener for what I would've done to her house.

After dinner, I wanted to talk to my mother about her life and her happiness. I knew she hadn't really been with a man in years because she was too busy raising me. My mother never brought men around when I was a kid. I often wondered if she was resentful because she didn't get a chance to live life like most women. If my mother had a boyfriend when I was a kid, I did not know about it. She must've been sneaking men in at night when I was sleeping because I never saw any.

I always worried about my mother being lonely. She was an attractive woman and was still in pretty good shape. Therefore, I asked her, "How come you don't have a boyfriend?" My mother responded, "Whoever said I didn't have one?" I was like "excuse me, player." I didn't know that I was about to find out that my mother was getting more play than I was, too. My mother explained to me that she has had a boyfriend for years, but she never felt comfortable enough to introduce me to him because the man was divorced and had three children by his ex-wife. She didn't know how I was going to react to it because I didn't grow up with my dad. My mother had been with this man since I was in high school and she's managed to keep it from me. I was wondering what else she was keeping from me. I asked her "Do you have any other secrets that you're keeping from me?" She answered "No." I said, "Are you sure?" She answered, "Of course I'm sure." I took her word for it.

I wanted to know how serious her relationship was with the man. She told me it was serious enough for her to keep seeing him, but not important enough for her to marry him. My mother never wanted to get married for some reason. She told me a little bit about the man and that he was a real-estate investor and a builder. However, the two of them enjoyed their space and they didn't want to get married or live together because the relationship worked better that way. My mother had been getting her freak on behind my back. "I could've walked in here one day and found you with this man," I said. "No you couldn't because he does not come over here like that. I told him that I have a son who comes by unannounced, sometimes. You might be a grown ass man, but you're still my son and I respect you" she said, "where do you see him then?" I asked. "We go out on dates and I spend time with him at his house. His children are still mad at him for divorcing their mom, so they don't come over his house like you come over here," she answered. I didn't want to know too much about my mother's relationship with this man, but from what she told me, I knew that he was not trying to get her money. My mother had gotten too smart to ever let another man use her again.

Part of me was really happy for my mother. I always wished she had a companion. I never yearned for a dad because Dexter's father had always been there for me. I wanted to meet this man that she had managed to keep a secret from me for so long. From what my mother told me about him, he seemed like a wonderful human being. He'd better be or else he'd have to face me for a beatdown.

I wanted to know about the rest of the family, Uncle Pete, Aunt Anne and Aunt Leslie. They were all married with children, but I didn't get to spend too much time with my cousins as a youngster. My mother informed me that she had mailed out checks to everyone for about one hundred thousand dollars each and they all called to thank her for the money. However, none of them took the time to come by to thank her in person. She couldn't figure out why they didn't come by to see her, but I knew why. My Aunt Leslie's husband was a controlling and abusive man who kept her away from the family because he always feared that she would one day leave him, and after receiving such a big check from my mother, she was definitely on lockdown. I knew that bastard felt threatened after she received that money. My Aunt Leslie never worked, she was a homemaker who relied on her husband for everything and he used that to control her. I wondered if she kept the money from him.

My Aunt Anne had moved to Virginia with her children after my grandparents passed. She wanted a slower pace, so she and her husband packed their bags and left. My Aunt Anne was an English teacher and her husband was a dentist. Last I heard, their two sons and two daughters were all about to become doctors and lawyers. He was and has always been a good husband to my aunt. They couldn't really help that much financially with my grandmother's funeral because their kids were attending private schools at the time.

Uncle Pete had left his high maintenance wife for an even higher maintenance woman who was younger. According to him, he never fathered any children. I'm sure a blood test would prove him wrong because there were rumors out there that he may have fathered half a dozen kids with half a dozen women that he didn't want to claim. Maybe it was just better for those children not to have that kind of man in their lives. He's probably going to leave this new girl soon after he received the money from my mother. Uncle Pete had always been a hustler who acted like he was in charge of situations when he really wasn't. He was a cool uncle because he never wanted to discipline anybody. Uncle Pete was the kind of uncle who would drink with his ten-year-old nephew. He wanted to make a man out of all of us. I never understood it because he didn't even know how to be a man himself.

My aunts and my mother never really had a chance to develop a relationship because she was the oldest of the three girls and three years older than the one who followed her. The fact that mother became pregnant at seventeen years old stretched the distance between her and her siblings even further. She grew up very fast after she had me and her sisters were still trying to be teenagers.

I don't think anyone in my grandparents' household ever figured out what Uncle Pete was ever up to. He was carefree and living life as if nothing in the world mattered to him. I don't recall him ever having a job or a profession, but he always had money. Uncle Pete was always a mystery to the family and he will remain a mystery. It won't be long before he'll come over to visit my mother. I'm sure his money will run out soon and he'll become my mother's best friend. I'm sure my mother knows this little piece of information too and that's probably why she only sent a one hundred thousand dollar check to each of her siblings. Family always comes back for more no matter how much you give them.

My mother also sent checks to each of my cousins for the same amount. She wanted to make sure that the immediate family members were taken care of. Most of my cousins were doing pretty well financially, but I'm sure they welcomed the money. My mother also tried to locate some of the women who claimed that they had children by Uncle Pete. She was able to locate one woman who had a fifteen-year-old son who looked just like Uncle Pete. She sent an anonymous money order to the woman for seventy-five thousand dollars. My mother is the type of woman who does things her way, and that's what's so special about her.

I was happy to see my mother and I was even happier to learn that she had a companion. You know she had to ask about my trip to Jamaica. I told her that I had a great time and that Dexter, Jessie and I made the best of our time. My mother looked at me funny after my statement. I was wondering what the hell was wrong with her. She turned to me and said, "So, it wasn't just you and Dexter, there was a Jessie too." I said, "Yes, you remember Jessie, one of my best friends from college." My mother shook her head and said, "I don't remember no Jessie. Don't act like I know everything about your freaky life. You don't tell your mother everything anymore." I was sitting there looking confused as hell because I had no idea what my mother was talking about.

After a long pensive moment, she turned to me and said, "As long as you and Dexter had fun and he didn't have any problem with you bringing Jessie along that's all that mattered." I said to her, "Of course, Dexter would never have gone if he knew that Jessie was coming, but I tricked them both into going without them knowing about it." My mother seemed a little too intrigued by my trip. She wanted to know if Dexter and Jessie got along once we got to Jamaica. I told her sure they got along and I think that they might be dating each other. She turned to me and asked, "You don't have a problem with that?" I told her "Of course not. Who am I to stand in the way of two people dating each other?" I continued, "I used to have a thing for Jessie, but I realized when we were in Jamaica, that Jessie is more suitable for Dexter." My mother turned to me and said, "As long as you guys are happy with your arrangement I have no problem with it."

I had been at my mother's house for close to four hours and I felt the conversation that we were having about my friends was starting to get a bit personal. So, I put an end to it because I needed to go home to see if Marjorie had finally called me. My mother never lets me leave her house without giving me a plate of food after having dinner. She packed a little bit of everything for me in a big Tupper-ware. I gave her a great kiss and a hug and told her that I'd call her the next day.

After I left my mother's house, while driving home, I realized that my mother must have mistaken my conversation about Jess and Dexter. My mother had never met Jess and I remembered that she thought Dexter and I was a gay couple. She must've thought that Jess was a man and I brought him in for a threesome. My mother thought I was a freak. I couldn't believe that I had to keep telling my mother that I was not gay. She continued to misinterpret every conversation I had with her and my dumb ass never picked up on it. I was starting to look real bad to my mother. I had to start fixing my image with her.

A Candid Moment

It had been a few days since I heard from Dexter, and I wanted to call him to see how he was doing. I knew he was busy trying to catch up on inventory at his garage, so I didn't bother him. We hadn't been to the gym since we came back from Jamaica because he was backed up at work and needed to catch up. Dexter didn't micro-manage his employees, but he was always involved in every decision regarding his business. Some of the business savvy that he possessed couldn't be taught at Harvard Business School. Business was in his blood, and he managed well.

I was sitting at home bored and wondering why I hadn't heard from Dexter about the gym. I was more enthusiastic about the gym than Dexter because I was a beginner and people took notice of my newly developed muscles. I wanted to get back to the weights; we had missed a whole week and more while we were in Jamaica. Also, part of me didn't want to go through the soreness that I went through the first time we started. My body hurt so badly after the first day I almost didn't go back to the gym. However, once the soreness went away, I started to enjoy the workouts.

I picked up the phone and called Dexter at home and surprisingly he picked up the phone. When he heard my voice, he immediately told me to hold on while he got rid of the person on the other line. I sensed excitement in Dexter's voice when he came back to the phone and I asked him what he was so happy about. He told me that he had been on the phone with Jess for the last couple of hours and they decided to go out on a date the upcoming Friday. I asked him what happened to the guy she was dating; he told me that, she told him the guy was playing too many games and she didn't have time for games. She was too old to be seeing somebody on their schedule, blah, blah, blah, blah. Dexter told me that he and Jess had been talking on the phone since we came back from Jamaica and he was starting to feel her.

I have to admit that I have never seen Dexter that excited about any woman, but I was cautious not to buy into his act completely. Because I was the person who sort of brought them together, I wanted to make sure that he understood the guidelines of dating my friend. I didn't have room in my heart for jealousy when it came to Jess anymore because Marjorie was occupying my mind. I wanted to be frank with Dexter and there was no sugar coating what I wanted to say. Dexter asked if I had a problem with him dating Jess seriously and I responded "No. However, before you can receive my blessings I need to set a few things straight with you first." "A few things like what?" he said. "If you're going to date Jess, there has to be a new set of rules. You can't be trying to use her to get your thrills then throw her to the side and I have to pick up the pieces after you. Jess is like a sister to me just like you're a brother to me. I know that sounds weird right now, but that's not the way I meant it. Anyway, just don't hurt her because I don't want to hurt us" I told him.

Dexter was silent on the phone for a long while. I called out his name to see if he was still there and he confirmed with a "yeah, I'm here." I don't know what Dexter read into my comment and I didn't really care. I just wanted to make sure that he wasn't trying to run games on Jess. There are plenty of women out there he could conquer and I had to make sure that there were certain rules that couldn't be broken and boundaries that couldn't be crossed. I understood that Dexter and Jess were adults, but I didn't want them to start something at the expense of my friendship with them.

Dexter must have been pondering what to say next because he came back at me strong and determined saying "Yo man, are you ever gonna give me any credit? I know that I used to mess around with a lot of women, but I told you I was getting tired of that shit and I wanted to find somebody nice to settle down with. You, of all people should know that when I say I'm ready to give up the game, that I mean it!" I didn't really know how to respond to Dexter's statement so I said, "Man, I do not doubt your motives, I just want to make sure we're on the same page. It's bad enough that I'm losing Jess to you, but I don't want you to hurt her." Dexter was a little shocked at my comment, but he asked me if it bothered me that he and Jess were going on a date and if it did, he would cancel the whole thing. After he said that, I knew for sure that Dexter and I were going to be best friends forever. He was willing to forgo his own feelings and possible happiness for the sake of our friendship. It was then that I realized that Dexter would not be such a bad guy for Jess.

Dexter was maturing as a man right before my eyes and I was still a virgin. The conversation between Dexter and I was starting to become a bit uncomfortable for both of us. Men aren't supposed to reveal their feelings and get all sentimental and stuff with each other. He decided to quickly end it with a "Yo everything's cool man. I'll holler at you later." I responded, "Aight, we'll talk later."

After I got off the phone with Dexter I felt gayer than Richard Simmons. I wondered if Dexter felt the same way. It's such a female thing to be revealing your feelings to other people so openly. Men will always be men when it comes to certain issues that we have to deal with. We usually check ourselves when the situation is becoming too uncomfortable. If we don't check ourselves, we at least run away from the situation because that's what we do as men. We don't have any excuse for doing it; it's just what we do. If women recognized that's the way men deal with their problems, they would never end up with those down low brothers. Whenever a brother starts to get too comfortable talking about sentimental issues with a woman, it's a big red flag that he might be swinging both ways. I understand that most women want to be with a man who's in touch with his feminine side, however, that man does not exist. And if he does exist, he's gay, queer, on the down low, funny, homosexual, or whatever you wanna call him. Okay maybe there might be a small percentage of straight men out there that are like that.

A Cross Cultural Encounter

A week and a half had gone by before I finally received a call from Marjorie. When the phone rang, I picked it up as nonchalantly as possible. I had no idea who the person on the other line was. Maybe she was expecting excitement in my voice, but I was not moved by her gesture. I was waiting in vain for this woman to call for over a week. I even cancelled my personal plans so I could be home to receive her phone call. The desperate part of me was happy that she had called, but the human part of me was angry because she had disregarded my feelings. Why be angry when I had no claim to her, right? I listened as Marjorie tried to explain her delayed phone call to me. She told me that she had had a hectic week trying to finalize her admission to Boston University's Medical School. I felt that she was sincere enough with her explanation, so I let down my guard to enjoy the conversation with the woman I had been dreaming about for the last week and a half.

I was glad to hear from Marjorie because there was so much that I wanted to know about her. Since she called me around nine o'clock that evening, I was already in a mellow mood and my voice tends to get sweet and sexy at night or so I've been told. As sexy as my voice supposedly sounds, it's never gotten me anywhere with the ladies. Marjorie took notice of the sensuality in my voice and commented, "You sound real sexy right now, what are you doing?" I was hoping her question was meant in a sexual way, but before I could give her an answer she followed with another question "Are you reading or something?" I was like damn! I thought she was gonna take it there with me on the phone and then she switched gears on me. So much for my sexy voice, huh?

I was actually watching television when she called, but I turned down the volume before I picked up the phone. Marjorie's voice reminded me of this woman that I called once from one of those 900 numbers. Yeah, I got horny one night and I called one of those numbers just to see if I could get my thrill, but it didn't work. The person had a sexy voice, but because I knew that it was costing me a dollar ninety-nine a minute, I felt like I was paying a prostitute. I ended up hanging up the phone on her after the first minute before my phone bill got too high. She wasn't that convincing either. Though she had a sexy voice on the phone, I imagined that she was this super fat woman that I had seen on one of those undercover sting operations on television for illegal sex hotlines.

It was different with Marjorie because I knew what she looked like, but she wasn't trying to talk dirty to me on the phone. I was turned on by her voice because I was horny. I think I was horny most of the time. As horny as I got, I was very particular about the type of woman I wanted to sleep with. I had plenty of opportunities in the past to sleep with women, but I couldn't justify sharing myself with just anybody. I know that statement sounds bitchy, but hey.

I was so caught up in Marjorie's sexy voice and my own fantasies I forgot to answer her question. She asked again "Are you doing something because your attention seems to be elsewhere." I told her that she had my full attention and that I was just caught-up momentarily in this football replay between Tom Brady and Troy Brown from the Patriots Super Bowl season that they were showing on ESPN. I told her that the TV was off and I was all hers. She said, "Good, because I don't want to fight the television for your attention." I liked the tone she used when she said that. Therefore, I asked how her day went and what she had been up to besides trying to finalize things with BU. She told me that's all she had had time to do and nothing else.

I was feeling the vibe that I was getting from Marjorie. I asked her when she and her family moved to the states, she told me that her parents fled Haiti amid all the unrest that was going on in the country in 1996. She told me that her family barely escaped and that all the looting and chaos that was going on almost cost them their lives. Her father was shot in the arm the day before they fled. She was in her first year of college when they left Haiti and moved to Boston. I could tell that Marjorie wasn't comfortable discussing that ordeal in her life, so I changed the subject to something light. I asked her if she had been to the movies lately. She told me all the spare time that she had was devoted to study for her MCAT and her application for medical school. So, she barely had time to breathe.

From our conversation, it felt like Marjorie had not been pampered in a while, so I decided to ask her out to dinner and a movie. She said yes without any hesitation. We set a date for the upcoming Friday at 7:00 pm. Marjorie asked if I could pick her up from her house on Stanton Street in Dorchester. She asked if I knew how to get there and I told her "of course." She was very surprised when I told her that I grew up a few blocks away from her on Fuller Street. We got through talking about the neighborhood and some of the changes that have taken place over the years since my mother moved to Fuller Street. She was surprised when I told her that we were one of a few Black families who lived on Fuller Street back in the late seventies. Even Stanton Street still had a few white residents back then. I painted a whole different picture of the neighborhood that she knew. I told her that my friends and I would sometimes go to Evans Park to try to play basketball with the older guys, but they would always chase us off the court. She laughed at my adolescent stories.

Marjorie seemed so mature while we were talking on the phone I never bothered to ask her age. However, from the way she looked I could tell that she was a mature twenty something. The plan was set to meet on Friday for dinner; I knew that we were on the phone for over an hour and I didn't want to seem overly anxious. I told her that it was nice talking to her and that I would call her on Friday to finalize our date. Surprisingly, Marjorie asked why I was getting off the phone so quickly. In my attempt to appear cool and not desperate or overly anxious, I might have offended Marjorie. I didn't really have an explanation for trying to abruptly end our conversation, but I needed to stick to my guns and act as if I was just as important as she was. I told her that I needed to take out my trash and catch up on my reading.

She surprised me even more after that statement. She said, "I just love a man who likes to read." I didn't know how to respond. Did I mention that I had no mack daddy vibe? I accepted her compliment as nonchalantly as possible with a "that's nice" remark. She got a little sarcastic with me before we hung up the phone. She said, "Well, if you gotta go, you gotta go. I guess I'll talk to you on Friday." I got a little cocky and said, "Yeah, we'll talk on Friday. Goodnight."

After I hung up the phone with Marjorie, I was asking myself "what the hell did I just do?" As if I had anything else better to do with my time. I was trying to follow something that I once heard from Dexter. He said, "A man should never wait until a woman asks to get off the phone first." I don't know where he came up with that crap, but why did I have to listen to it? It made no sense to me that I got off the phone with Marjorie because I still wanted to talk to her. And in my haste to try to get off the phone to earn cool points, I forgot to ask for her number. So, once again I'm at her mercy. I blame all this awkwardness with women on my dad not being a part of my life. I'm sure if he were around, he would have schooled me about women from the time I was a young man. But what's a man to do?

If I Could Turn Back Time

It really bothered me that I didn't get Marjorie's phone number. I was trying to keep my mind occupied by watching reruns of the Soprano's and Sex and The City before going to bed. The shows didn't seem that interesting to me anymore. I couldn't miss an episode of the Soprano's in the past because I felt it was one of the best shows on television. I would always go to Dexter's house to watch it on Sundays before I got my own cable. I was too cheap to get cable before I won the money. I didn't mind if I missed Sex in the City occasionally, but I loved the Sopranos somewhere along the way, that show started to lose its luster to me. I didn't find the storylines as interesting anymore. I was bored with the episode that I watched that night.

I started flipping through the channels to find something to watch because I was bored and bothered by the mishap with Marjorie. While flipping through the channels, my phone rang. I was praying to God that it was Marjorie calling me back after realizing that she didn't give me her number. It felt like I had just done three back flips and five somersaults like I was in a Jackie Chan Kung Fu flick to get to the phone. I picked it up on the second ring and almost out of breath and said, "Marjorie!" all excitedly. To my disappointment, it was Dexter calling to say what's up. However, not before he cracked a few jokes first. The first words out of his mouth were "Oh, you're getting ass from Marjorie and you didn't tell me." I told him that I was not getting any ass yet and if I got some ass, he'd be the first to know.

Dexter had more to say of course, he went on "I feel sorry for the woman who lets you get your hands on her. You're going to tear her ass up like your life depends on it. You got all this virgin rage inside of you that's waiting to come out. Ooh, I feel bad for her." All I could say was "whatever man" because Dexter was right. I was ready to explode if I didn't get my first experience with a woman soon, but I also didn't want to compromise my standards in the process.

I said what's up to Dexter with an attitude because he had just dashed all my hopes. He asked why I was still waiting on that girl to call me. I told him that she had already called but I forgot to ask for her number. Dexter was like "Yo, it's simple, man. Just star 69 her on your phone." What Dexter said made sense, but the problem was that I was so cheap that I had never gotten any of those features on my phone and forgot to get them even after I won the money. Damn me! I felt worse telling Dexter that I didn't get a chance to add that feature to my phone even after I got all this money.

I knew he was going to rub my frugality in my face. I just kept quiet for a second to hear it come out of his mouth. And he went there hard too. "I told your cheap ass to stop being cheap a long time ago, but no. Now you can potentially lose your first piece of ass because you were being cheap. How do you plan on having a girl when you're so far behind technologically because you're cheap? Now that girl probably figures you have caller ID and she won't call you back and you'll be there jerking off all by yourself and whose fault is that? Your own damn fault, that's who!" said Dexter.

I didn't really want to hear anymore from Dexter, but he was right. I lived my life so niggardly, I missed out on a lot of opportunities. I had to explain to Dexter that my frugality didn't just spring up out of nowhere. I got tired of watching my mom bust her ass everyday to make ends meet when I was a child. I decided that I never wanted to be in a situation where I didn't have any money in case I needed something for an emergency.

My grandmother died because my grandfather didn't plan well financially. I learned a lot watching my family deal with their adversities. I made it a rule to save at least twenty-five percent of my income every year and invest another five percent. I never want to repeat what my grandparents and my mother went through. Planning is essential to financial freedom no matter how small a salary a person has.

Dexter sat there and listened to what he perceived as mumbo jumbo at the time coming out of my mouth, but he was just as financially astute as I was. The only difference between Dexter and I was that he lived for the moment and believed that old saying "There's only one life to live." I believed in that too, but I also believed in my future and the future of my family.

I left it up to the possibility that she might remember that she didn't give me her number and she would call me back sometime between then and Friday. It was a lot of hoping on my part, but that's all I could do at the time. Dexter asked if I knew her last name and I told him that unfortunately I didn't get that either. I felt like Dexter was trying to school me, but at the same time it was one of his lessons that forced me to get off the phone with Marjorie so quickly. I wanted to talk about the positive aspect of my conversation with Marjorie. I told Dexter that Marjorie and I set a date for Friday evening and I would appreciate a few suggestions for a nice restaurant.

Since Dexter was a lot more outgoing than I was, I figured he might know where the better restaurants were. Dexter thought about my request for a few minutes and I could tell that he was running a few places up in his head. He asked what kind of girl she was and I told him that she was wholesome, beautiful, educated and classy. "I haven't been out with too many of those, but the few that I did take out, I took them all to Top of the Hub. Are you trying to be casual or dressy?" he said. I told him that I wanted it to be a casual date, but not that casual. He suggested the Cheesecake Factory in Chestnut Hill. I had never been there myself, but Dexter explained how easy it was to get to on route 9. Dexter told me that it wasn't too far from the mall, but I had also never been to that mall. From what he told me, I knew it wouldn't be hard to find because I had driven past that place on my way to Brandeis University many times.

Dexter was happy to hear that I was going on a date with a woman that I had met without his help. For the record, I told Dexter that I could've slept with many of the women that he introduced me to in the past; I just found that most of them wouldn't be anything more than a cheap thrill. The fact that my father left my mother after she became pregnant with me might have a lot to do with the way I deal with women. I have always been careful enough not to lie down with just anybody. I respected my mother as a woman too much to sleep around with a bunch of women. It could've been a subconscious thing, you never know.

It was getting late and my eyes were starting to burn, so I decided to get off the phone to catch some much needed sleep. He had to make one last comment before he got off the phone with me. "Play on… Player," were his last words before we hung up the phone.

A Possible Obsession

Three days had come and gone and I didn't hear from Marjorie. I was starting to conjure up all kinds of stories in my head as to why she didn't call. I started telling myself that maybe I was too forceful or moved too quickly; I felt that I tried to dictate to her when our conversation should have ended. Maybe Marjorie took it as sign that I was not really into her or maybe I was trying to act too conceited for her. I was going crazy trying to figure out the reasons. It was almost like an obsession by 4:00 o'clock that Friday afternoon. I only had three and half hours left to hear from her before our date. Even earlier that day when I went to the barbershop to get my haircut, the guys there thought something was wrong with me. One of them came straight out and said that I had pussy problems on my mind. I never realized that I was so easy to read. Everyone just kept reading me like an open book.

Normally, when I go to the barbershop, I try to take part in their conversations even though I was lying most of the time. These guys were often talking about women and how good this woman's pussy was or how bad that woman's pussy was. I would always jump right in as if I had been getting pussy myself. I never went too far with my exaggerations because I didn't want to be found out. I kept my lying to a minimum just to act like one of the guys. If those guys at the barbershop knew I was a virgin, they would have had a field day with me and I would need to find a new barbershop to go to. And I couldn't do that. It took my barber years to become the perfect barber for me even though I only went there once a month before I became rich. I didn't want to start all over with someone new. I didn't want to hear what those guys were saying in the barbershop that day, so I went home right after my haircut was done. Usually, I would stay a few minutes longer after I get my cut, but not that day. I was worried too much about seeing Marjorie.

To make matters worse, I had a wet dream about Marjorie the night before our date. I was hoping that I was not obsessed with this woman, but she dominated my every thought. My dream was so disturbing, I felt ashamed for having it. It took me back to the train where I initially met Marjorie. I entered the same car and I sat down in the same seat, but in my dream, Marjorie was wearing a trench coat with nothing underneath. She was sitting across from me with her legs slightly spread open so I could see her goods.

I couldn't believe what I was seeing. I became excited almost instantly from peeking at her nicely manicured lawn that was cut into a heart shape right above her clitoris. Part of me wanted to go in there and just stick my mouth on her pussy and start eating her like my mama's fried chicken, but she could sense my hesitation. Even in my dreams, I didn't have any balls when it came to women. She took one look at my overgrown and rising manhood and asked if I planned to use it. I looked behind me to see if there was someone else standing behind me. I pointed at myself to make sure that she was talking to me and she confirmed with a seductive "Yeah, I'm talking to you, bad boy. I've been a bad girl and I want you to punish me." Man, I got all shy and acted like I didn't know what to do with myself.

Marjorie spread her legs wide open even more, exposing the pinkness of her kitty cat right in front of me on the train and told me to come and get it. I wanted to get up and get it so bad, but for some reason I couldn't move my legs. Something was holding me back and I couldn't see it or fight it. Marjorie continued to play with herself, licking her nipples one at a time slowly and asking me if I wanted to get a taste. I was salivating like a little puppy, but my tongue couldn't make its way to her tits. I started rubbing my own chest emulating her every move in anticipation that she might actually get up from her seat to come across to me, but she remained put in her seat teasing me more.

Marjorie took one her finger's from inside her mouth then pulled it out and started rubbing her clit with it. She was moaning, groaning, and rolling her eyes in the back of her head during a voyage in seventh heaven. The only thing I could do was watch her and pull out my own toy out of my pants and do what I knew how to do best. I was staring at Marjorie while I jerked off stroking my meat back and forth with my two favorite girls Leftonia and Rightina Hand. The twins never let me down. Marjorie slowly started to insert one of her fingers inside of her then two and three while screaming at the top of her lungs with pleasure. It was painful for me to be so close to her kitty cat and could not even get a taste of it in my dream, but I wanted to come in unison with her. I started stroking my meat harder and harder. As she and I were reaching ecstasy, my phone rang and it was my mother on the other line when I picked up. She just had to interrupt my dream at that moment. I could never catch a break!

I felt dirty talking to my mother on the phone while I had semen all over me and holding my nine-inch tool in my hand. I told my mother I would call her back and ran to the bathroom to wash up and take a cold shower. I also had to change my sheets because I had bust all over them.

Prayer Answered

While waiting for Marjorie to call I decided to pick up this book called Neglected Souls by this young author that I had bought and taken with me to Jamaica. I didn't get a chance to open the book while I was in Jamaica, but when I got home I started reading the book and the storyline pulled me right in from the beginning to the point where I didn't even realize that it was six o'clock when my phone rang. I was so caught up in the book I almost missed the call. It was Marjorie calling to make sure that I was still coming to pick her up at 7:30. She wanted to give me her exact address. I don't think God created a happier soul after I received that phone call. Before Marjorie got off the phone, I made sure I asked for her number just in case I got lost.

Honestly, I had driven through the street where Marjorie lived so many times that I could guide Ray Charles to her house with blindfolds on. I just wanted to make sure that I got the digits. I did not want to put myself through this kind of torment anymore. I was also not sure if Marjorie remembered that I had told her that Stanton Street was my old stomping ground. I wondered who was fooling whom. I was so excited about the prospect of our date that I could not be contained. If I listened to what most people have to say about life, I would hear that old proverb "You have to crawl before you walk." If they saw Marjorie, to that I would say "not always." Some of us do get lucky, sometimes. I was one of those lucky people. Most virgins lose their virginity to the girls that nobody else wanted to sleep with or the girl who hadn't been to the dentist since birth, but not me. There was a chance that I might lose my virginity to a fine woman.

I know what I'm saying sounds selfish, but I was not just looking forward to sleeping with Marjorie. I wanted to get to know her and fall in love with her. Was I lusting? Yeah, but any man would lust after her. She reminded me of Kenya Moore, but her knockout ability was more like Robin Givens, a sexy Vixen. Most men know that she's no good for them, but they would drop their pants in a minute to sleep with her. I didn't know if Marjorie was no good for me yet.

It was about 6:30pm when I jumped in the shower to make sure that I washed the crack of my ass, my balls, inside my ears, my arms, my feet and pretty much every nook and cranny of my body as clean as I possibly could. I felt like I was rejuvenated when I came out of the shower. I was so clean even a person who suffered from obsessive-compulsive disorder could've eaten off my body. I wanted to wear something that was casual but dressy just in case she wanted to hang out at a club later. I developed a new habit of laying my clothes on the bed before I got dressed ever since I became rich. I laid out a nice pair of black pants, a bright orange linen shirt and black shoes to match. Last time I wore the orange shirt I received quite a few compliments, so I wanted to see Marjorie's reaction. Because I have a dark brown complexion, people tell me that bright color shirts complement my skin.

I was not sure if I wanted to blind Marjorie's vision with a bright ass orange shirt just yet, though. I did not want her to be thinking, "Where's Mr. Rainbow Bright going with that bright ass shirt," when I pulled up to her house. I decided to wear my dark tan linen pants from French Connection, a white short-sleeved button down linen shirt with brown shoes and brown belt to match. Before I got dressed, I rubbed lotion on my entire body with Alfred Dunhill's Desire body lotion and lightly sprayed my chest, behind my ears, and wrist with the cologne. It was a light scented cologne, so I knew it would have the right effect by the time I got to Marjorie's house. I threw on my favorite Sean John briefs and undershirt to match before I put on my clothes.

I was dressed by 7:00 o'clock and ready to go pick up my date. I checked the mirror to make sure everything was in its proper place including my hair. I ran the brush over my hair a couple more times just for sanity's sake. I went downstairs to my car and came out the parking lot the happiest man on earth. I was blasting Biggie's hit Hypnotized because it was still my favorite jam. As I made a turn about a few of blocks away from Marjorie's house, I reached for my ashtray to grab a piece of my favorite Wrigley's spearmint gum, I noticed that there was no gum in the ashtray and all my loose change had been taken. I couldn't believe those bastards at the car wash robbed me again. Every time I got a full-service car wash from those knuckleheads, they stole my gum and loose change. One day I'm gonna set their asses up with some gum that'll send their thieving asses to the bathroom all day.

I always like to make sure that my breath is fresh at all times, so I pulled up at the corner grocery store on Milton avenue and Norfolk street to get a pack of gum before I reached Marjorie's house. I never take chances with my breath. This girl once told me when I was fourteen years old that my breath was tart and I wasn't sure if she was trying to be mean or not. Ever since, I have kept a pack of gum with me all the time. I was only fourteen years old and she could've just been talking shit at the time. I was in a good mood, and was hoping to have a great time with Marjorie. I looked at my watch and noticed that I was still a few minutes early. I drove down to my favorite florist on Walk Hill and picked up a dozen yellow roses for Marjorie. By the time I drove to the florist and back to Stanton Street where Marjorie lived, it was about 7:35. I was five minutes late, but I was hoping the roses would make up for my tardiness.

I pulled up to this red and white house, parked my car and walked up to the front porch and rang the doorbell. A man with a thick and heavy accent came to the door and told me that Marjorie would be right out. I could hear Marjorie telling the person to let me in. This mean looking older guy came to the door and seemed angry as hell. I figured the guy was either her father or an uncle. He favored her a little bit and he was tall, dark and big. Marjorie yelled from the top of the stairs "Malcolm, did you meet my dad?" I was like damn! Her dad was mean as hell. How the hell was I going to break the ice with this dude? He left me standing by the front door and went to the back. I wanted to scream back at her that I didn't really meet him, but I didn't want him to know that I thought he was rude.

As I was standing there waiting for Marjorie I could hear them talking in their native tongue. Her father had an angry tone in his voice. "Mwen we'w gin ou foli soti ak amerikin. Mwen pa konn depi kile mwen te gin amerikin nan fanmi'm. Sak fe'w pa chache ou bon ti Ayisien pou'w soti?" he said. I didn't understand what the hell he was saying to her, but he was not happy. She ignored him for the most part and didn't say much in response. Before we left the house she turned to her dad and said, " Papi, misie se ou bon ti gason li ye. Bali ou ti chans avan'w jige'l. Paske li pa ayisien yan pa vle di ke li pa ou bon moune." Marjorie walked down the stairs looking like a beauty pageant queen. I gave her a quick hug and handed her the roses. She put them straight to her nose and smiled as if the aroma of the roses had just lightened her mood. She walked towards what I presumed was the living room and placed them in a vase. She said good-bye to her father and I screamed, "It was nice meeting you, sir" as we walked out the door.

I opened the passenger side door of the car for Marjorie and as I was walking back to the driver's side, I saw her father standing by the window looking just as angry as ever. I was a little bothered by her father's demeanor, so I asked Marjorie what that was all about. She told me it was nothing but her father's strong determination to run her life. She was his only daughter, and he had worked hard to send her to college and nobody was ever going to be good enough for his little girl. Her mother passed away after she graduated from high school and her father has been doing it all for her ever since. She told me not to worry about him and that he'd come around after he got to know me. I wasn't sure if I wanted to get to know him.

After I saw how mean her father looked, all those perverted thoughts that I had about Marjorie took a brief vacation from my mind. That man looked like he could kill a bull with his bare hands. I wanted to be on my best behavior because I knew that she had a crazy ass father at home who made it known that he didn't want his daughter going out with anybody. However, there was nothing he could do about it, because she was over 18 years old, which reminded me to ask Marjorie how old she was. I said to her "If you don't mind me asking, how old are you?" She said to me "How old do I look?" I didn't know whether to be generous, polite or kind, so I told her it's never polite to guess a woman's age. She said, "In that case, I'm twenty four years old." I had figured that she was about twenty-four years old based on the conversations, but I didn't want to make the wrong guess and be rude.

I was so scared when I was inside Marjorie's house, I didn't get a chance to take full inventory of what she was wearing. I grew eyes in the back of my head momentarily as I left her house. I wanted to keep track of her father at all times. I didn't want this guy to come out of nowhere and jump me. She was walking in front of me, but I didn't want to make it obvious that I was enjoying the view fearing that her father may have been looking at us and he was.

While we were in the car, I took the time to glance over to see what Marjorie had on. For some reason, I was drawn to her legs first. Her legs were bare and sexy and she was wearing a nice black open toe sandal and one of those wrap around black dresses that tie on the side. The dress fit her body just right and accentuated her very curvaceous body. Her hair was combed back, exposing her African features like a queen from the motherland. It didn't seem like she was wearing much make-up as I could only make out the eyeliner and the lipstick. Everything else was natural. She was wearing a sweet smelling perfume that was so inviting that I wanted to jump her bones in the car. However, I remembered how angry daddy was before we left.

As part of my small talk with Marjorie, I asked her what kind of perfume she was wearing. She told me it was called "Un Amour De Patou" by Jean Patou of Paris. She also told me that she liked the cologne I was wearing; she smelled it when I hugged her at the house. Of course, she enquired about it and I told her it was Desire by Alfred Dunhill. I was hoping that she might want to get a little whiff of it later on by getting closer to me. I was trying to keep my mind out of the gutter. Marjorie looked so scrumptious and smelled so delicious I couldn't help myself.

I wanted to know if she had been looking forward to our date as much as I was and she told me that she was in a way. I accepted what she said. It was better than not looking forward to it at all. As I was driving, I couldn't help the occasional glance at Marjorie's legs because they were so smooth and toned. I'm sure she noticed the interest that I took in her legs as she kept crossing them like she was inviting me to touch them. I found her flirting with me entertaining for the most part. Marjorie's primary interest was the sciences and she was so passionate when she talked about biology. I didn't get a quarter of what she was talking about, but I acted like I was interested giving her the occasional nod and "wow" to show how impressed I was. I was never a science guy and I did what I needed to do to pass my science classes in high school so I could graduate. If I had to take one science course in college, I would've dropped out. It just wasn't my thing.

I may not have liked science, but I loved the biological creation that was before me. We arrived at the restaurant around eight o'clock and there was a bunch of people ahead of us waiting to be seated. The place was crowded and every waitress who walked by carrying someone's food order, only confirmed that the food was going to be good. The hostess took our name and asked if we wanted to wait at the bar until our name was called. I looked at Marjorie and she shook her head and said, "Sure, we can wait at the bar." We went to the bar and ordered a couple of drinks. I have always liked kamikazes and I hadn't had one in a while. I ordered a kamikaze and she ordered an apple martini. The drinks were huge. We were at the bar for about fifteen minutes sipping our drinks having a good time waiting for our names to be called for a table.

Most of the men who were at the restaurant with other women couldn't help sneaking a glance at Marjorie. She looked that good and her beauty crossed all color lines; White, Black, Hispanic and Asian men were all looking at her. I was so proud and happy that she was with me. I was giggling inside knowing that all these men were admiring her. It's not as if she didn't know that she had admirers, she knew and the more they looked, the tighter she held on to me. She demonstrated that she was proud to be out with her average looking guy, by rubbing my head and holding on to me every chance she got. I knew that most of these men were probably thinking, "What the hell was she doing with him" as I had done myself in the past with some other guys, but I didn't care. Marjorie was confident enough in herself that she didn't need to be with a man who looked a certain way, be a certain height or have a certain amount of wealth. She knew that I was a teacher, she looked to be about an inch taller than me with heels and I was not a head turner and it was all good. I was no Boris Kodjoe, Denzel Washington, Shemar Moore or Morris Chestnut look alike. She was just happy with plain regular Malcolm.

That night, we had great conversation, a great dinner and a great time all around, but a part of me felt guilty because I was so caught up in Marjorie's beauty. I'm usually the biggest complainer when it comes to vanity, but here I was getting caught up in it. I always wanted a woman who liked me because of who I was, but I wasn't sure if I could be with a woman who wasn't beautiful. I was the biggest hypocrite that night. Everything about Marjorie seemed so real that I felt like I was phony. I wanted something that I couldn't even offer and I might have made it a priority without realizing it. I wanted an intelligent woman with great beauty first.

After Marjorie and I had dinner, we went down by the Charles River to enjoy the skylight of Boston. It was a clear night with a full moon and the sky was filled with stars. She held on to my arm as we walked across the bridge on Massachusetts Avenue like a couple in love. We were conversing about the simple things in life like our future goals and the difference we hoped to make in the world. As a physician, or specifically a heart surgeon, Marjorie knew that she was going to be saving lives and giving people hope. She had always wanted to do that. I was already making a difference as a teacher and she thought it was the greatest job in the world because teachers are the ones who mold the future doctors, lawyers, stockbrokers and every other profession on this earth. She held my profession in high esteem and I appreciated her for that.

Marjorie and I must've walked about three miles up and down Memorial Drive and Massachusetts Avenue. Her feet were starting to hurt, so we took a seat on one the benches to watch the seagulls fly around the river. It was the right mood for me to at least attempt to get a kiss from Marjorie. She could sense that I wanted to kiss her and instead of me trying, she pulled me closer to her and planted a big wet kiss on me. My toes were curling like a little girl who just had her first kiss. I couldn't believe it! I kissed her back with a voracity that scared the hell out of her. She had to ask me to take it easy because my aggression was scaring her. She wanted me to take my time and enjoy the kiss. My desperation couldn't be contained anymore.

After making out on the bench for about fifteen minutes, Marjorie told me that she wanted to get to know me better and all the kissing we were doing was getting in the way of it. I agreed and asked her what she wanted to know. She told me that she wanted to know about Malcolm, the man, and what I was all about. I told her I was a simple man who led a simple life and wanted to be with a woman who was not too complicated. I asked Marjorie how complicated she was and she told me that she was not complicated at all. She was comfortable talking about her experiences with men and that she found it hard to keep a boyfriend because everybody was trying to rush her into bed. She still had never slept with a man and she wanted to lose her virginity to someone special. She didn't care about being married, but she wanted to be in love with the man who would take her virginity. After she revealed that little bit of information to me, I couldn't believe how she's managed to stay a virgin for so long as fine as she was. I could definitely understand why I was a virgin, but a goddess like her, there was no acceptable explanation for it.

Talking to Marjorie about her past experiences also put things in perspective for me. I knew that I had to be respectful, patient and appreciate what she had to offer. I didn't want to come straight out with the fact that I was also a virgin, fearing that she might have thought it was just a line to get in her panties. I alluded to the fact in not so many words, but she thought I was being overly modest. She believed that there were enough hoochie mamas out there in the world who were willing to give a man like me a piece whenever I needed it. What she didn't realize was that I was very choosy and selective when it came to sex. Okay, I may not have had too many choices, but I was very selective with the limited choices that I had. I have been so selective that I've remained a virgin.

It was getting close to midnight and for some reason the only picture that would pop up in my head was that of her angry father. I decided to take her home so that I would not be greeted with a shotgun barrel in my face, but not before I got one long kiss goodnight from Marjorie. On a scale of 1-10, I couldn't rate her kiss because neither of us were great kissers. We somehow managed to enjoy all the tongue movement we were doing for about five more minutes before I took her home. Marjorie turned me on in a way that I couldn't fully describe. It was not the usual turn on that I got when I watched my favorite porno flicks, it was more stimulating than that. Although Marjorie was probably the finest woman that I had ever been out with, after our date I was drawn more to her intelligence than anything. She was no longer only a sex goddess and I wanted to take my time to get to know her.

We arrived at Marjorie's house about a half hour after midnight and as expected her father was at the window looking out for her. I was starting to think that her father might be a bit too controlling for me. I didn't want to date someone whose father seemed to be so overbearing. I walked her up to her door and attempted to give her a hug and she backed off making me feel very uncomfortable. I felt like I was a teenager all over again when Marjorie didn't embrace me. "We're not teenagers," I thought. I was a grown ass man and she was a grown woman and I couldn't even give her a hug, because daddy was lurking in the background. We said our goodnight and I was on my way.

While driving home, I couldn't help but wonder what to make of the cultural differences between Marjorie and me. I could almost imagine my mother's reaction to the fact that she was Haitian. At the hospital where my mother worked, she didn't like some of the Haitian workers who worked there because they were rude. Some of them did not like to greet people and they acted as if they owned the world. My mother was always complaining that they thought they were better than African Americans. I wasn't sure about the conversation that took place between Marjorie and her father, but I'm almost certain that it had something to do with me being African American and dating his daughter.

It's sad that Black people from all over the world come to this country, expect us to be as determined, and driven as they are without realizing first the struggle that we had to face in America. The differences between black people from all over the world continue to create a great divide that makes it so easy for us to be conquered. I have heard the comparisons between some of the West Indian and African Blacks to African Americans and they have not all been positive. The Black immigrants don't understand that if people like Martin Luther King and Malcolm X didn't fight to open doors for Blacks here that they wouldn't be able to achieve the success that they have when they come to this country.

Some of the Black immigrants even buy into the idea that African Americans are lazy. However, I don't totally blame them for accepting that fact. We mostly ridicule them because we make fun of their language and heritage when they first get here. Because we don't understand their assimilation into the American mainstream, we look at their culture in a negative way. They also have to deal with the fact that the media here does not paint a good picture of us most of the time. However, after traveling to Barbados and Jamaica, I realized that we're faced with the same issues in the ghettos of Jamaica and Barbados. When I was in Jamaica, Ballo was afraid to take us to Kingston because of the danger that was prevalent there.

I have watched news footage of Haiti and I understand the plight of the people. I think Black people in general need to create a united front where our bond can't be broken, in order to change the world for Black folks everywhere. I never hear about the Europeans fighting over their differences in the States. Instead, they embrace the common fact that they're all white and we need to do the same. Divide and conquer seems to be the philosophy that we fall trap to.

With all that said, I had to consider the possibility of my own relationship with Marjorie. Though we liked each other and I could see her in my world, I could not see myself trying to be cool with her dad. And for that reason alone I decided that I was not going to go out with Marjorie again. The fact that he spoke to her in their native tongue didn't even bother me that much; I just wished he had said what he needed to say about me to my face in English. As scared as I was of him, I would have respected him more.

Moving On

A week had gone by and I didn't hear from Marjorie. I didn't bother calling her either because I figured that her father had put a stop to our relationship before it even started. All the little signs were there and my mother was right to a certain extent. Her father probably thought that she was too good for me. We tend to think that we're better than most foreigners too, so I wasn't surprised.

I didn't speak to Dexter for about a week after my date with Marjorie and I wanted to know what was up with him. I called Dexter to say what's up but a girl picked up the phone. It was a voice that sounded familiar. When I asked who it was, the voice answered, "It's me, silly." I thought it sounded like Jess but I was wondering what she was doing answering Dexter's phone. She told me that Dexter was in the bathroom and he had asked her to answer the phone for him. I almost fainted because Dexter usually took his phone off the hook when he had company. "Could he really be that serious about Jess? Was Dexter up to a new trick?" I wondered. There was no way that Dexter would ask a woman to pick up his phone unless he was ready to change his life and make that woman part of it. Jess handed the phone to Dexter after we chatted for a few minutes.

My nosey ass wanted to hear the details of Dexter's date with Jess. So I asked him to divulge as much as he possibly could and that, he did. Yeah, men do talk and we talk about all of it just like women do. Are women the only people who have the right to get excited about a new relationship? Dexter couldn't tell me anything right away because Jess was standing right in front of him. He excused himself to the den so we could talk. Anyway, Dexter told me that he ended up taking Jess to The

Top of the Hub restaurant and they had great conversation and a nice meal. He also took her down by the Charles River around the same time that I was there with Marjorie. He said he never felt so connected to a woman his entire life. He realized that he and Jess could never stand each other in the past because they were such a good match for each other.

Unlike the Dexter of the past, this time around he didn't even try to sleep with Jess, despite the fact they had been spending every moment together since their date the previous Friday. Dexter told me that he and Jess decided to take things slow because he wanted this relationship to work. I asked Dexter about the knucklehead that Jess was seeing, he told me it was over when she discovered that he was still very married to his wife and they were expecting their second child. She happened to run into homeboy with his wife at the supermarket and she confronted him. His wife was dumbfounded because she had no idea that her husband was cheating on her with another woman. Jess didn't want to cause a scene, so she left the supermarket without saying a word to his wife.

Dexter also told me that this asshole had the nerve, the audacity and the balls to call Jess later that evening to tell her that he was still gonna leave his wife because he believed in their relationship. She couldn't stop laughing after he made that comment, then she hung up the phone. Dexter and Jess seemed to be happy that they finally got together and now I felt like I was going to be the third leg.

I also told Dexter about the differences between Marjorie and me. Of course, he said fuck what her father thought about me as long as she and I got along, but I had to explain to him the kind of influence and grip that her father had on her. "I hate these West Indians! They act like they should be the ones to choose who their daughters should date. I was trying to date this girl from Jamaica and her parents had a problem with me too. I tore that ass up when I finally got it just because I knew her father didn't want me to date her," he said. "So, you took your rage out on his daughter?" I asked. "Nah, I didn't do it just because of that, the ass was good too," he said. Dexter was an asshole when he wanted to be. Before he got off the phone he said, "If this is any consolation, I think you're a great guy and there's a girl out there waiting for you to make her the happiest woman on the planet. Keep your head up, dawg."

Before I got off the phone, I wanted to talk to Jess so I could tease her about Dexter, and I asked him to put her back on the phone. He handed the phone to her and from the sound of her voice, I knew that she knew I was going to tease her. Instead, I asked if she was happy and if everything was going well with Dexter. She told me that she has never been happier and Dexter had been a total gentleman since they went out. I said, "Well, you're at his house now and it's a matter of minutes before he has you in your drawers and begging for mercy." She answered, "I can't wait for him to make the move because a sister is frustrated and needs to release the tension." That's all I needed to hear. I told her that I'd call her later and to take care. I thought of the possibility of calling Marjorie after my conversation with Dexter, but I knew it was best to leave her alone.

A tiny little part of me was envious after I hung up the phone with Jess. I have always liked Jess, but I also came to the realization that we were too different to be together and I never had enough guts to seriously ask her out. I didn't really want to believe that Dexter betrayed me, but the jealousy and envy was eating at me like a cancer. I didn't want to be around them and I didn't want to speak to them. I wanted to be in my own world for a while without any friends.

Finding Myself

It took me a few weeks before I got over Dexter and Jess's new relationship. They tried to reach out to me and I brushed them off every time without letting them know that I was mad at them. I needed to find myself as an individual. I took up running and I made up an excuse for Dexter as to why I couldn't go to the gym to work out with him anymore. I knew Dexter usually went to the gym in the evening, instead, I went in the morning by myself. I ran about five miles three times a week and went to the gym four times a week that summer.

I needed to build my confidence and the more I worked out and jogged, the better I felt about myself. I didn't have to compare myself to Dexter for almost two months and that gave me a lot more motivation to do some work on me. By the end of August, I had developed a washboard stomach and I had put on about ten pounds of muscle. My body was really defined and I felt great as a person. I was looking forward to the new school year and I bought a few shirts that complemented my new physique. I had not seen Dexter and Jess in about two months, Labor Day weekend was coming up and I wanted to show off my new body down in Martha's Vineyard.

Dexter called me the week prior to Labor Day to see if we were still going to the Vineyard as we did for the past three years. By then, I had gotten over my anger with him and Jess and I needed to be out there and be seen. Dexter told me that he was bringing Jess along and if I minded. Of course, I didn't mind that Jess was coming along because I wanted them both to see the new Malcolm.

I could always count on Labor Day at the Vineyard to meet some of the most stimulating, intelligent and beautiful women from all over the Northeast. Since I only had a week before the actual day, I decided to work out twice as hard so I could get buff enough to turn a few heads. In the past, I watched how some women salivate over Dexter when he took off his shirt and I wanted to see if I'd get the same reaction. I wasn't trying to be like Dexter or anything, but I wanted to see if his method worked. Maybe some women are shallow enough to like a man because he has a nice body like most men do with women.

The week went by quickly and Dexter, Jess and I drove down to Woods Hole in his Mercedes Benz the Thursday evening before the long weekend. Dexter and Jess tried their best to make me feel comfortable with their new situation. I felt a little bit awkward because I couldn't joke around with Jess the way that I used to anymore without offending Dexter. No matter how close two friends are, one would still get territorial when the other jokes around with his girlfriend in a way he might deem inappropriate. We parked the car at a lot because we didn't make reservations early enough to take it across on the boat to Oak Bluffs. It was still early when we got to Oak Bluffs and we caught a cab to our destination which was a house located not too far from the port. The streets were filled with people and there was this festive mood all over the town under the warm autumn sun. I couldn't wait to go over to Ocean Avenue to hang out.

Our conversation during the ride from Boston in the car and on the boat to Oak Bluffs was limited. When we got to the house, I changed into one of those ribbed Gap t-shirts displaying my biceps and chest. I was looking buff and Jess took notice. She lightheartedly made a comment that I was getting almost as big as Dexter. I tried brushing it off, but Dexter followed through with his own comment "Damn, man, what you've been hitting the gym everyday for the last two months?" That basically confirmed the positive change in my body. I felt good hearing those words from Jess and Dexter. I was ready to go out and show all of my hard work to the world. I was in a rush to get to Ocean Avenue and I didn't want to waste any more time. I told Dexter and Jess to hurry it up.

We went outside and attempted to flag down a cab to take us to our destination. It was still daylight when we left the house, but finding a cab was a chore in itself. We couldn't get a cab to save our lives. By the time an empty cab drove by us, we were only a couple of blocks from Ocean Avenue. We ended up walking the whole way there. We made it there in no time because we were engaged in a deep conversation about my new workout regimen. I was happy to flaunt it to Jess and Dexter. They boosted my self-confidence as much as they could with words of encouragement.

As fun as that walk might have been from the house to Ocean Avenue, we didn't want to do it again. We went straight to this luxury car, rental place and rented a couple of convertibles. At first, I wanted to rent the Mercedes CLK coupe convertible for all three of us, then Jess and Dexter started fighting over the front seat, so they decided to get the SL 500 convertible model for the two of them. I was riding solo. I had never really driven a Mercedes before, but after driving that CLK, I was sold. I wanted to get one almost immediately. The car definitely had a different feel to it than my Honda Accord. My Honda was nice, but it was not a Mercedes. I was starting to understand why Dexter was so particular about the car he drove. I enjoyed riding in Dexter's car when we go out, but driving the car made me want to own one.

We finally got our cars and we were ready to go do our thing. One by one, we pulled out of the parking lot and we headed up the hill to Ocean Avenue. I needed to get some shades because the sun was beaming down on my forehead and the glare was really hurting my eyes. I pulled up in front of this little boutique where they only sold t-shirts and sunglasses. I purchased a nice pair of Kenneth Cole sunglasses that looked so good that they could've easily used a person with the same nose as me as the model when they designed them. Dexter and Jess went about their way to see the rest of the island. As many times as we had been to the Vineyard, we never really explored the whole island. Dexter took the opportunity while he was with Jess to explore the whole island. Before, when we would go to the Vineyards, we didn't have much time to dedicate to the island because ninety eight percent of our time was dedicated to the women on the island. Whether we were watching them, talking to them or just plain admiring them from afar, we enjoyed it.

I walked out of the store with my shades on feeling like the world was mine. I caught a few glimpses from people looking at me, but I was only interested in the young ladies who suddenly took interest in me. As fly as I thought I was, I still had a problem approaching women. So many women were smiling at me that whole weekend; I didn't know what to do with myself. I tried to bask in the glory for as long as I could without letting it go to my head.

I hit the club every night that weekend and I had dinner with a bunch of women whom I found out later were not only interested in fly Malcolm, but also the fly car that Malcolm was driving. All that just sent me back to square one because I refused to date any woman who was into the kind of car I drove, the brand name clothes I wore, my bling bling, the location of my house and its size and the size of my wallet. I was attracting all the wrong type of women that weekend. There were a few among the many that I could have probably slept with, but I didn't want to embarrass myself like that. I was willing to wait for the right person. They say "you can't miss what you never had" and I found that to be true. I was intrigued by the idea of having sex, but the act itself was too important to me to do it with just anybody.

Being at the Vineyard that weekend and spending the bulk of the time alone really boosted my confidence. I was really starting to enjoy the new changes in me and I was willing to accept them as they made me a better person all around. I was also thankful that I had friends like Jess and Dexter who sympathized and respected me for who I was. I had a whole new outlook on the world and its vision of me.

The Right Place

When I came back from the Vineyard that Monday night, I had to catch up on my sleep from all the partying that I did. As a matter of fact, I really needed to get some sleep because I had to be up early the next day for the first day of school. I must've fallen asleep around nine o'clock that evening and I didn't wake up until the next morning to the sound of my alarm clock around six o'clock. I got up and took a shower in no time. I put on one of my favorite navy blue suit that I had purchased in the spring that I didn't get a chance to wear. I wore a sky blue shirt, a yellow tie, black belt and shoes to match. I was looking rather spiffy. If GQ saw me that morning, they would've wanted to put me on their cover.

I got to the school early as usual because I liked to usher my kids into class before the bell rang. I was familiar with a few of the students from the previous year, but there were also a lot of new faces. The school received the most transfer students that fall and the freshmen class was bigger than ever with more kids with attitudes.

I usually try to set the tone in my classroom the first day of school by handing out the syllabus and my class rules to the students, but this time I wanted to get to know them first. Because I noticed a change in their attitudes, I took a different approach. I cracked a few jokes for the first few minutes of class, then I asked each student to get up and tell the class something about them that we would never know. We went down row by row and every student was trying to top the last one. When we got to Timmy, I was in shock. He told the class that someone had killed both of his parents and the person was only sentenced to a few years in jail for the murder. I didn't know what to make of Timmy's revelation. I could only imagine all the strife that he had been going through during the holidays, birthdays and any other special days in his life.

That whole day was routine for me and with each one of my classes, I asked the students to do the same thing repeatedly. No one ever topped Timmy's story and I couldn't stop thinking about it. When I was leaving the school that day, I tried to imagine life without my mother and I just couldn't picture it. My mother had been my cornerstone my whole life and I don't know if I'd still be sane if she were gone. Timmy had to be a strong kid to even continue to go to school.

It was a beautiful sunny afternoon that Tuesday in September and I decided to take a ride to my mother's house after work. After hearing Timmy's story, I had to go home to give my mother a hug for being around for me. On my way to my mother's house, I made a right turn from Dorchester Avenue onto Fuller Street when I noticed the nice derrière of this corporate looking young lady on my left walking up Fuller Street. She was wearing a dark tan business suit with a white-collar shirt, and nice three-inch heel black shoes that accentuated her beautifully toned legs. She was carrying a black shoulder bag over her left shoulder and a black briefcase in her right hand. I couldn't help but notice her body and strut. She was working it in a way that was classy, but yet sexy.

At first, my eyes took inventory from her legs all the way past her shoulders and I liked every inch of what I saw. I was just hoping she wasn't one of those "Butter Face" women. You know the type that has a killer body "but her face" is scary. To my surprise, she was not a "Butter Face." She was the whole package physically. She wore her hair in a bob; she had slanted eyes like one of her great grandparents was of Asian descent or something close to it. She had the dark brown complexion of an

Ethiopian goddess. Her little button nose accentuated the deep outline of her lips and her elongated face. Her brown skin was flawless and lightly outfitted with just enough make up to make a brother lose his mind.

Although I was shy, this was one opportunity I couldn't allow to pass me by. Since my confidence was on the rise, my shyness had subsided tremendously as well. I had to talk to her. I didn't know what I wanted to say, but I knew I needed to say something. For some reason, I woke up that morning feeling pretty good about myself when I left my house and I also had just had my hair cut the past Friday. It was as if I was having a déjà vu. The situation seemed very familiar to me, but whatever result I had in the past I did not want it to be the same this time around. I pulled the car over a few feet ahead of her. I checked my breath to make sure it was fresh because you never know! I popped a piece of peppermint gum in my mouth to make certain that a bad case of halitosis didn't sneak up on me. I also checked my nose in the mirror to make sure there weren't any green or foreign objects hanging out. I felt like Dexter for a few minutes in the car checking myself over.

As the young lady approached the car, I stepped out to introduce myself and extended my hand to her. She politely shook my hand and told me that her name was Eileen Jobson. She gave me all the confidence I needed when she actually shook my hand. I never paid attention in the past, but I realized that day that most professional women are easier to talk to than some of the hoochie mamas. Hoochie mamas have more prerequisites than professional women do. Hoochie mamas are like puppies; they'll follow a man around or are affectionate for as long as the man has something he can give them.

In the case of the hoochie mamas, they have to see the bling bling and 24-inch spinning wheels on a high price luxury car right away. I had never stepped to a hoochie mama in my Honda Accord and received any play from any of them. My plain Honda Accord was never good enough for them. The hoochie mamas have the loyalty of a dog; as long as you possess something that they want, they'll stick around. It just so happened that I'm usually driving when I spot what I perceive to be interesting women, sometimes.

As I was saying, Eileen boosted my confidence when she decided to be polite and shook my hand. I didn't have to guess that she was professional because it was written all over her face and the way she carried herself. The moment I laid eyes on her, I felt this tingling feeling in the pit of my stomach, it was the kind of feeling that could send a man into a daydream bonanza. And you know how I like to daydream. We hadn't even exchanged but a few words and this woman had captivated me. She was gorgeous and most of all she was friendly and receptive.

Eileen was of a different breed. She didn't look me up and down like most of the women I met in the past. She was watching my demeanor the whole time while I was trying to start a conversation with her. I was confident and nervous at the same time while I gazed at her beautiful brown eyes. She kept biting her bottom lip like she wanted to flirt with me. I didn't know if she was in one of those LL Cool J moments or not, so I didn't really want to assume she was flirting with me. Sometimes, it seems like LL can't stop licking his lips, not that I pay that much attention to LL, but this woman couldn't keep from biting her bottom lip sensually while talking to me. I didn't know how to contain myself. It was like a test of will she had planned to administer on the next guy who approached her and I was the guinea pig. However, this was one experiment that I didn't mind being a guinea pig for.

Eileen stopped biting her lip just long enough to ask me if I was going to say anything to her. The only thing I could say was actually what I was thinking silently in my mind. I told her that I found what she was doing with her lip very sexy and provocative. Unfortunately, she told me it was a bad habit she developed as a teenager. When she gets nervous around men, she bites her bottom lip. "So, it has nothing to do with me?" I asked. "Not entirely" she said. I was crushed and relieved at the same time. I was crushed that she wasn't flirting with me, and I was relieved that it was just a habit. I have never seen such a sexy habit in my entire life, and it was something I could get used to.

I asked Eileen where was she headed and she pointed toward the hill on Fuller Street. I was trying to be sarcastic so I told her "You about to go over the hill, huh?" She smiled at me and told me "that was cute, but I live on Fuller Street between Washington Street and Milton Avenue." I offered to give her a ride home, but she declined. She told me that she would never get in a car with a total stranger even though I had a trusting face. Kudos! I asked if I could walk her home and she told me it was a free country and that I could do whatever I wanted to because she didn't own the street. I went back to my car to properly lock the doors and close the window because I didn't trust the two knuckleheads who were staring at me from across the street while I was trying to get my mack on with Eileen. I was finally developing macking skills. Hooray!

So, we started walking up the hill and I asked Eileen what she did for living. She told me that most guys who asked that question in the past were always intimidated by the answer. By this time, I was thinking that she was about to tell me that she was a stripper and I was ready to dash back to my car while she headed for the hill. Deep in my gut, I knew that there was no way that she could be a stripper because she was too friendly outside of a strip club. Strippers are overly friendly when they're working because it's part of their customer service requirement. A lot of strippers are very defensive outside of work. Believe me, I know. Dexter and I visited quite a few strip clubs when we went down south and for some reason, I always thought the strippers were nice to me because they liked me. I had to learn the hard way that it was part of their job when one of them told me to "fuck off "outside of a club after I had just spent fifty dollars on lap dances. I said I was cheap didn't I? She was lucky that night because thirty of those fifty dollars came from Dexter. He treated me to a few lap dances.

Eileen had the kind of body that could make a man drool. I was hoping and praying to God that she wasn't going to spit out the word stripper. I was so caught up with my own assumption in my head I didn't even hear when Eileen told me that she was a lawyer. I said, "Excuse me, what did you say you were?" She told me "are you gonna run too because I'm an attorney?" She didn't know how happy and relieved I was when I heard the word attorney roll off her tongue. It was like hitting the lottery all over again. I was already mesmerized with her character and the fact that she was also educated and professional was the icing on the cake for me.

I was impressed with Eileen to say the least. I wanted to know what kind of law she practiced and she told me she was a corporate lawyer working at a prestigious law firm downtown Boston. I could see why she would intimidate most men, but I wanted to give her the benefit of the doubt. Eileen was very confident and proud and some people might misread her as arrogant. Because I had been around Dexter and Jess who are very confident, I didn't misinterpret her that way at all. I welcomed her confidence because I couldn't bring a woman who's apprehensive around my mother and my friends.

When Eileen asked me, "What do you do for work?" I paused for a second then I looked her straight in her beautiful eyes and said, "Are you gonna run from me now?" She smiled and said, "You're not a pimp or drug dealer are you?" I said, "No, nothing like that." She then asked, "What is it that you do?" I told her I was a teacher at the Jeremiah Burk High School. Her face lit up and then she said, "That's commendable! I always wanted to teach, but I didn't have the patience. I admire teachers and without them we wouldn't have doctors and lawyers or any other professionals" I looked at her and I was like "wow." I couldn't believe I met an intelligent, beautiful and sexy goddess in the hood who looked beyond my paycheck and admired my profession as a teacher for the second time in my life. Most of the broke ass women I met in the past were quick to tell me that teachers made no money or they'd make comments like "What you're earning about thirty five thousand dollars a year?" And most of the time, these hoochies didn't even have a GED themselves. Sometimes I think that women live in two different worlds even though they're on the same planet.

We were getting pretty close to Eileen's house as she pointed it out to me with her hand and I wanted to make sure I got her phone number so I could see her again. The conversation was flowing so well, I didn't want my asking for her number to sound like an intrusion. However, I could not let this great opportunity pass me by. As I mustered the confidence and courage to ask Eileen for her phone number, the coward in me started to emerge again. I wanted to find the Dexter in me who got out of the car when I first saw Eileen, but he went on vacation. At this point, being a coward was not an option.

Before I could ask Eileen if it was possible for us to keep in touch, she reached into her bag, she grabbed one of her business cards, flipped it over to write her personal number on the back, and handed it to me. She followed with "I really gotta go because I'm meeting my girlfriends in Cancun for a short vacation and my flight leaves in three hours. But, I would like to continue our conversation when I get back." I was so elated that I got her number; I forgot to give her mine. I told her it was nice meeting her and that I looked forward to seeing her the next day, not realizing she had just told me she was leaving the country in three hours. I didn't know what the hell I was saying, but I was excited!

Conditioned Reaction

The whole time I was walking Eileen up the hill I was thinking to myself "Were those two punks going to try to rob me when I got back to my car?" The way they were looking at me seemed like there was more than one opportunity on Fuller Street that day for more than one person. Eileen was mine and I was gonna be theirs. I placed Eileen's card in my pants pocket as I rushed back down the hill on Fuller Street and just as I expected, the two guys were both leaning against my car waiting for me to appear. I could see them leaning against the car from up the hill, I walked into someone's yard and grabbed a piece of two by four and hid it under my jacket.

As I got closer to my car, I asked them what they were doing leaning on my car like that. One of them took one look at me and told me that they didn't mean any harm. When they saw me walk up the street trying to talk to Eileen and the Parking Enforcement agent came around to ticket cars for not having a resident permit sticker, they had to pretend my car was theirs so I wouldn't get tagged. I was relieved that these brothers were looking out for me. I thanked them as I eased my way back into the car to place the two by four down without them noticing. I was so enthralled by Eileen, I didn't even notice the "Resident parking only" sign on the street.

As I took off in my car, I realized that I made one of the worse assumptions about the two brothers that most white people and sometimes, Black people made about me all my life. I wanted to make up for my preconceived notions of guilt because I felt bad. I drove back around the block to find the two brothers and handed a one hundred dollar bill to each of them for looking out for me. Even though a parking ticket was only going to cost fifty dollars, the gesture they made to save me a few bucks I felt was worth more than the two hundred dollars that I gave to them, and it also eased the guilt that I felt just a little.

I had fallen into a trap that was set for me by other people and I was ashamed of it. Black and White people alike have been conditioned to believe or perceive certain stereotypes when it comes to black men, and I allowed those perceptions to get the best of me. So many brothers go through life everyday being judged by other people and in most cases, it's just not fair. I don't think that all brothers would act the same way these two brothers did, but I think I should have at least given these brothers the benefit of the doubt before jumping to conclusions.

The shame that I felt that day raised my awareness of how I have viewed other black men and the way people have viewed me. I felt ashamed for thinking that I was better than these brothers just because they were standing on the street. The fact that they could've possibly lived in the house from which they were standing never even crossed my mind. I was intimidated by my own peers, and as a result, I made a bad judgment call. I often heard that young black men were intimidating, but I never understood why. It's not like I took inventory of their clothes or anything. I simply looked at them and assumed the worst. I now was wondering how many people must've thought the worse about Dexter and me when we stood around the corner from our house just to talk.

Someone created the notion that when more than one black man is standing on a corner, it must have something to do with some type of illegal activity and that notion is ridiculous to me. Someone who must have been suspicious of their own criminal activities must have created that mind set. How can anybody assume that something illegal is happening on every corner of America where Black men are gathering? I never questioned it before because I was asleep like the rest of the world. However, I'm glad that these two brothers awaked me and I vowed not to ever sleep like that again.

I also realized how much paranoia money could bring. In the past, I probably wouldn't have worried about those guys, but because I had a lot of money, I had my guard up. We react to situations in many different ways sometimes and we allow our fortune to also cloud our judgment. It was almost a subconscious thing that I did.

My Longing Heart

Eileen only lived a block from my mother's house. When I got to my mother's house, I was so excited about Eileen I started ranting about how gorgeous, fine, sexy and intelligent she was to my mother without giving my mother her customary hug and kiss. My mother was looking at me from the corner of her eyes and I could tell that she was wondering if I made this girl up. As much as my mother loved me, I knew she would have been disappointed if I were truly gay. She wanted grandchildren from me. She turned to me and said, "You're not gonna be one of those LD or DL brothers are you, Mal?" Whenever there was a concern, my mother referred to me as Mal. I knew she was concerned when she made that comment. I assured her that I was not on the DL or down low and that I really met a beautiful woman that I was hoping to get involved with romantically.

Though she didn't completely believe me at the time, my mother was content with the fact that I could possibly be interested in women. I was happy to see my mother, but I didn't want to wait another week to see Eileen. She told me that she was going to be in Cancun until the following Sunday, which would have been six days. I wanted to call her to offer a ride to the airport. I didn't want to act desperate, but I was. I posed an hypothetical question to my mother. I asked her, as a woman how she would feel if she had just met a man and he called her almost immediately after they met; would she think he was desperate? My mother told me it would depend on the situation and what kind of vibes that she got from the man. With that said, I knew that I wanted to call Eileen.

After dialing her number, I waited patiently while the phone rang about four times before she finally picked up. She sounded like she was preoccupied with something else. She was also surprised to hear my voice on the other line. I told her that I was calling to see if I could offer a ride to the airport because I didn't want to wait five days to see her again. She was very receptive and found my offer generous. She told me that she only had about an hour to get to the airport and she would call me back as soon as she was ready. I gave her my cell phone number and waited for her call.

While I was sitting in my mother's living room waiting for Eileen to call, my mother came in with some home made brownies and sat next to me. I knew that she was about to give me one of those lectures again about being true to myself because she refused to believe that I was not gay. As she started with "Mal, you know that you're my only son and that I will always love you no matter what," before she could finish her statement I was saved by the phone. My cell phone started ringing and it was Eileen calling to tell me that she was ready. I grabbed a couple of brownies and a bottle of water from the fridge and told my mother that I'd call her later because I had to go.

I dashed out that door faster than Carl Lewis ran the 100-meter dash at the Olympics in 1984. I wished my mother would let up already with all that gay crap. My mother could be very irritating sometimes and that's something I always wished that I could change about her. She just never knew when to quit.

I reached Eileen's house in less than five minutes and she was surprised that I got there so quickly when I called her from my cell phone in front of her house. I failed to tell her that she only lived a block away from my mother's when we met earlier. I didn't want her to think that I was stalking her or anything, so I told her that I grew up one block up the street from where she lived. She told me that she had only been living on Fuller Street for about three years and that she wasn't too familiar with her neighbors. She also said that she didn't spend much time at her house since she bought it. With such a demanding job, she spent most of her time at work. Eileen asked me to come in and help her with her luggage because she was pressed for time.

We didn't have too much time for small talk at her house as it was getting close to her flight departure time. I grabbed her suitcase, placed it in my trunk, and waited for her in the car. It took all but five minutes for Eileen to emerge wearing the tightest pair of jeans that her body would allow with a light cream color fitted sweater, a blue sport coat and nice pair of sexy pointy light brown boots and a brown belt to match. She had on a nice pair of Gucci sunglasses and a handbag that matched her boots. She was looking so good I had to slow down the image in my head as she walked towards the car from the staircase at her house. I kept replaying that image repeatedly in my head.

When Eileen got in the car, the only thing I could say was, "Wow." Not the same wow that I said when I saw Marjorie, this wow was on a whole different level. Eileen was a complete woman in my eyes. Everything in her life seemed to be in order. She smelled so good I had to put my window down to catch my breath so I wouldn't hyperventilate. Eileen was without a doubt, the most beautiful woman in the world to me. While driving to the airport, I wanted to see how down to earth she really was, so I asked what her favorite food was. She couldn't believe that I was interested in the kind of food she ate. She thought I was sweet for asking and for that, I earned a few brownie points. She told me that she liked Simco's hot dogs. I was a little taken back by her answer because Eileen looked glamorous without trying and there was no way in the world that I would associate her with Simco's. My mouth almost dropped to the floor when she said that.

Simco's was my favorite place to get a sub or a hot dog after the club let out. They offered the best of everything. Their fried clams, hot dogs, fried chicken, subs and fish were the best. Unfortunately, some knucklehead gang members decided to settle their beef in front of Simco's one night after the club and the city placed a curfew on the place. They had to close by a certain time in order to avoid another gang violence disturbance. I jokingly promised that I would take her to Simco's for dinner when she got back from her vacation. She laughed and told me that as long as they had her favorite hot dogs there she didn't mind. We also discussed our upbringing briefly and I told Eileen I was an only child. She told me that she once had a sister, but she passed away. She didn't go into too much detail about her sister, though.

I had never been so impressed with a woman my whole life. Everything that came out of Eileen's mouth made her more appealing to me. She could easily be mistaken for one of those high maintenance women, but she was as down to earth as can be. I could not wait to get to know her. Eileen was able to roll with the punches and she had a few jokes of her own, which I found very amusing. I knew I couldn't wait to see her again and her smile would stay on my mind until we saw each other again.

I finally made it to the Delta Terminal at Logan airport. I pulled up by the curb and one of the bag handlers asked if we needed help. I told him to please take the lady's luggage inside and I handed him a ten-dollar bill. I really didn't want to see Eileen go, but she had made her plans before she met me and I highly doubted that she would have changed them for me. She gave me a nice hug and promised to call me when she got back. I stood back for about three minutes watching Eileen walk away from me. There was a little bounce to her walk that ran my imagination wild for a few minutes.

During the drive back home from the airport, I was hoping and praying that Eileen was going to be the right woman for me. I was imagining her and me on my couch wearing sweats, kicking back or just watching a movie together. I only had good thoughts about her. I imagined holding her in my arms and laughing at her silly jokes. I saw us in a pillow fight with the feathers from the pillow are all over our faces while we roll around on the floor in front of a fireplace. I also saw us skiing in the mountains of Vermont and sipping cocoa in a small isolated cabin after a long fun-filled day. I was having thoughts about this woman that I never had about anyone before. I also saw complete happiness in a family setting.

I wanted to have Eileen at all cost as long as I was still myself. This woman brought warmth to my heart and made me experience feelings that I didn't know existed. I could see myself waking up to a woman like Eileen for the rest of my life and I could see her with my children in a big black house with the black picket fence somewhere in the suburb. Yes, that's right! I'd get a black house just to piss off the white people. Okay maybe that's too over the top. I'd get a white house, but everyone who lived in it would have to be black. Eileen was it for me and I was focused.

Love Calls

It had been a couple of days since Eileen left and I was missing her like I had known her for years. For some reason, I felt like she was now a part of my life. I wanted to spend every moment with her. I was consumed by her in all but one day. There was something about Eileen that captivated me in a way that only the Lord could understand. I don't even know the right words to use to describe it. I was thankful for the experience. Most Thursdays I would sit in front of the television to watch some of my favorite shows like Frasier and Will and Grace, but I didn't want to do that anymore. I wanted to be somewhere with Eileen spending time with her. I wanted to give her all of my attention. I was falling for a woman that I barely knew and I wondered if I was a fool.

If I were a fool, was I the only fool to ever fall for a woman the first time that I laid eyes on her, I wondered. Was she missing me as much as I was missing her? Was she yearning to see me as much as I yearned to see her? Did I even cross her mind after her flight landed in Mexico? I wondered, and then my phone rang. It was Eileen calling to tell me how much she has been thinking about me and how she wished that her vacation was shorter so that she could be in Boston spending time with me. I wanted to do better than that. I told her that I missed her so much that I was willing to fly to Cancun to meet with her the next day. She thought I was kidding at first, but when I told her that I could be on the five o'clock flight the next day to Cancun, she thought I might've been serious.

Eileen and her girlfriends had planned this trip a few months ago and they had planned to live it up in Mexico. For some reason, after meeting me, her vacation was not as fun anymore and she was no longer interested in her girlfriends' plans. Yeah they were partying from the time they got there, but Eileen's agenda had changed. She didn't want to have a good time with some Rico Suave guy for five days anymore. She wanted to be with me and her girlfriends thought she was spoiling their vacation because she met the man of her dreams. Eileen stayed on the phone with me that night for about two hours. I knew she paid a bundle for that international phone call, but she didn't care because she was talking to her future husband. You heard me right, I said her future husband.

After Eileen ran up her phone bill at the hotel for about two hours, she realized that it was getting a little bit too expensive for her. She wanted to get off the phone but I insisted on continuing our conversation. I asked for the number at the hotel and I called her right back. We stayed on the phone for an additional two hours talking about everything we liked and disliked. We found out that we had a lot more in common than we initially thought. The chemistry between us could not be denied and we wanted to see if a scientific experiment between the two of us would work.

Eileen was also sympathetic, she understood that I was a teacher and I didn't have the kind of money to just give away to the phone company. She suggested that we end our call for the sake of my pockets. It was hard saying goodbye to her because I knew that the money for the phone call didn't mean much to me. However, I couldn't let the cat out of the bag about my wealth just yet. So, I obliged and hung up the phone, but not before I told her a thousand times how much I was gonna be thinking about her.

I barely got any sleep after I hung up the phone with her. It was about three o'clock in the morning when we got off the phone and I needed to get up for work by six o'clock. I dozed off somewhere in the night planning a wedding with Eileen. It was my imagination at work again. I must've had the biggest smile on my face when I fell asleep that night.

I woke up the next morning feeling tired and a little worn, but I didn't want to disappoint my students. I went to work as planned but I acted like a young kid waiting for the bell to ring after each period. By the time the last period bell rung, I was almost halfway out the door. I peeled out of the school parking lot so fast that day even the Indy 500 speedway couldn't handle my speed. I couldn't wait to get home to pack a suitcase to go to Cancun for the weekend. It was Friday and I did not want to wait until Sunday to see Eileen again. I told her that I was gonna get on the five o'clock flight to Mexico and I meant it.

I went home and packed my bag in no time. I drove my car to the airport and made it to the ticket counter just in time to get the last available seat in first class. All of the regular coach seats were sold out anyway. It was an expensive flight and I definitely wouldn't have been able to afford it on my teacher's salary, but Eileen didn't have to know that I was rich yet. I wanted to see her and she wanted to see me that was all that mattered. Before I boarded the plane, I placed a call to my mother to let her know that I was going to Mexico for the weekend. I also called Dexter to tell him that I was gonna be in Cancun with Eileen for the weekend too. Dexter had plans of his own with Jess. They were headed to the Berkshires to check out the fall foliage.

I took my carry-on bag on the plane with me and asked one of the flight attendant for a pillow. I was knocked out in five minutes and I slept the whole way to Mexico. By the time the plane landed, I was well rested and ready to take Eileen out for a good time. I wasn't sure if Eileen really took me seriously when I told her I was going to get on the five o'clock flight to Cancun, but there I was in Cancun ready to surprise her. Eileen had mentioned that she was staying at the Hilton, so I called up the hotel to see if they had any rooms available. I was told that all the regular rooms were sold out and only their suites were available. These people were making it harder and harder for me to conceal my wealth from Eileen. I needed a place to stay, so I took the suite.

When I got to the room, I changed into some baggy cargo shorts and a tank top for comfort, and the heat in Cancun was killing a brother. I grabbed a towel and went down by the pool to chill out. I didn't want to call Eileen just yet because I knew that she was probably out somewhere with her girlfriends. I wanted to surprise her face to face. I was chilling by the pool with a towel over my face basking in the evening heat. I ordered a couple of complimentary drinks to loosen me up a little. I don't know why most black people go on vacation and sit by the pool. We rarely get in the pool, but I guess it's cool just to sit by it. At least that's the way it was for me, anyway.

An hour had gone by and I knew that Eileen was probably going to try to call me at home. I went up to my room and called her directly. She picked up the phone and told me that she was getting ready to go out with her girlfriends because they had been calling her a party pooper all week. She was very excited to hear my voice, but she had to hurry downstairs to meet her girlfriends. I told her that I understood the situation and that I would call her later.

After hanging up the phone, I ran downstairs to the souvenir shop located in the hotel lobby to grab a dozen roses for Eileen. I stood right in the middle of the lobby with the roses in front my face concealing it waiting for Eileen to appear. I noticed two other gorgeous black females waiting down on the other end. I caught them trying to get a glimpse of me, but they couldn't see my face as it was concealed by the roses. They must've seen something they liked because they couldn't keep their eyes off my body.

After waiting for about five minutes, it was time for the moment of truth. Eileen appeared from the elevator wearing white drawstring linen pants that were almost see-through, with a white tank top and white sandals. She was wearing a nice thong underwear to prevent lining in her pants.

As usual, my baby was looking good, and better than all the people in that resort. I ran to her as if I was floating on a cloud and effortlessly making my way to the other end of the lobby with my face still hidden behind the roses. She had her back to me as she headed towards her girlfriends. I whispered in her ear "Can I please have a moment of your time?" The first thing out her mouth was "No way, it can't be!" Yes, it was! Me in the flesh in Cancun to surprise the woman I was lusting after. She was so happy to see me that I didn't even get a chance to hand the flowers to her. She jumped on me and gave me the nicest hug and the longest kiss that I could imagine. She totally caught me off guard with the kiss. I was happy to say the least. I told her that I couldn't wait any longer to see her and that I decided to come down there. Her girlfriends didn't even get mad that she wasn't coming with them anymore because they thought my gesture was so romantic.

As the two women walked away from Eileen, they screamed, "We'll see you later girlfriend!" I didn't even get a chance to meet them and I didn't even care. I was there for my baby. For some reason, there appeared to be an instant connection between Eileen and me. Since I had never fallen in love with anyone before, I wondered if it was normal for us to discover love at first sight. I always thought it was some made-up fantasy for good television stories from Hollywood, but it was happening to me.

I actually didn't want to stay in with Eileen. I wanted to take her out for a good time. We went back upstairs to my suite and Eileen's jaw almost dropped to the floor. She asked how I could afford something like that and I told her that I found a way because I wanted to see her. I explained to her that the reason I was in that suite was because there were no more rooms available at the hotel. She was thoroughly impressed with my efforts. She was also careful to tell me not to ever act that foolishly again in the future because she didn't believe in wasting money. I told her she was worth every dime. I was still holding on to the roses and she finally extended her hand to take them from me in the room. She raised them to her nose, told me that they were nice, and thanked me. I told her it was no big deal because my woman was worth all of it. "Your woman, huh?" she replied. "Did I say that?" I asked. "You did," she said. I was like "well then."

I didn't want it to seem like I was rushing things, but I got the feeling that Eileen was right along with me on this one. She was feeling me just as much as I was feeling her and I got the sense that it was the first time that she'd also met someone and clicked with him almost instantly. I needed to jump in the shower to wash up before heading out with Eileen. I told her she could wait in the living room area while I showered. I took a quick shower and when I came out from the bathroom, I found Eileen sitting on the bed. I had the towel wrapped around my waist and her eyes were directed straight at my tool. I didn't want to embarrass myself, by allowing my tool to stand erect; I grabbed my bag and ran back to the bathroom.

I knew if I started anything with Eileen, we'd be staying in watching movies all night. I allowed her to watch the water drip off my rippled chest and washboard stomach for only a quick second. Eileen was doing that thing with her lip again as she was watching me and I knew that gesture alone could've gotten me erected in no time. While in the bathroom, I threw on a fresh pair of briefs with my shorts and a t-shirt. My clothes were all wrinkled in the bag and I didn't want to go out looking wrinkled. I plugged in the iron, I quickly ran it over my cream-colored drawstring linen pants, and a white ribbed sleeveless t-shirt. Eileen was sitting on the bed watching me get dressed the whole time. She nervously bit her bottom lip a few times, but I turned my head before I allowed myself to get hooked.

It took me less than fifteen minutes to get ready. I was ready to take on the town with my lovely queen. Eileen had planned to go to Senor Frog's with her girlfriends and I didn't really see any reason to change those plans. First, I was hungry and I needed to get a bite to eat. We went to this nice restaurant by the water and I had the best lobster that I had ever eaten. Eileen had sautéed scallops, as she was not very hungry. We conversed a little during dinner, but we mostly expressed our gratitude for having met each other. I found out that Eileen was at a point in her life where she was going to focus strictly on her career and if a good man happened to be part of the plan then good, and if not, she was okay with that as well. I happened to be the good man at the right place on Fuller Street on that day.

We left the restaurant after we ate and walked to Senor Frog's, which was about a mile away from the restaurant. We needed the walk to help digest some of the food. Eileen held on to my hand the whole walk to the club and she was very affectionate. I love an affectionate woman and I was starting to fall in love with Eileen right away. Of course, I reciprocated the affection that I received from her because she deserved it. I was like a little kid who was falling in love for the first time. Though Eileen mentioned that she had a couple of boyfriends in the past, I still felt like she was also falling in love for the first time. What she felt for me was different than her two previous relationships, she explained. "This feels like nothing I have ever felt before and it seems more real," she said.

I had a great time with Eileen and her girlfriends at Senor Frog's that evening. We put on a show for all the white tourists who thought we were the next best things to Michael Jackson on the dance floor. All my inhibitions went away and I let loose like I was on some kind of amphetamine. It seemed like white people would never let the electric slide die no matter what part of the world they're in. We led the charge for the electric side very smoothly then one by one rhythmically challenged white folks got on the floor and started messing it up. People started bumping into each other creating a domino effect all over. Eileen and I stepped back to watch these people make fools of themselves. One thing for sure, drunk white folks know how to have a good time. They would dance to a presidential speech if music were added to it.

Eileen and I left the club around two o'clock in the morning because we were tired and we wanted to spend a little private time together. When I reached my room at the hotel, I noticed the red message button on the phone was flashing. I told Eileen to have a seat on the couch while I checked my messages. I dialed into the voicemail to see who it was. Dexter left me an urgent message to call him. I called him on his cell phone and he was in Williamstown, Massachusetts with Jess. Dexter wanted to talk to me because he felt something that he had never felt before. He told me he was falling for Jess and he didn't know how to stop it. I asked him why would he want to stop it and he told me that he really didn't.

Dexter had gone up to the Berkshires to check out the fall foliage, but somehow he managed to fall in love in the process. He couldn't really talk to me because Jess was sitting next to him, but he promised to call the following day with the details.

It was just as well because I needed to spend some quality time with Eileen.

Eileen and I spent most of the night in each other's arms cuddling, kissing and necking on the couch until we fell asleep. I woke up around five in the morning because I needed to take a leak. I went to the bathroom to relieve myself and when I came back, I couldn't help but notice how beautiful Eileen was even in her sleep. I carried her from the couch to the bedroom, laid her down on the bed then I pulled the covers on her. I went back to the living room to sleep on the couch.

Getting to Know the Friends

Eileen and I were having a wonderful time in Cancun. I got to meet her two best friends Carla and Diana. All three women grew up together and they all wanted to be lawyers since they were kids. All three of them were practicing attorneys and single. Carla was a bombshell, but from talking to her, I could tell she was high maintenance. That could've been one of the reasons why she was still single. It would take a professional athlete to satisfy all of that woman's material needs. She was all about Fendi this, Gucci that, and Versace this. For a moment there, I thought she was going to start speaking Italian. She clearly had her priorities all screwed up. But, there's always a man out there looking for eye candy who wouldn't mind putting up with the headache.

Diana was sophisticated to the point where she was very judgmental of everyone who didn't speak well or act properly. Etiquette was very important to her and I could easily see a guy like Dexter playing her for getting on his nerves. She had set the standards so high for her man that God himself was having a hard time creating that man. Every time God started creating a man for her, she had an additional request and he had to start from scratch all over again. He figured that he would have her man ready for her by the time she's forty-nine and unable to be nothing more than a sugar mommy to some young lover boy.

I was so happy that I got the sane one out of the crew. I wondered how Eileen managed to stay friends with these women. Then I thought about it and realized that most people said the same thing about Dexter and me. Eileen's friends had their flaws, but they were no concerns of mine. Eileen was perfect as far as I could see and that's all that mattered to me. I was going to be courteous to her friends and keep it moving.

We hung out at the beach all day Saturday and I took the girls out to dinner at the Hard Rock Cafe later that night. Eileen was staring at me with this curious look on her face all through dinner. I knew she was wondering how I was going to pay for this dinner on my teacher's salary. I appreciated her concern, but I gave her the nod that everything was okay. We sat through dinner for about an hour and it was the same thing that I was hearing all day from her friends. They kept complaining that there were no good Black men out there, but they never stopped once to take a look at themselves. Any brother who came into contact with these women would run for his life. They were looking for all the wrong things in a man. They might've been professional and earning great money, but their standards went way up along with their lifestyles and salaries. They were the type who hate on the brothers who end up with white women. The brothers with the big salaries just wouldn't put up with all the attitude, requirements and extremely high standards. They needed to come back down to Earth. I'm not condoning the fact that some brothers do sell out after they make it.

There was a lot to be said about Eileen when I compared her to her friends. She was grounded, and she didn't think that she deserved to be with a man who was earning a six-figure salary just because she earned one. She wanted a man, who could make her smile, feel appreciated, wanted and sexy, but most of all she wanted a man who could add to her own happiness. She didn't rely on a man to make her happy because she was already happy when I met her. I'm sure her friends were making her miserable and that's probably why she missed me so much. Her friends were like boat anchors holding her down with them.

I planned to treat Eileen with the same respect that I gave my mother. I was hoping that I could make her laugh, cry in a good way and appreciate her for being a wonderful person. We all deserve to be happy with our mates, but we must also find happiness within ourselves first. Maybe one day Carla and Diana will realize the source of their unhappiness, but for now, I was going to pull Eileen away from them as much as I possibly could. Not that I thought they could somehow manage to manipulate our relationship, but I didn't want to take that chance.

The Right Time

It was getting late, the two hopeless singles wanted to go out to the clubs and scour whatever they could find. Eileen and I wanted to retreat to my room for a great night of conversation. I paid the tab for our dinner and drinks and we told the girls that we'd catch them in the morning. Eileen and I caught a cab back to the hotel because we didn't feel like walking and it was a little far. The cab driver was very nice. He started to tell us about a few places to visit, but unfortunately, we were leaving the following day. We thanked him for all his help and I gave him twenty US dollars for the ride. After paying the cab fare, Eileen pulled me to the side and told me that she hoped that I wasn't trying to impress her by throwing away money I didn't have. I told her that was not my intention and the money for the trip had been saved from a while back.

Eileen was very practical and genuine. I didn't feel frugal around her because she was just as financially conscious as I was. A part of me wanted to be honest with her, but good sense told me to wait and see how the relationship developed. We went upstairs and ordered a few movies on the cable station that we ended up not watching at all. We were all over each other the minute we sat down on the couch. The night before we didn't take off any clothing items, but not this time around. Eileen pulled my shirt off me and started rubbing my chest.

I got a rise out of the touch of her sensual hands and she could see my manhood growing. We were kissing and rubbing each other's chest, but Eileen was still wearing her bra. Not being an expert, I was trying to sneak the bra off Eileen's chest and she sensed that I didn't know what I was doing, so she offered to help. She unclasped her bra and pulled her shirt off. Her c-cups were standing in front of me begging to be sucked. Eileen had the firmest breasts. I kept kissing her and rubbing her tits, but my lips were trying to make their way down to her nipples. I started kissing her neck and she was moaning and giving me directions on how to do it better. Of course, I obliged. I needed all the direction I could get.

Eileen told me straight up that she wanted me to suck on her breasts. It was like hitting the jackpot all over again. This was the first time that I was about to suck on tits that I really wanted to taste. Man, I almost devoured her tits like a hungry lion, she had to tell me to take it easy and take my time. She told me that we had all night and there was no need to rush. I asked her how she wanted it as I motioned my tongue slowly around her nipples and she started moaning. She kept telling me to suck harder on her nipples and the harder I sucked, the louder she became. I brought her tities together so I could have both of them in my mouth at the same time. I was sucking the hell out of them and I could feel that Eileen was getting even hotter. Every little direction I received from her made it more pleasurable for both of us.

She got up and grabbed my hand to lead me to the bedroom. Just like a little boy who obeyed his orders, I followed behind her. When we got to the room, Eileen pulled off my belt and pulled down my pants. She pulled out my hard dick and said, "Scrumptious." I could tell that she was impressed with my nine-incher. She took it in her mouth and started licking the head like a giant popsicle. The sensation was too great for me to bear; I came within seconds all over the floor. I didn't want to disappoint Eileen, but I needed to come. She asked why did I come so quickly and I had to tell her that she was the first woman that I had ever gone this far with. Surprisingly, Eileen told me "Mama's gonna have to show you her tricks." I was thinking that "Mama's gonna have to wait because my dick is too sensitive to be touched right now."

Even though I came, I was still as hard as ever and I just needed a few second for that sensitive sensation to go away. Eileen kept stroking my dick with her hand back and forth until all the semen came out. She took it back in her mouth and she started doing things to me that I could not describe. I had never been to heaven, but if it felt anything like that, I was going to be on my knees praying every night so I could reserve my spot up there. Eileen was sitting on the edge of the bed while I was standing, I felt like my knees were about to buckle from under me, so I asked to switch places with her. I was on the edge of the bed and she was on her knees giving me the blowjob of a lifetime. I tried as best as I could to contain myself, but I had to scream to her that the shit was good!

She told me to lie down on my back as she took off her pants and underwear. I was thinking that I didn't have a condom for what she was about to do, but Eileen came prepared. I understood clearly where she was coming from. Who was I to judge her, anyway? Eileen came and sat on my chest near my face and told me to eat her pussy. I had never eaten anyone before and I needed a little direction. She took one of her fingers and pulled back the skin to expose her clit. She told me to lick it as gently as possible. I was licking Eileen's clit as gently as I could and she tasted very good. She must've been reaching orgasms on top of orgasms because she was screaming at the top of her lung and telling me "Right there, keep going, don't stop" every time she was about to come. With Eileen's directions, I ate her just right. I wanted to taste her juices too, so occasionally I stuck my tongue inside of her to taste her flowing juices. I developed a little rhythm after a while and I was able to figure out when Eileen was about to come. Each time she was about to come, I stuck a finger inside of her while I ate her to maximize her pleasure. What can I say? Watching a lot of porno flicks helped me out a little, too.

After eating Eileen for about forty-five minutes, it was time to let her feel my nine-inches inside of her. She ripped open a condom and rolled it down on my dick like an expert. I was lying on my back and all of my nine inches sprung up like a flagpole on top of a state building. Eileen mounted me like a horse and started winding on me like she was possessed. She grabbed a hold of my chest and was screaming, "Yes, keep it going baby." My intent was to keep it going, but if she continued to wind on me like she was, I was gonna come very quickly again. I slowed down a little bit just to pace myself and to keep from ejaculating too soon. I was trying my best to keep up with her. She was good and I wanted to be better even though it was my first time. The faster she was winding on me, the harder I became. I wanted to make sure that Eileen was pleased.

I flipped her over so I could watch her beautiful round ass while I slid in and out of her. I was banging Eileen like a newly released ex-con who hadn't had pussy in years. Sweat was pouring down my whole body as I stroked her gently back and forth and then hard. I stroked her so hard my knees were starting to burn from the sheet. I asked her to kneel on the edge of the bed so we could continue. With every motion and every stroke, I knew that I wanted to be with Eileen forever. I didn't need to compare her to any body else. She was good enough for me. And with one last stroke and Eileen rubbing her clit with her finger, we both came at the same time.

That night marked the first time that I ever had sex with a woman and she was worth every minute of it. While we were lying down in the bed, we fell asleep with our bodies wrapped around each other. We felt so comfortable sleeping together we didn't even bother putting on any clothes. The warmth of Eileen's body sent me to sleep like a little baby.

I woke up the next morning sprung on Eileen and it was just a matter of time before she was sprung on me too. That weekend was the best weekend in my life. I discovered things that weekend that I would've never learned had I stayed home. Eileen and I became an item the night after we slept together. We've been together now for a few months and everything has gotten better with each passing day. Eileen and I have gotten closer; she has become a friend and a confidant. She taught me how to be a great lover to her and she has helped me make up for lost time every chance we get in the bedroom and all over my house and hers.

It had been a few months since Eileen and I were together and I wanted to make it official to my friends and family. A part of me felt bad that I was keeping my fortune a secret from Eileen, but I had hoped that she would forgive me when she found out the truth. Eileen was a dreamer who hoped to one day have a family and her own law firm. She was working hard towards that goal and I didn't want to get in the way. Eileen's financial forecast would allow her to start a family in two years. She and I were getting pretty serious and I knew that I didn't want to wait two years to start my life with her. She was all I ever wanted in a woman and there was no need to look further.

Offering a Helping Hand

Through the course of my relationship with Eileen I had also decided to help Timmy deal with his past ordeal. The brutal slaying of his parents left him scarred and Timmy didn't know how to release his anger and frustration. Timmy was living with his maternal aunt, but she couldn't afford to pay for Timmy to receive counseling. I took it upon myself to call his aunt to suggest and offer to pay for counseling for him. I knew a great child psychologist who was able to help Timmy deal with his trials and tribulations in a proper manner. Within months of treatment, Timmy's grades started improving and he was able to get along better with his peers. Occasionally, I would pick him up and take him out as part of his treatment prescribed by the doctor.

Timmy's aunt had three kids of her own and she barely had enough time to do anything with any of them. Although she received a monthly check for Timmy from the state, it was not enough to cover all of his monthly expenses. Timmy enjoyed hanging out with me because we spent a lot of time at the mall buying some of his favorite games and clothing items. Everything was done with the consent of his aunt and the approval of the psychologist. Timmy had made tremendous progress and his road to full recovery was getting closer by the day.

Timmy was such a very likable kid that I sometimes wished he were my son. He and I developed a close enough relationship that I knew I would be in his life forever. I want to be there for Timmy when it is time for him to graduate from high school, go to college, and get married and so on. He brought joy to my heart and peace to my mind and he was the epitome of determination. I see in him a kid with tremendous potential and ability. I know that Timmy will become a great man one day.

One of the arrangements that I made with Timmy was that if he worked hard enough in school to get a scholarship to college, I would buy him a brand new car. However, if he's not able to earn a scholarship and is accepted to any college in the country, I would pay his tuition in full. I was trying to get him motivated in the right direction and to push himself harder in school. We all need a little motivation at some point in our lives and children are no different.

Timmy has become part of my extended family. He's met my mother and my friends and everybody thinks highly of him. He's slowly tearing down the wall that he had put up to protect himself against the world. I'm very happy with the great strides that Timmy has made and he's very happy with himself as well.

The First Supper

We were now at the sixth month mark in our relationship and I was ready to introduce Eileen to the important people in my life. Sure, they all heard about her, but no one had met her, not even Dexter. I wanted to invite everyone out to dinner for a formal introduction, but my mother insisted on cooking at her house and who am I to turn down a home cooked meal, right?

A dinner was scheduled for 8:00 pm at my mother's house. I told my mother to make it special because I was bringing a special friend. I also told Dexter and Jess to get there on time because they had a bad habit of getting into it sexually after they got dressed. Those two freaks had more sex than a whole farm full of rabbits. I asked Eileen to wear a sexy, but conservative dress because she was going to meet my mom. I also asked my mother to invite her boyfriend to the dinner because I wanted to meet him. It was a night where everybody was going to meet for the first time.

I went to Eileen's house at 7:45 pm to pick her up. She stepped out in this little black dress that I hadn't seen, with a nice scarf around her neck and a full-length wool coat. This one was a special number for my friends and family. I knew that I was gonna be everyone's envy that night because my baby was looking good. I didn't want to mess up her lipstick, but I couldn't pass up kissing her beautiful lips. First, I had to tell Eileen that she looked great and I appreciated her efforts. She also told me how great I looked in my black suit, sky blue shirt, black belt and shoes with a solid sky blue tie. I wore my Ralph Lauren black overcoat. I briefed Eileen about my mother in the car just in case something odd came up. She was looking forward to meeting my friends and family and I was looking forward to showing her off. I knew that I hit one of the biggest jackpots in lottery history, but I considered Eileen to be the biggest jackpot of my life. She made me feel complete as a person and I was extremely grateful and happy.

Eileen and I were the first people to arrive at my mother's house. As usual, I used my key to enter after ringing the doorbell. As I was making my way in, my mother was walking towards the door and when she saw Eileen her mouth dropped. I knew this wasn't one of the good mouth drops, so I signaled for my mom to chill out. I knew that my mother was probably thinking that Eileen was a transvestite of some sort and she was surprised to see how good she looked as a woman. My mom still thought I was gay and I would have to set her straight that day. She was checking Eileen all out, as she extended her hand to introduce herself. I knew that Eileen felt kind of strange and uncomfortable with my mother's scrutiny.

My mother asked if she could take Eileen's coat and scarf to hang in the closet for her. She handed her coat and scarf to my mom and as my mom walked away I could hear her whisper "she has great taste too" referring to Eileen's coat and scarf. I wanted to ask Eileen to help my mother in the kitchen, but I knew that she would be all up in Eileen's face and neck searching for an Adam's apple. Instead, I sat in the living room with her to keep my mom from embarrassing herself. After a while, I left Eileen in the living room for a few seconds to check with mom. The first words out of her mouth when I entered the kitchen was "great job," I was thinking that she's finally accepted Eileen as a beautiful woman and was congratulating me, but she followed with "Who's her doctor and how much did it cost?" I was starting to lose patience with my mom and all her homosexual innuendos. I stormed out of the kitchen back to the living room to sit with Eileen.

About ten minutes later, I heard the doorbell ring and it was none other than Jess and Dexter looking dazzling as usual. Dexter was wearing a dark gray suit coordinated with everything from his handkerchief to his tie, down to his socks. Jess was wearing a nice little body fitted dress that barely reached her knees. I ushered them to the living room and took their overcoats to the closet. I could not wait to introduce them to my prize. I was looking at Jess and Dexter's faces when they first laid eyes on Eileen and from Dexter's reaction, I knew I had the thumbs up from him. From Jess's discomfort, I knew that she felt that she was not the only beautiful person in the room. I couldn't wait to tell them that she was a practicing attorney at only twenty-seven years old.

I noticed that Dexter kept staring at Eileen as if she looked familiar to him. He looked at her and shook his head couple of times, as if he had seen her somewhere before. Eileen didn't seem at all familiar with Dexter. After shaking hands with Dexter and Jess, she went back to her seat. I didn't make too big a deal of what took place between Dexter and Eileen.

Before totally breaking the ice with Eileen, Dexter needed to introduce Jess to my mother as his girlfriend. My mother often heard me talk about Jess, but she never actually met her. I took Dexter and Jess to the kitchen to my mother and my mother gave me the same look she gave to Eileen when she first saw her. Dexter introduced Jess and my mother took inventory of Jess's whole body before she whispered to me "You all could've fooled me with your dates. What kind of doctors on earth is changing God's work like that?" I had to tell my mother to chill. All of her homosexual suspicions of Dexter and me had to be put to rest once and for all before her boyfriend arrived.

I asked my mother to come into the living room to prove to her that our girlfriends were real and that they were born female. I sat everyone down in the living room and asked for everyone's attention for a minute. I told them that I needed to put to rest something that's been on my mother's mind for a while, but I needed their help. I took the floor and said, "Mother, I know that you think that Dexter and I have been secretly dating each other since we were kids and you think that we're gay because of our close relationship. I'm standing before you today to tell you that we're not gay, we've never been gay, and we don't want to be gay and if I were gay Dexter wouldn't be my type. And furthermore, these are real women who were born female and there isn't a doctor in the world who could do work of this great quality" while pointing at Jess and Eileen. Eileen and Jess's faces almost hit the floor. They had no idea what they were in for. We had to explain to them later our little confusion with my mom.

I could sense that my mother was a little embarrassed because I put her on the spot, but she refused to believe that I wasn't gay and left me no choice. She didn't have much to say other than, "I'm happy I'll get to have some grand children in the future. They can have kids, can't they?" We all just shook our heads because my mother was a trip. I apologized to Jess and Eileen, but I told them that I had to do that to prove to my mother that Dexter and I weren't a couple. Stupid ass Dexter had the nerve to ask, "You really don't think that I would be your type?" I rolled my eyes and shook my head in disbelief as I left the living room to go to the dining room to help my mother set the table.

As my mother and I were setting the table, I could tell that she had a smile on her face. She was happy that I had found someone that made me happy. My mother thought Eileen and Jess were both pretty, but as my mother, she told me that Eileen was a knockout. My mother's boyfriend was about to make an impression of his own. The bell rang again and my mother ran to get it because she knew it could only be her boyfriend. He came in with a dozen red roses in hand. He pulled two roses out of the bunch and handed one to each of the girls after greeting my mother with a hug and kiss. He handed the other ten roses to my mother. He introduced himself as Clifford and we all told him that we were waiting on him to eat after introducing ourselves.

Clifford was a tall and handsome brown-skinned man and he spoke with the same tone as James Earl Jones, but a little more hip. I could tell he was quite the charmer and I could understand why my mother would fall for him. We all headed to the dining room and took our seats to start feasting on this great dinner that my mother prepared. She made sweet ham, collard green, macaroni and cheese, rice and beans, fried chicken, potato salad and she broke out a couple of bottles of wine that she'd stored since I was a kid. Before we could all dig into our plates, Clifford offered to bless the food. We all bowed our heads as he led us into prayer. Clifford took longer than necessary to bless the food; he was obviously a religious man who was very serious about God.

I think Clifford might have heard my stomach growling during his prayer and decided to cut it short so we could start feasting. My mother's food had never tasted better. Everything was delicious and I watched Eileen's face as she tried each dish and was delighted by them all. I hope that she took a cue from my mother. Through dinner, everyone talked about their backgrounds and what their plans were in life and where they wanted to be in a few years. It was very interesting conversation, but I had to come clean with Eileen.

I raised my glass and asked everyone to toast Eileen and me on our six-month anniversary I wanted to give a short speech and let the cat out of the bag at the same time. I stood up with my glass still raised and said, "Eileen, I want to take this moment to thank the Lord for bringing you into my life. You have brought me happiness, joy, excitement and most of all, love. I have waited my whole life for a woman like you and at one point, I really didn't think that people like you exist. I know this is the first time that you're meeting my family and friends, so I'd like to take this opportunity to ask you to marry me" as I knelt down on one knee in front of her. Eileen was shocked and she didn't know what to say at first because she was overcome with emotion and joy. She shook her head saying yes to me before I got a chance to pull the ring out of my pocket. I pulled out a five-carat solitaire diamond ring and placed it on her finger and her eyes lit up like a little girl on Christmas.

I didn't want to make Eileen wait any longer because I knew she was gonna start questioning how I was able to afford that ring. I asked everyone to quiet down so I could tell Eileen that I was also a multi-millionaire by luck when I won the big lottery jackpot the previous year. Eileen never really paid attention to stuff like that on TV and she had no idea that my mother had been on television accepting the check. I told her that I was sorry for keeping that big of a secret from her, but I was happy that she accepted me as Malcolm the Regular Guy instead of Malcolm the Millionaire.

Eileen gave me the biggest hug and kisses and made me promise to never keep secrets from her again. I looked in her eyes that day and saw a glow that I had never seen before. Dexter gave me a big congratulatory hug and Jess was just in tears. She walked over to me and gave me the tightest hug since I've known her. Everyone in the room congratulated Eileen and welcomed her into the family. My mother was very happy that she was finally getting a daughter in law.

The women gathered around Eileen to talk about her ring, while the men headed to the living room to watch ESPN. I found out that Clifford was a big Patriots fan as were Dexter and I. I told them that I'd get season tickets for the upcoming season and that we'd get to hang out every other Sunday when the Patriots played at home. We stayed at my mother's house until midnight that evening talking about just anything and everything. Of course, she had to break out with the photo album to embarrass me further in front of my new fiancé. I took it all in stride and Eileen didn't mind hearing the stories from my mother and Dexter.

That night I took Eileen to my house and we made love all night long. Eileen taught me quite a few tricks with strawberries and chocolate. I felt like I was in the Garden of Eden with her that night. I prayed to God everyday that the relationship between Eileen and I got stronger. She was learning to adjust to my ways as I was with her and we had planned to marry the following summer. Dexter would be my best man without a doubt and hopefully he'll realize that he'll need to take the leap of faith with Jess in the near future.

The Recollection

Dexter called me a few days after the dinner to tell me that he needed to talk to me about something important. He made it sound so urgent that I dropped everything that I was doing to head over to his house. On my way to Dexter's house, I was wondering what was so important that he couldn't talk to me about it over the phone. I ran a few things in my head, but I drew a blank. I couldn't figure out what it was.

When I arrived at Dexter's house, I had no idea what I was in for. I rang the doorbell and he answered in his pajamas. I was wondering why he was home in the middle of the week still wearing his pajamas. Dexter looked like his mother died and he hadn't shaved in days. Something was hurting him and I wanted to know what it was. I asked Dexter why he wasn't at work. He told me he was too tired to go to work because he hadn't slept in a few days. I was wondering what he was trying to get at.

Dexter asked me to take a seat in his living room so we could talk. "First of all, I want you to know that I love you like a brother and I would never do anything to hurt you" he said. I was like get on with it already. "Eileen, the girl that you introduced me to as your girlfriend and now fiancé, I think I slept with her," he said. I couldn't believe what I was hearing. Just when I thought that everything in my life was perfect, Dexter had to hit me where it hurt the most. I didn't how to react to his confession. A part of me was torn, but I wanted to know the whole story. "I met her at a college party at Harvard and we were both drunk at the time. I ended up staying the night at her off campus apartment in Cambridge. I'm not trying to hurt you, but as my best friend, I think you need to know the truth before you marry her," he said. I wanted to run up on Dexter and punch him in his mouth, but I knew that he would probably kick my ass and I had no right to be mad at him. However, I had every right to be mad at Eileen for keeping that secret from me after I introduced her to Dexter.

Dexter wanted to know if she said anything to me and I told him no. He told me that she might not have recognized or remembered him because they were drunk and he left her house early that morning before she even woke up. He also said that he only slept with her once and they never kept in touch. A part of me was fuming because I gave Eileen more respect than she deserved. I never pictured her as the type of woman who would sleep with just anybody on the first night. All kinds of shit was running through my mind, but the first thing I wanted to do was to take my ring back from her and call off the engagement.

Regardless of the fact that she acted like she didn't remember Dexter, she was no different than all the other hoes that I didn't want to get with. I should've suspected something because she didn't take long to sleep with me. She made me feel like I was special that night and that she had never done anything like that in her life. Dexter told me not to react in haste and that she probably thought nothing of him or that night. It was easy for Dexter to come up with all these excuses for her trifling ass because he wasn't in love with her and she wasn't his woman.

As much as I hated to have Dexter's leftovers, I hated the idea of losing Eileen even more. However, I didn't know if I could forgive and forget. I didn't want to be with a woman who screwed my best friend the first night they met. I was feeling like a loser once again. "She took the pretty boy home the first night she met him and probably fucked his brains out, but she wants to settle down with me, the loser," I thought. Of all the women in the world that I could've met that day, why did it have to be Eileen? Why did I have to fall in love with a woman that Dexter had slept with? It was nothing against Dexter, but I wanted to find a woman that I could call my own.

I didn't want to hear anymore that Dexter had to say. I got up and left his house feeling pissed. As I was driving home that day, I was trying to figure out what to do with the whole situation. My heart was in pain because I was in love with Eileen, but my ego couldn't stand the fact that she had slept with my best friend. I started banging my head against the steering wheel of my car and tears started flowing down my face like I was a wimp of a man. I had never been hurt like that.

A Hasty Decision

I didn't eat anything that entire day and I didn't want to speak to Eileen. I was feeling like a lost soul. The pain hurt me directly in the pit of my stomach and I couldn't bear it. I was able to deal with rejection in the past, but I couldn't deal with deception. I felt like I had been deceived by Eileen and I didn't want anything to do with her anymore. I stayed in bed all day watching television. I turned my cell phone and my home phone off because I didn't want to speak to her. I didn't want to hear her explanation.

What hurt the most was the fact that she acted as if she had never met Dexter before. Nobody, no matter how drunk they were could tell me that they were able to find their way home, but not being able to remember the person they brought home with them. I refused to believe that. It would have been an entirely different story if Dexter took her to his house. But she gave him directions to her own house, she unlocked the door, brought him to her bedroom and now she wanted to act like she didn't remember him. I couldn't be a sucker anymore and I didn't want to be one.

I wasn't going to allow love to make a fool of me. I picked up the phone later that evening and I called Eileen. At first, she was trying to make small talk and wondered why I hadn't picked up my phone all day. She wanted to know if I ate and so on, but I cut her off before she could lay all her sweetness on me. I told her that I didn't want to see her anymore and that the engagement was off and I wanted my ring back. She wanted an explanation and I told her that I didn't like people keeping secrets from me and especially secrets that they know could hurt me. Eileen acted as if she didn't know what the hell I was talking about. She didn't understand why I wanted to end our relationship so abruptly. She told me she'd come by my house after work to talk.

After I hung up the phone with Eileen, I knew that I wasn't going to be able to handle not being with her anymore. It hurt so bad for me to tell her that I didn't want to see her, but it hurt even more that she tried to hurt me by keeping secrets from me. I was torn between my feelings and my ego. If I stayed with Eileen, I felt that she would never respect me. However, if I stopped seeing her, I knew that I was losing the best thing that ever happened to me.

A Simple Mistake

My doorbell rang at exactly 9:00 that evening. I went to the intercom to find out who it was, it was Eileen and she was in tears. I pressed the buzzer to unlock the door for her. She walked up to my apartment wondering why I was acting like an ass and she wanted an explanation. She made it clear to me that she didn't mind ending our relationship, but for her own sanity, she wanted to know why. I felt like she was still acting and I told her to stop acting like she didn't know what I was talking about in a tone filled with hate and pain. Eileen had never seen that side of me and she was rather shocked that I had so much animosity in my heart.

She didn't want the situation to escalate further, she handed me the ring and told me to have a nice life. I took the ring from Eileen and I slammed the door shut. After shutting the door, I stood leaning against it with my back and my face buried in my chest on my folded arms. I felt my heart being pulled from my chest that night. A part of me almost wanted to cry like a little baby, but I only shed the few tears that my manhood would allow. I ran to the side window to see if Eileen had pulled out the parking lot, but she was still there. She was sitting in her car crying and I felt bad because I was in pain myself.

I wanted to go downstairs to console her, but I abhorred her too much to even look at her. I went back to the living room to watch ESPN. After about ten minutes into the Celtics game, I heard someone banging on my door. Eileen was somehow able to manage to sneak into the building as someone was leaving. She kept banging on my door and told me that she wasn't going to leave until I opened the door and spoke to her. I saw a feisty side of Eileen for the first time. I opened the door and she came inside and demanded an explanation. "I'm not going to walk out of here without an explanation after I felt like I've given you the best six months of my life. I'm not just gonna walk away from this without hearing from you the reasons that our relationship is ending," she said. In a way, I felt she was right and she deserved an explanation for my sudden change of heart. I told her that I found out from Dexter that she had a one-night stand with him. Her mouth almost hit the floor after I said that. She couldn't believe that I was accusing her of having a one-night stand with someone she had never seen before. She told me that Dexter was lying and that she had never met him.

I had known Dexter all my life and the one thing that he had never done was lie about the women he slept with. I was giving Dexter more credit than Eileen, because I had known him longer. Eileen was furious that I didn't believe her. "Where did he say we met?" she asked. I told her that Dexter said he met her at a party at Harvard and that she was drunk when she took him to her place that night. Eileen looked deep into my eyes as tears welled up in her own eyes and told me that Dexter didn't meet her and that he met her sister. She started pulling a picture out of her wallet. "I know I never mentioned this to you before, but the sister that I told you that I had who passed away was my identical twin sister" she said and handed the picture to me so I could see it. "My sister was in her last year of law school at Harvard when she and a few friends went to a party to celebrate the end of their final semester. Unfortunately, she had developed a bad drinking habit while she was in school and that night after the party, against her better judgment, she got behind the wheel of her car after drinking. My sister was a wonderful person, but she was not perfect. She got into a fatal car accident that night and I never had a chance to say goodbye to her," she said.

After hearing that, I didn't know what to say or do other than cry along with my woman. I took Eileen in my arms and apologized to her over a million times. "I'm sorry that I jumped to conclusions. I knew that you weren't that kind of person. Let me start over, I didn't mean for it to come out like that. I just want to tell you that I'm very sorry about your sister and everything that happened between us. I never wanted to hurt you, but I didn't want to be hurt myself. I hope that you can forgive me and allow me to make it up to you," I said.

I had awakened something that Eileen had buried deep inside her soul and it was too painful for her to bear. She said goodbye to me and went home. I made many attempts to reach Eileen for two days, but she never picked up her phone. I finally decided to go to her job to ask for forgiveness. I brought a car loaded with roses with me and rented one of those Goodyear blimps that spelled the words "I'm sorry, will you marry me again?" in the sky. I had called her job ahead of time to arrange for her to be outside when I arrived. I got on one knee in front of everybody and begged her to marry me again and with the encouragement of her co-workers she told me "yes" again. I ran to my woman and gave her a long kiss.

Making Up is Nice to Do

I knew that I messed up very badly and though Eileen had forgiven me, I wanted to do something special for her. I also wanted to call Dexter to give him a piece of my mind, but I realized that Dexter made an honest mistake and he was trying to watch out for me as a friend. I called Dexter anyway to explain the whole thing and he apologized to me for causing so much chaos in my relationship.

Since Dexter was the one who messed up my relationship with Eileen to start with, he needed to help me make up for it. Dexter asked me for Eileen's number so he could apologize to her for the misunderstanding. But he had more than that planned. He called first to apologize to Eileen, but also to ask her to report to the Boston Park Plaza Hotel because he was planning a surprised party for me. Dexter told her that a key to access the room would be left at the front desk. Dexter arranged for a suite at the hotel for Eileen and me. He had roses delivered and rose petals thrown all over the bed for us. Dexter had also ordered a bottle of Dom Perignon on ice and he made a CD with all of my favorite slow jams. He left a nice black lace teddy on the bed for Eileen and a pair of silk boxers for me.

He also went to his favorite jeweler, The Jewelry Store in Sudbury, Massachusetts and bought a nice pearl necklace for Eileen. He left the necklace on the armoire so that she wouldn't miss it. Dexter had asked Eileen to get to the room at 9:00 pm, about a half hour before the time that he told me to get there. There was soft lighting, soft music a bowl of fresh fruit, a bottle of bubbly and a nice Jacuzzi filled with warm water.

The mood was set, Dexter left the suite before Eileen, and I showed up. He left special instructions with the front desk clerk to only give keys to Eileen and I. Dexter knew that I didn't have much experience making up with women, so he took it upon himself to get it started for me and the rest would be up to me. It was also his way to rid himself of his guilt.

I walked in the room at 9:30 as scheduled and I found Eileen on the bed wearing a lace teddy, a pearl necklace around her neck with a glass of champagne in one hand and half of a strawberry hanging out of her mouth. Before I could say anything, she used her finger to motion me towards her. She took the strawberry from her mouth to my mouth and I tell you, strawberries never tasted so good. She started kissing me and biting her bottom lip the same way she did when we first met. I knew it wasn't because she was nervous this time. She took the silk boxers and handed it to me. I took it to the bathroom and put it on.

When I came out the bathroom, I found Eileen on her back with a strawberry in one hand and a glass of champagne in the other. She sensually placed the strawberry between her breasts and asked me to fetch it. I brought my mouth down to her chest and took one of her nipples into my mouth along with the strawberry like I was about to make strawberry milkshake. I leisurely sucked on her breasts as I effortlessly unclasped her teddy and pulled it off her. She told me to get on my stomach. She poured a little bit of the champagne down my back and started to gently lick it, savoring every drop. The movement of her tongue sent chills up and down my spine. She started kissing and rubbing my back in a way that no masseuse in any spa ever could. She went up and down my back with her tongue and when she got near my ass, she used her teeth to pull my boxers off.

After slowly pulling off my boxers with her mouth then dropped them to the floor, she started licking me from my feet up to my butt cheeks. The sensation was so good, I felt like people should be banned from experiencing that kind of pleasure. She licked all around my ass cheek and up my back until I couldn't take it anymore. She turned me around and went up and down my chest with her tongue until all of my nine inches stood erected in her face. She grabbed it and took the tip of her tongue to the head of my tool licking it slowly forcing my whole body to jerk like I was about to catch the Holy Spirit. She licked all nine inches of me up and down like her favorite chocolate ice cream then took half of it in her mouth. The warmth of her mouth and the motion of her tongue almost drove me insane. She sucked me real hard and then blew on it softly with her mouth. The sensation was very pleasant.

She was making me feel too good and I wanted to return the favor. I turned her around so her goods would rest on my face in a sixty-nine position. I started licking her clit slowly and as her pussy became wetter and wetter, her juices started to flow down her thigh to my face. I stuck my tongue inside of her to taste her sweet juices. She was moaning and groaning and I was making all kinds of sexual faces that she couldn't see. I did not want to pull my dick out of her mouth. I kept screaming, "Suck it baby, and don't stop." I grabbed her ass like a soft cuddly pillow and took her pussy in my mouth again like a sweet piece of watermelon. I ate her until her clit became erect to the point where she was trembling and winding all over my face.

I felt my dick extending to more than its regular nine inches inside Eileen's mouth as she sucked on it well. I wanted to be inside of her. I flipped her over on her back and I took the head of my dick and brushed it up and down her clit like a painter using a paintbrush on a masterpiece. She was shaking and grabbing me like the sensation was too much for her to bear. I slowly slid my nine inches inside of her and started humping her softly. Her rhythmic movements brought joy to my eyes and every time I looked at her face, I wanted to please her more. I buried my head in her chest while I was still inside of her and I sucked on her breasts until she couldn't take it any more. She was holding on to my head, screaming out the Lord's name as she reached the best, and longest orgasm since we had been having sex.

Eileen knew that doggy style was my favorite position and she enjoyed when I stroked her from the back. She brought her ass halfway up to my waist and I inserted my whole manhood inside of her. I grabbed on to her ass like I was on a roller coaster ride holding on for dear life as I stroked her as hard as I could. I stroked her back and forth, fast and slow for about thirty minutes until we were both about to explode together in ecstasy. However, I didn't want to cum just yet. I wanted to maximize Eileen's pleasure, so I slowed down. I pulled her legs back so she could lie on her stomach as I continued to stroke her from behind. As I was sliding back and forth inside Eileen, I couldn't help spanking her nice round ass. I started spanking her in a way that felt like I was caressing her ass and Eileen enjoyed every minute of it. She kept telling me to do it harder and with her every request I was losing control. I gently raised Eileen's ass up so I could get my hand around her stomach down to her clit so I could rub it. The harder I stroked her, the more she wanted it. After about the last five of my best strokes, I held on to her ass as we both exploded in pleasure. It was the best sex we ever had.

After sex, during pillow talk, Eileen started thanking me for the nice gesture and she told me how much she loved the pearl necklace. I didn't really want to disappoint her so I took credit for the whole thing. I knew that Dexter was the one who set it up and I was grateful. We told each other how much we loved, treasured and cherished one another. Eileen and I made up that night and we've never looked back.

Conclusion

No one has the right formula for love. Love creeps up on us when we least expect it. I have heard people mention that some of the best places to meet people are the workplace, through friends, singles' social gatherings, nightclubs and church. The day I met Eileen I realized that meeting a partner could literally take place anywhere and sometimes we have to take advantage of the opportunities presented to us when they arise. I could've walked past Eileen without saying anything that day and I would've missed out on the love of my life. There's no specific place to meet Ms., Mr. or Mrs. Right. They sometimes work with us, they're a friend of a friend, they're sometimes our enemies first, and they can be our longtime close friends. All the formulas might work in their own way, but none is guaranteed.

I also realized that all is fair in love. Denying Dexter and Jessie the opportunity to share a lifetime together because I had a crush on her would've been impossible for me to live with after seeing how their relationship has flourished. I could not let my feelings for Jessie get in the way of her love for Dexter and his for her. Sometimes we have to look beyond our own personal feelings in order to allow love to blossom for the ones we love. Keeping a person from exploring love for selfish reasons is worse than to never allow them to discover love at all.

Love is the most impossible word to define as it changes through the course of time in every relationship. Some people grow to love each other while others allow their love to fade away. Love sometimes drives us and it can also make us stagnant. Love will continue to exist until the end of time and no one will be able to escape it. Love has its way of finding us when we least expect it and sometimes it forces us to fight for her even when we have no more strength left within. No four-letter word in the dictionary is so powerful and has so many meanings to so many different people. No four-letter word evokes so many emotions and makes us act so foolishly sometimes. No four-letter word in the dictionary is as indiscriminately powerful to the young, the old, and it crosses all racial and ethnic lines.

Sometimes, we have to be careful not to force love because it should not be so complicated all the time. I believe that love should be natural and those people involved in a loving relationship are usually surrounded by enough positive people to help reinforce the love. Some people choose their mates to spite their parents, friends or society, but that kind of love rarely lasts long enough to simmer into the real thing. The best love for me was Eileen whom I simply discovered by chance just as I have discovered wealth. I can never say that good luck doesn't strike more than once in a lifetime.

I happened to get lucky twice within a year and from what I've noticed around me, many others got lucky as well, including my best friend. Good luck has a way of rubbing off on good people. We should not take for granted the wonderful things in life such as friendship, family, love and life itself. We're put on this earth to live life to its fullest in a positive way and when we do good things, we're sometimes rewarded justly. However, life shouldn't always be about the rewards we get. Life is about helping your fellow man to become better citizens to build better communities. Allow your friends to love and show love. Life is about forgiveness and great health. That's what I've discovered during my thirty-two years of life.

NEGLECTED SOULS
Motherhood and the trials of loving too hard and not enough frame this story...The realism of these characters will bring tears to your spirit as you discover the hero in the villain you never saw coming...
Neglected Souls is a gritty, honest and heart-stirring story of hope and personal triumph set in the ghettos of Boston.
In Stores!!!

Jimmy and Nina continue to feel a void in their lives because they haven't a clue about their genealogical make-up. Jimmy falls victims to a life threatening illness and only the right organ donor can save his life. Will the donor be the bridge to reconnect Jimmy and Nina to their biological family? Will Nina be the strength for her brother in his time of need? Will they ever find out what really happened to their mother?

In Stores!!!

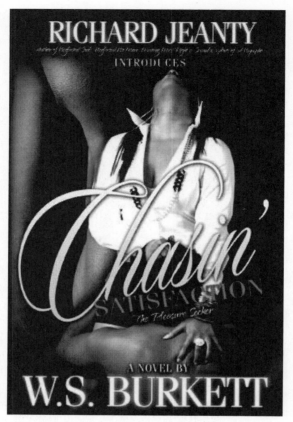

Betrayal, lust, lies, murder, deception, sex and tainted love frame this story...
Julian Stevens lacks the ambition and freak ability that Miko looks for in a
man, but she married him despite his flaws to spite an ex-boyfriend. When
Miko least expects it, the old boyfriend shows up and ready to sweep her off
her feet again. Suddenly the grass grows greener on the other side, but Miko
is not an easily satisfied woman. She wants to have her cake and eat it too.
While Miko's doing her own thing, Julian is determined to become
everything Miko ever wanted in a man and more, but will he go to extreme
lengths to prove he's worthy of Miko's love? Julian Stevens soon finds out
that he's capable of being more than he could ever imagine as he embarks on
a journey that will change his life forever.

In Stores!!!

The police in New York and other major cities around the country are increasingly victimizing black men. The violence has escalated to deadly force, most of the time without justification. In this controversial book, noted author Richard Jeanty, tackles the problem of police brutality and the unfair treatment of Black men at the hands of police in New York City and the rest of the country. The conflict between the Police and Black men will continue on a downward spiral until the mayors of every city hold accountable the members of their police force who use unnecessary deadly force against unarmed victims.

In Stores!!!

Just when Darren thinks his relationship with Tina is flourishing, there is yet another hurdle on the road hindering their bliss. Tina saw a therapist for months to deal with her sexual addiction, but now Darren is wondering if she was ever treated completely. Darren has not been taking care of home and Tina's frustrated and agrees to a break-up with Darren. Will Darren lose Tina for good? Will Tina ever realize that Darren is the best man for her?

In Stores!!

Ronald Murphy was a player all his life until he and his best friend, Myles, met the women of their dreams during a brief vacation in South Beach, Florida. Sexual Jeopardy is story of trust, betrayal, forgiveness, friendship and hope.

Coming February 2008

Tina develops an insatiable sexual appetite very early in life. She only loves her boyfriend, Darren, but he's too far away in college to satisfy her sexual needs.
Tina decides to get buck wild away in college
Will her sexual trysts jeopardize the lives of the men in her life?

In Stores!!!

Faith Jones, a woman in her mid-thirties, has given up on ever finding love again until she met her son's best friend, Darius. Faith Jones is walking a thin line of betrayal against her son for the love of Darius. Will Faith allow her emotions to outweigh her common sense?

In Stores!!!

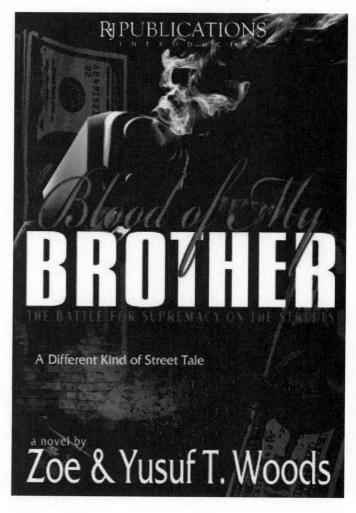

Roc was the man on the streets of Philadelphia, until his younger brother decided it was time to become his own man by wreaking havoc on Roc's crew without any regards for the blood relation they share. Drug, murder, mayhem and the pursuit of happiness can lead to deadly consequences. This story can only be told by a person who has lived it.

In Stores!!!

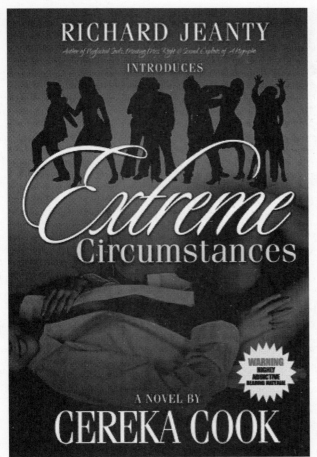

What happens when a devoted woman is betrayed? Come take a ride with Chanel as she takes her boyfriend, Donnell, to circumstances beyond belief after he betrays her trust with his endless infidelities. How long can Chanel's friend, Janai, use her looks to get what she wants from men before it catches up to her? Find out as Janai's gold-digging ways catch up with and she has to face the consequences of her extreme actions.

In Stores!!!

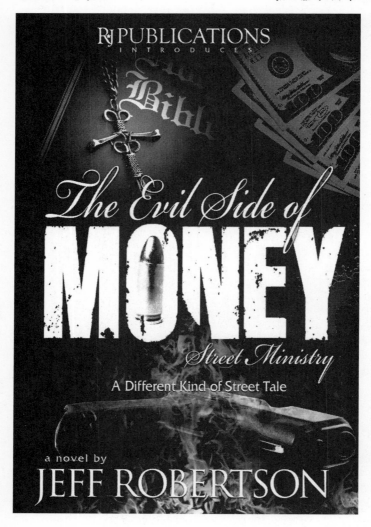

Violence, Intimidation and carnage are the order as Nathan and his brother set out to build the most powerful drug empires in Chicago. However, when God comes knocking, Nathan's conscience starts to surface. Will his haunted criminal past get the best of him?

In Stores!!

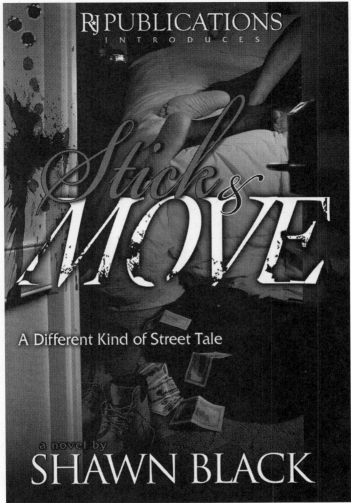

Yasmina witnessed the brutal murder of her parents at a young age at the hand of a drug dealer. This event stained her mind and upbringing as a result. Will Yamina's life come full circle with her past? Find out as Yasmina's crew, The Platinum Chicks, set out to make a name for themselves on the street.

In stores!!

RICHARD JEANTY

Author of Neglected Souls, Meeting Ms. Right & Sexual Exploits of Nympho

INTRODUCES

Too Many
SECRETS
& Too Many Lies

WARNING
HIGHLY
ADDICTIVE
READING MATERIAL

A NOVEL BY

SONYA SPARKS

Ashland's mother, Bianca, fights hard to suppress the truth from her daughter because she doesn't want her to marry Jordan, the grandson of an ex-lover she loathes. Ashland soon finds out how cruel and vengeful her mother can be, but what price will Bianca pay for redemption?

In stores!!

What happens when a woman's devotion to her fiancee is tested weeks before she gets married? What if her fiancee is just hiding behind the veil of ministry to deceive her? Find out as Sean Mitchell takes you on a journey you'll never forget into the lives of Angelica, Titus and Aurelius.

Coming March 2008!!

PUBLICATIONS
BRINGING EXCITEMENT, FUN AND JOY TO READING

Use this coupon to order by mail

1. Neglected Souls, Richard Jeanty $14.95
2. Neglected No More, Richard Jeanty $14.95
3. Sexual Exploits of Nympho, Richard Jeanty $14.95
4. Meeting Ms. Right's Whip Appeal, Richard Jeanty $14.95
5. Me and Mrs. Jones, K.M Thompson ($14.95) Available
6. Chasin' Satisfaction, W.S Burkett ($14.95) Available
7. Extreme Circumstances, Cereka Cook ($14.95) Available
8. The Most Dangerous Gang In America, R. Jeanty $15.00
9. Sexual Exploits of a Nympho II, Richard Jeanty $15.00
10. Sexual Jeopardy, Richard Jeanty $14.95 Coming: 2/15/ 2008
11. Too Many Secrets, Too Many Lies, Sonya Sparks $15.00
12. Stick And Move, Shawn Black ($15.00) Coming 1/15/ 2008
13. Evil Side Of Money, Jeff Robertson $15.00
14. Cater To Her, W.S Burkett $15.00 Coming 3/30/ 2008
15. Blood of my Brother, Zoe & Ysuf Woods $15.00
16. Hoodfellas, Richard Jeanty $15.00 11/30/2008
17. The Bedroom Bandit, Richard Jeanty $15.00 January 2009

Name_____
Address_____
City_____State_____Zip Code_____

Please send the novels that I have circled above.

Shipping and Handling $1.99
Total Number of Books_____
Total Amount Due_____

This offer is subject to change without notice.

Send check or money order (no cash or CODs) to:
RJ Publications
290 Dune Street
Far Rockaway, NY 11691

For more information please call 718-471-2926, or visit www.rjpublications.com

Please allow 2-3 weeks for delivery.